GHOST IN TRAINING

NEARLY DEPARTED - BOOK 1

TERI PETZOLD

DEDICATION

In loving memory of:

Claire Jordan Taylor

An angel whose sweet disposition left a lasting impact on her family.

ACKNOWLEDGMENTS

Becky, Becky, Lynn, Chris, Janice, Kristy, and Lynette - my beta readers, for your valuable feedback and encouragement. I hope the masses enjoy it as much as you all did.

David, editor and publisher of the first edition, collaborator and best of all, son. I couldn't have done it without you.

My late husband Dexter, for listening patiently as David and I discussed the characters at the dinner table like they were real people.

Sarah W., for bravely wading into the first edits with David. Your persistence and humor have been an inspiration.

Yasmine, and the team at Everest Press, for giving the book a professional polish, and a wider audience.

CONTENTS

CHAPTER

ONE

Outside Food Fresh, Ann Miller's breath steamed in the brisk air as she pulled on her gloves. *I hope Nick changes his mind about this weekend. He's working so hard for us. The mountains would do him good.*

Moments earlier, a fellow shopper had held her place while she jogged from the checkout line for a jar of Kalamata olives—her husband's favorite. On her way back, she spotted pecans. *Claire and I can make cookies after dinner.*

She coupled her shopping cart with another in the stall by the sliding doors, gathered her bags, and started across the snow-flurried lot to her car.

She briefly lost her footing on a patch of ice, flailing her arms with grocery bags in both hands. Laughing at her awkward dance, she recalled their trip to a friend's cabin last winter, teaching six-and-a-half-year-old Claire to skate on the frozen pond. Weary from a day in the snow with her family, she had donned a sweater knit by her grandmother, warming herself in front of the cast-iron stove, sipping hot chocolate, and laughing with Nick and her daughter.

1

Under her parka, she now felt the soft warmth of the same sweater from that weekend, and at that moment, she had never felt more connected to those she loved.

Albert Cunningham tapped the wheel to a jazz beat. He usually shopped with Rosie, but she didn't feel well today. So, he donned a sporty tweed driving cap, trimmed his white mustache, and drove his Caddy to the market while the snow was still light. He warmed his fingers in the flow from the heater vent and turned into the parking lot.

Today's errand was for tonight's dessert: pistachio ice cream. Rosie loved pistachio, and so did he. He smiled at a memory from nearly sixty years ago; they had strolled with youthful grace on a crowded pier, eating their cones and plotting fanciful adventures—maybe sailing around the world or raising quarter horses. He'd wiped a drop of pale green from her chin, realizing from the surprise on her face that she was 'the one'. The memory was so vivid he could almost taste it. But then the taste turned metallic, and he couldn't catch his breath or feel his hands on the wheel. The winter day dissolved into white.

Bags flew onto the hood of the car, oranges rolled down the walkway. Glass shattered, and olives scattered on the pavement. Metal crumpled.

Ann gasped as the world fell away. One moment, she slipped on the ice; the next, she hovered outside her body.

"Oh, no!" the shopper who had held Ann's place in line shouted, falling to her knees beside her. Ann watched the woman's cart roll towards the parked cars, retrieved by a man rushing in to help. He stopped to check on the Cadillac's driver. Eyes downcast, he turned to the shopper and shook his head.

Ann rose, the scene below her blurring, and floated through a prism of brilliant light. Her senses sharpened as confusion gave way to wonder, then awe. The spectrum of colors merged with her being, glowing from within. A profound peace, like an ocean wave, washed away her doubts as she entered a clearing.

Faces appeared in the mist. *Grandma? Grandpa?* Other relatives encircled her in welcome. She saw Nick and Claire in the unfathomable distance and understood—they would be all right. She'd fulfilled her purpose on Earth, and her soul had come home. The love for her husband and daughter swelled within her like joyful music, warm and rich. She appealed to the divine glow surrounding her—*Please help them heal and find their happiness again.*

Far beyond the reach of Earth's atmosphere—somewhere between the dimensions—floated a busy afterlife agency nestled among the stars, with views of constellations no living human had named.

Inside its Control Room, rows of alerts blinked in organized chaos. Monitors and meters tracked souls, timelines, and corresponding events with the calm efficiency of a skilled but overworked IT department.

Two technicians, Larry and Joey, hovered near the central feed. One studied the monitor; the other slouched in a chair with a steaming mug labeled *"Judgment is Above My Paygrade."*

On screen: a snowy parking lot in Mapleton, Utah. A dark blue Cadillac rolled without guidance through a grocery store driveway.

The satellite feed zoomed in, tracking the collision, and a woman's fall—a spilled bag of oranges, a burst jar of olives, and a moment of stillness too quiet for mortal ears.

A blinking light marked her soul's transition, in this case, to somewhere else.

A new alert lit the board. A man's heart had failed behind the Cadillac's wheel, and two souls diverged on separate paths to their afterlives.

A line of text scrolled across the main monitor:

"INCOMING: A. CUNNINGHAM — CASE STATUS: PENDING ORIENTATION."

A printer spat out forms into a plastic tray.

Larry adjusted his glasses and reached for the paper, muttering about the system lag and Earth's time zones. He ran a hand through his wispy hair. "Check out display seven, Joey. Zoom in on the grocery store on Chestnut Avenue, Mapleton, Utah. Dark blue Cadillac."

Today, in the Control Room, they operated a satellite feed with keyboards and mice and something like Google Earth. The hologram displays and gesture controllers were down for repairs again.

"Got it." With a practiced eye and a flurry of keystrokes, Joey recorded the trajectory of the car and the path of the young woman in jeans and a blue parka.

Larry glanced at his partner, then back to his monitor. He keyed the intercom. "Boss, we have Incoming, one eighty-year-old male." Just then, he glanced through the glass wall as the elderly man materialized, noticeably disoriented.

Albert found himself sitting on the hard floor of an unfamiliar lobby—clean, functional, and intriguing in a way he couldn't place. He rose to find his bearings, noting the ease and absence of pain when he moved. *This doesn't feel like my body.*

Turning to his left, he saw two men working at consoles through a glass wall with a sign marked 'Control Room.' To his right were double doors, and mounted on the wall, a screen powered on, displaying the scene in front of Food Fresh, where his beloved Eldorado's front end steamed, caved in by a building pillar. People gathered near a pair of ambulances, while paramedics rolled his body on a gurney into the back of one.

Albert stared at the image in his strange new environment when a slender young man, no more than twenty, with faint acne scars and a concert T-shirt pushed through the double doors and approached him, hand extended.

"Hi there, I'm Edward. You must be Albert."

"I'm pretty sure that's me." He looked at Edward, then pointed to the screen. "I think that's me, too."

"Yes, that's where you were before you got here."

"Okay," Albert said, unconvinced. "Where's here?"

"It's, um, where you are now. Will you please come with me? I'll escort you to where we're going."

"Sure. Where are we going, Edward?" He shook the young man's hand, playing along.

"Orientation."

"Orientation?" Albert chuckled, baffled. "I guess that makes sense. I'm about as disoriented as I've ever been." He took two steps and stopped, looking again at the display. "Wait, how can I see the market from here?"

An alarm chirped, and a shout came from the Control Room. Albert and Edward turned to see the balding man stand and press buttons on a panel. The lights in the lobby dimmed, and the TV snapped off. The lights brightened.

"What was that all about?"

"We've had some technical issues lately." He led Albert to a hallway. "You'll be fully briefed when you sign the release forms."

Albert frowned. "Forms? Signatures? I'm retired; I'm not applying for a job." He raised a bushy eyebrow.

Albert and his wife, Rosie, lived a comfortable, simple life. She tinkered on her piano, and he tinkered in his workshop and hit a bucket of balls now and then. He hadn't punched a clock in over fifteen years. He put in his time and retired from the USDA at sixty-five to invent gadgets that challenged and stimulated him. Now this. Unease rippled through him as he thought, *Rosie knows what to do if anything happens to me. Maybe something has.*

Turning to the youth, he asked, "Edward, can you at least tell me what happened to the lady? Was she...?"

"I'm just the receiving clerk, Albert, here to escort you to the next department. They don't give me access to classified material. I'm only GS-2."

"A GS-2? No offense, but you must be pretty new. I used to be a GS-12 designing systems for the U.S. government." He stroked the smooth wall of the corridor as they walked, unfamiliar with the material.

"None taken." He brushed a lock of unruly hair from his forehead. "Here 'GS' means something different. It's not the same as in government service."

"What does it mean?"

"I'm not at liberty to say—it's classified." Edward grinned.

They reached a door that read "Orientation." Edward knocked and ushered Albert inside. They approached an attractive redhead behind a counter, and he introduced Albert. "She'll take over now. I should get back to my post. Good luck."

Albert thanked him and frowned as Edward vanished down the hall. *This is the wildest dream...* He sighed and looked at the redhead behind the counter. "Okay, what's next?"

Back in the Control Room, lights blinked and equipment reset as Joey and Larry pondered the events unfolding on Earth. They operated the communication and extraction hub, alerting other departments to incoming souls.

They had a few minutes to kill while the system rebooted after the crash. As former first responders, dark humor and bad puns helped smooth the jagged edges of the job.

Joey stretched, leaning back in his chair. "Yep. She would have made it to her car, except for the olive delay. Now she's off to the Pearly Gates, and we get the old-timer."

"Well, they're both gonna be late for dinner," Larry deadpanned, scanning the alarm panel and resetting meters. A live image of the accident lit up display seven. Red and blue emergency lights strobed over the thin white blanket on the asphalt. A stocky, middle-aged woman swept spilled food and broken glass into a long-handled dustpan. "Ah, back online." He glanced at the clock. "Shift's almost over. I guess *olive* to serve another day. But they won't."

"Bad, Larry. Even for you," Joey replied. "*Orange* you glad we don't have to die again?" They chuckled half-heartedly. Any shift could bring a dozen new arrivals with their psychic baggage, but the guys were pros and knew how to take care of themselves.

"C'mon, I'll finish the shift report." Joey entered the readings from the software malfunction, and his laptop pinged with an incoming message. "Oh, here's the old guy's file: Albert Cunningham, retired systems engineer for the government. Maybe he can help with our tech issues."

"Forward it to The Boss. Wouldn't hurt to ask."

After completing the logs, Larry waved a wand resembling a curling iron around his head, then around Joey's, releasing the energy of departed souls that could cling to them like static. Otherwise, they might not get any rest. They briefed their relief and headed for the cafeteria.

Back on Earth, other professionals managing the scene at the grocery store wrapped up their interviews. Albert's Eldorado was towed. Next of kin were notified. Ambulances rolled away without lights or sirens, and the world kept turning.

In the Orientation room, Albert stood before a woman, hands clasped behind his back. She smiled. "Have a seat. This will take a while. I've already filled in the pertinent information: name, address, next of kin, DOB, and DOD..."

"Wait, what?"

"Name, address..."

"No, that last part."

"Date of birth, date of death?"

Albert stared at her for a moment, his mind swirling with questions. "So, it's official? That's how I went? I never felt a thing. Ah, poor Rosie." He sat heavily on a folding chair.

"You kicked the bucket, all right," she said with a smile. "Now, please sign here and here." She pointed to another line, "and here."

"How can you be so casual about this? You're telling me I died like you'd say it might snow tomorrow." Tension constricted his chest. "I won't do it. This is just a terrible dream. I want to wake up now. Rosie!" He closed his eyes, willing himself awake, his hands searching for a bed that wasn't there, and his wife, who was very, very far away.

The woman behind the counter sighed. She smiled and spoke to him in a soft, clear voice. "It's only a transition, Albert. You were alive, you died, now you're a ghost."

"A ghost? Come on!" Albert sprang to his feet, levitating a few inches off the floor. *Whoa*, he thought, *that was cool.* "Huh." He felt for his keys. Not there. *Did I leave them in the car?* He twisted, taking his time. To the left, to the right. No pain. "Can you show me some proof?"

She fanned the papers on the counter between them. "It takes a minute to get settled. It happened to all of us, but trust me, it could be a lot worse. You can read the disclaimer and terms of service if you like."

He glanced at the documents, overwhelmed by the finality of it all. Finding no recourse and no good reason to hesitate, he accepted his fate. Grumbling, he signed the forms.

"When we're done here, we'll get you to Wardrobe for a change of clothes, then someone will escort you to see The Boss."

In Wardrobe, he exchanged his coat and thermals for a casual shirt and khakis. "Mr. Cunningham," another staffer appeared. "It seems The Boss will be tied up in meetings until this afternoon, so let me show you to our lounge. You can have a cup of coffee or a cold drink while you wait."

"Is there ice cream?"

Albert liked the lounge, even if it didn't serve ice cream. The chairs were comfortable. He found a recent issue of Popular Mechanics and waited.

Edward led Albert into the C-suite, where HD monitors covered the sleek, paneled walls, each flickering with scenes of Earth. Through a massive bay window, the planet spun in breathtaking detail. As Albert stepped inside, a group of executives exited, nodding politely as they *passed.* He sat at a worn but sturdy conference table with The Boss.

"Albert, I believe we have a position for you if you'll accept. We've been short-staffed for some time, so there's quite a backlog, and our tech team is way behind. But with your background—and lots of time on your hands—I'm sure you could bring it up to snuff. You'd be doing us a great service."

Why not? I might as well keep busy. "Thank you, sir. I'll do my best."

CHAPTER
TWO

Fourteen Months Later

After work, Ron enjoyed flying his kite at the beach. He'd practiced for years and loved showing off his skills—from a distance. His latest rig was an eight-foot dual-line red and black stunt kite he imagined as a wicked bird of prey. His day job as an air traffic controller at LAX was stressful, the level of focus intense, even during monotonous times. This was his well-earned reward.

He launched the kite into a gust of wind. It bucked and strained against the leash, raw power coiled, aching to break free. Ron tugged the lines, and it climbed, scouting the thermals. Unspooling the reel, the beast soared gracefully, daring the wind. Smiling smugly, he mumbled, "Yes, my lovely, let's dance."

The wind was perfect. His arms and shoulders strained as the lines hummed with tension. He yanked into an upward spiral, looping into a slow roll that traced a powerful arc across the afternoon sky.

A group of young teens watched. There was only one other serious flyer, further down the beach. Ron talked to the wind, coaxing his kite to perform for his audience. He ran toward the rocks that separated the sand from the road, climbing a boulder as he flipped the kite into a hesitation spin. A hard twist into a corkscrew dive.

Damn, I'm good.

Ron stood tall on the boulder, the lines taut in his hand. The sea air pushed against him, crisp and wild. Below, the waves crashed against the rocky outcrop like applause. He raised one arm, balancing with practiced flair. The kite dipped low, then soared again, riding the gusts like a trained hawk.

This is it, he thought. *This is the kind of moment you frame. Freeze it. Stick it on a retirement plaque.*

Behind him, a few beachgoers gathered. A father pointed. A child clapped.

Ron grinned. "Showtime."

He glanced at the nearby kids feeding Cheetos to the seagulls—which annoyed him. He didn't like the birds flying too close. He drifted further from the group, drawing the kite into a tight pattern. The kids turned their attention to the other flyer. "Good," he muttered. "Go bother the amateurs."

The reel jerked in his hand. *Snag. Damn, gotta bring her in.* The braided line frayed as he reeled, struggling for control. He leaned forward, shifting his weight to guide the kite's arc. But then—

Snap.

What the hell? A seagull flew toward him with an orange Cheeto in its mouth, tangling in the slack line. He scrambled to land the expensive kite with one line and dislodge the bird from the other. The kite fluttered and strained in a wild arc under the weight of the gull. A rogue gust of wind, the velocity of the kite, and the panicked bird created a momentum that turned into a tightening spin. Ron's expensive kite circled him and attacked the back of his head like a predatory condor swooping on a tasty forest creature, causing him to lose his footing.

The gull shrieked as it tangled in the tail, flapping wildly. The kite dipped, spiraled, caught an updraft—and yanked him forward.

Ron slipped.

He pitched sideways, arms windmilling. The rocks didn't move, but his world tilted.

He heard a shout, maybe his own, maybe someone else's.

Then came the fall.

Time warped. Seconds seemed to stretch into minutes. Sea spray rose to meet him. His sunglasses flew off, and the gull squawked, freeing itself and rejoining the flock. For a brief, absurd instant, he thought: *I hope someone caught that on video.*

And then—

Impact.

Not pain, exactly. More like... sound and light collapsing inward.

The noise of the crowd dimmed. The seagulls blurred into vapor trails.

Even the wind seemed to hush.

Ron blinked.

He was no longer falling. But he wasn't standing either.

He hovered, somehow, above the scene. Below him, a man lay crumpled between rocks. His own khaki shorts. His own legs. Unmoving.

"Wait... what?"

And then the world as he knew it disappeared.

Control Room Feed – Moments Before

A blinking red light pinged above Monitor Seven.

Larry leaned in, brushing muffin crumbs from his shirt. "We've got a live one, Joey. Chest puffed out like he owns the coastline."

Joey swiveled in his chair, slurping a blue energy drink. "The beautiful California beach. Okay, I see him—the kite guy." Larry tapped a key, zooming in on the screen: Ron stood on a boulder, arms raised as if commanding the weather.

"What's that old proverb?" Joey asked, already grinning.

"Pride goeth before the... oh, there it is." Larry winced as Ron slipped. "It goeth right before the splat."

Joey watched him fall, along with the escaping seagull. "Man, I feel bad for the bird, having to witness that. What's kite guy's status?"

"Still alive," Larry said, checking the soul arrival queue. "Though not for long."

They waited in silence until a soft chime confirmed what they already knew.

"Incoming: Richardson, Ronald," read the display. "Escort pending."

Larry held up a dollar bill between his fingers. "Think he's going to be trouble?"

"A hundred percent," Joey replied. "I'll take that bet."

"Not if Gayle takes him. She can handle it."

"Fair enough." Joey leaned back and sipped his drink as the printer clattered in the background. "If these mortals knew how ridiculous their exits could be, they'd never leave the house."

"Incoming," Larry keyed the microphone for the general announcement and read the printout. "Ron Richardson, 46-year-old male, from Playa del Rey, the beach just north of the volleyball courts." He finished and turned to Joey. "This one's a shoo-in for the Triple D pool."

Joey glared at him. "Be careful, Larry. The Boss might be listening."

"Yeah, I lost my head. Sorry." He chuckled, recalling his own victory in the Triple D, or Dumbest Deaths of the Day pool. His decapitation occurred while goofing off at a museum. The vintage guillotine was supposed to be disabled.

Fortunately, policy stated that employee bodies were restored to near-normal appearance, regardless of the circumstances of their demise.

"Hey, Gayle," Joey called out to a blonde woman who appeared in the nearby lobby. "We've got a live one for you. Here's your chance to earn those wings. Have fun."

The guys laughed, and Larry added, "Yeah, we need some comic relief; it's been pretty dead. Hah."

"That never gets old, fellas." She smiled. The boys in the Control Room were her afterlife buddies. Another day, she might have wisecracked with them, but she had a deadline.

Edward stood over Ron, their newest arrival, who sat on the platform with his arms crossed as Gayle floated over. "Can I help, Edward?" she asked.

"I was trying to explain to this gentleman that he needs to follow me to Orientation, but he's a bit resistant." Edward stood, hands on hips, regarding the newcomer.

"Hello, I'm right here, you know. Who *are* you people?" Ron said.

"It's okay, Edward. They sent me to pick up this one." Gayle placed her hand lightly on Ron's arm. "Will you come with me, please? Others are waiting, and I'm escorting you all to meet The Boss."

Ron swiveled his head between them, more confused and riled as they spoke. "What Boss? What's going on here? This is ridiculous. I have things to do. I need to find my kite and—would you stop tugging on me?" Bits and pieces of his day came back to him in no sensible order, and his head ached.

"Let's go, Ron. We've got to be there in ten minutes. No time for questions." She pushed a lock of hair behind her ear and smiled.

For a moment, Ron thought she glowed, like an angel. *But wait, this can't be happening. What is this?*

"How do you know my name?" His mouth dropped open. "Oh my god, are you aliens? Wait—would you just stop for a minute?"

"Dude," she sighed. "Those are questions. The Boss will explain everything, but we can't be late."

Her eyes flashed, and he felt it, like a jolt to his unfamiliar body. "Lady, I'm not going anywhere until you tell me where the hell I am and who you are."

"Fine. This is not Hell, and we're not aliens. I'm Gayle. Your mentor." She waved a graceful arm over her head.

He rolled his eyes. "My mentor? Oh, Lord. I'm a dead man."

"I know. A stubborn one, too." She laughed with a little snort.

Ron's face was blank; he still didn't get it.

"Okey dokey." She pursed her lips. "Do you know why you're here?"

"Not at all. I looked up and saw this guy. Then you—did you fly over here? Now I have to go to some meeting? I was just at the beach." He blinked and swayed, looking woozy. "Hell, I'm still wearing my shorts! Dammit, I didn't sign up for this…whatever this is…" They stood face-to-face; he noticed she was a little taller than him.

"Alright, don't get all bent out of shape. Sorry to break this to you, Ron. Um, do you remember what you did today?" He tried to piece it together, looking around and squinting at the serene artwork on the corridor walls. Then he scoffed.

"Of course I do. There was a stupid construction detour, and I barely made it to work by seven. I did my job very well, as usual. If they could handle traffic like I handle my planes, L.A. would be a lot better off. My relief finally came in five minutes late, sniveling about her boyfriend or something. She looked like she'd been crying. Please, we're supposed to be professionals!" Tension tightened his jaw, and he tried to pace, but his legs wobbled.

"I told her to pull herself together, and she said they had a fight, blah, blah. I just held up my hand to shut her up because I don't have to listen to anyone's problems. Like I cared about her boyfriend. I had four planes on three runways, and I needed to concentrate 100%, because I do not make mistakes. I get the job done flawlessly every time. So, I briefed the little crybaby and took off. My shift was over."

Gayle winked at Edward and turned to Ron. "Sounds quite professional."

The sarcasm didn't penetrate. He continued. "So, I went home, grabbed my kite, and headed for the beach. I had a beer, and no one bothered me, so I could relax and wait for the wind to pick up." His lip curled in a tiny smile as he gazed into the distance.

"That's nice. What happened next?" Gayle guided him forward down the hallway.

"Why are you quizzing me about my day? I'm really not in the mood to talk."

"And yet, here we are. Do you want to know where 'here' is?"

"Must I go through my whole day?" he grumbled, turning his palms up.

Gayle remained silent, her gaze steady. "If it helps you remember, yes."

"Sheesh, whatever. So, I launched my kite. She's a real beauty, and so graceful under my command."

"And…?"

"And what? I ran up the beach to my spot by the rocks." He paused. "The seagulls—they were everywhere, circling too close."

Gayle waited patiently, which annoyed him.

Something tugged at Ron's memory. "The kids watched me. They were feeding the birds."

"And…?"

"Would you stop saying 'and'? I did a couple stunts."

"Okay."

"Okay, what?" Ron demanded, frustration edging his voice.

"Where were you when you did your tricks?"

"They're not tricks." He rolled his eyes. "They're stunts. There's a difference. Oh, why am I explaining? You wouldn't understand." A chill formed in his belly.

Gayle sighed. "Do you remember climbing the rocks, Ron?" She crooked an eyebrow.

Frowning, Ron searched his memory, afraid of what he might find. "There was this damn seagull." His eyes darted around his strange, new surroundings as realization dawned on him.

"And?"

"The stupid bird got tangled in my line. I think I fell."

"Yes, you did. You fell pretty hard. On the rocks. Remember?"

"No," he growled. "As a matter of fact, I don't. So?"

Gayle looked at her watch. "Ron, you didn't make it."

"What do you mean? I didn't make what?"

"You died, Ron. You fell so hard you fractured your skull. Massive brain damage. Cerebral hemorrhaging, hematoma..."

Ron stared at her. "What? You can't be right! I always climb those rocks. Dead? Listen, I have things to do. I just paid for three days in Vegas. Get this: I told my boss I was going to a self-improvement seminar. I'm not going for that, but it's Vegas. I like the shows. The buffets, free drinks..." His voice trailed off as he stopped for a breath and, not needing one, frowned. At a loss, he asked, "Dead?"

"There you go, slugger. Now you get the picture."

"Just wait a second, there's been some mistake. I'm up for a promotion—do you know how long I've been waiting? Let me speak with your supervisor..." He stopped talking and looked at her, fingers probing the dent in his head. "I really am dead, aren't I?"

"As a doornail." She smiled. "Now that we've got that out of the way, again, my name is Gayle. I'm your mentor." Her eyes twinkled. "Your supervisor, if you will."

"You're not an angel?"

She shook her head. "Nope, I haven't earned my wings yet. Hopefully, after you graduate, I will."

"Oh, this is just great. You're gonna teach me how to be dead? What's there to learn, anyway?" He threw his hands up. "I need a beer. Where can I get one?"

"Newbies don't get beer. Too much liability. HR would have a fit."

"HR—what? Never mind." He sighed, his tone softening. "You must have been young when you..."

"Died?" She twirled a few inches off the floor. "You can say it out loud, Ron. We're all dead here. I died at the same age I am now. That's one perk about this job—we don't age."

"Oh," Ron said as other people joined them in the lobby, as confused as he was. Gayle waved them over.

"All right, everyone, please stay together and follow me." She waved a little yellow flag over her head. "We don't want to lose anyone."

Eavesdropping from the Control Room, the guys chuckled while Joey waved away Larry's dollar.

⋅⟩⟩✳⟨⟨⋅

Gayle led the group to a meeting room where a very tall ghost sat at a long table, flanked by three ghosts on either side. Two wore flowing white robes; the others were dressed in business casual.

"Welcome," The Boss announced in a booming voice. "Glad you could make it, though I don't suppose you are." His chuckle rumbled in the cavernous room.

"Funny," Ron mumbled, his voice louder than expected. *He reminds me of Gandalf.*

"Let's get down to business, shall we? Some of you are waiting for your assignments, and my team has decided where you will go." He turned to them. "Please collect your new arrivals and get them prepped. My, we have quite a group this week."

The Boss glanced from the assembly to Ron. "You can stay where you are." He called out to the small groups filing out. "Good luck, people." An aide approached him with paperwork, which he signed.

"Ron, I have a mission for you that needs to be handled quickly. You have one week to prepare. Gayle, can you have him ready by then?"

"Yes, sir. No problem," Gayle replied, though her forced smile suggested she might regret her confidence. "All right, Ron. We're not getting any younger. Let's get started. Follow me." She floated to a door and passed right through.

Shrugging his shoulders, Ron attempted the same and slammed into the door, bouncing off like a marshmallow. On the other side, Gayle laughed—a hoot and a snort. He wasn't sure if it was endearing or annoying. *She is a hoot, all right.*

He pulled himself up, put on his game face, and tried again. He pictured himself as an airplane preparing for takeoff. Staring at the door and blocking everything else from sight, he ran at it and passed through— plowing into Gayle. She fell back into the ghost behind her, giggling. Ron helped her up. Not that she needed it, but it made him feel a little better.

"How was that, Teach?"

"You move pretty well for a guy in his forties," she said. Ron sucked in his gut a little. *Maybe she's not so bad.*

Ron brushed off his shorts. The dried sand itched. With an uncomfortable grin, he said, "By the way, Gayle, any chance of getting a change of clothes? This sand is getting... Well, you've been to the beach."

"Yes, I have." She made a face. "Yeah, I'll get you to Wardrobe soon. Hang in there." They floated into a room without furniture. Ghosts in uniform, hospital gowns, and even business suits hovered a few inches off the floor like they were skydiving. Arms out and knees bent, they tried to form a circle while holding hands, but kept bumping into each other. Another group leaped about like slapstick acrobats, falling, laughing, and getting up again.

Ron stood frozen, horrified by the incompetence. He tolerated no less than perfection in his work and hated the thought of looking foolish. Anxiety crept into his throat like a desire to flee. It reminded him of going to a three-ring circus as a child. Overwhelmed by the spectacle, he remembered when a woman fell from the trapeze and tumbled from the net to the floor below. Clowns, dancers, and men on stilts rushed over to help, stumbling over each other. Ron almost fainted. It was too much for him. Now he was dead and surrounded by chaos.

His heart—or whatever was pounding in his chest—raced. The absurdity and confusion squeezed like a cold, bony hand, amplifying his dread. The sense of loss and displacement crept up on him like malevolent shadows.

A dark-haired woman in jeans and a red blouse appeared, her head and shoulders protruding from the wall. She laughed in childlike delight, but Ron's head spun. His relaxing afternoon at the beach had morphed into this frightening world where he had no control. He looked around for Gayle.

His eyes landed on a man in a tuxedo, dragging a chain clamped to his ankle; drag, slide, drag, slide. Ron thought, *Come on, really?* Sounds echoed in the room—boos, screams, and long, drawn-out moans.

Ron stood frozen, unsure what to make of it all. *Why do ghosts have to be scary, anyway?* The noise crawled under his skin. A mission with living people? *I couldn't handle them while I was alive. What if I mess this up?*

The man with the chain felt like a warning—a reminder of the weight Ron was carrying, even now. The eerie scene felt ridiculous and unsettling all at once, leaving him torn between laughter and panic. *Maybe if I can stop being scared of how strange this is, I'll figure out what to do.*

"Boo!" Gayle's breath tickled his neck. He shot around the room like a balloon releasing air. Regaining his footing on the floor, he felt gooseflesh rise on his arms. He hung his head, at a loss. *Great. I'm dead and I got scared. What the hell am I afraid of? This is awful.*

"Looks like you're at about stage three or four," she said. "Just ride it out. You'll be okay."

"Huh?" Ron spun to face her, realizing he was floating.

"Stages of grief. We all go through it. Denial, anger, bargaining. You look like you're somewhere between bargaining and depression. Acceptance comes last."

Some of his panic subsided, and he took a deep breath, out of habit. "Okay, what's next?"

"So, here in Ghostland—that's what everybody calls it—we can wear what we want. We can see and touch one another, but gravity and the density of matter are optional." She pointed to the woman in the wall.

"On missions, you can wear clothes from when you were alive or the robes. But you need to stay invisible unless you get consent from The Boss."

Gayle told Ron that once he learned the basics, he would be tested. If he passed, he'd become a full-fledged ghost and leave for his first mission.

As a mortal man, Ron organized his life with the mundane precision of someone who avoided existential matters. He didn't ponder those things. Yet, he felt compelled to ask this woman, his strange new colleague, questions he suddenly needed to understand. "Why haven't I gone to Heaven? Or Hell, for that matter? Why do I have to be a ghost?" Deep down, he knew it wouldn't be Heaven.

"Good questions. It's about your unresolved life and how you lived it. The man upstairs has a plan for you. The Boss, I mean. He's not God; he just runs things here."

He didn't want to confront his unresolved life just yet, so he pivoted. "How did you get this job, teaching me?"

"On Earth, I married Jim. For twenty-one years, he couldn't make a decision to save his life. The best one he made was, you guessed it, marrying me." She grinned. "He's a good man, but a mama's boy. He expected to be taken care of. I'd like to think I straightened him out, but not really. We never had children, and I ran the roost. When I got sick, I went pretty fast. I couldn't even make my own arrangements, like I wanted, anyway. That's my unresolved thing: letting people learn their own way, not mine." She sighed, as if accepting her role. "So, this training is for me, too."

"Is your husband still alive?"

"Yes, bless his heart. He's finally learned how to make a pot of coffee and is working on white or wheat toast. See, we all can learn something new, whether we like it or not."

"I hope I won't have to rattle any chains or scare anyone. I don't see myself doing that."

"You should learn all the aspects of being a ghost; what you use depends on the situation. Acting scary or nice, materializing, blowing things across the room—these are your tools. If they help you resolve a major issue from your earthly life, you move forward. Here, that comes by assisting those you're sent to help. The Boss knows how to set things up." She vanished and returned with two cups of hot tea.

"Just do your best. I'll be watching and evaluating, too. Think about how you'd fix your life on Earth if you were smarter." She winked. "And friendlier, and less stubborn, and followed directions..."

"Okay, I get it."

"Hey, it's your afterlife. Just saying." She clinked his teacup with hers.

Ron sipped his tea, feeling more than a little uneasy about examining his life.

CHAPTER
THREE

Gayle worked with Ron all week—a long, grueling stretch of training. He grumbled, fumbled, and fell—easily frustrated despite her calm encouragement. He wanted to quit. He wanted to scream. He needed much more practice, but time was running out.

Gayle smiled, but with only a few days left to achieve the impossible, her smile was strained. On day five, however, during telekinesis training, Ron challenged a saltshaker with newfound determination. He stared at it until his eyes watered, imagining it moving two inches. On the first try, it wiggled. On the second, it fell over. Then, on the third attempt, it moved—just half an inch—but it moved, thrilling them both. Yet, he knew he was barely passing, and from Gayle's expression, so did she.

After the final, tedious day of dragging chains, the time had come.

Ron stood outside the heavy doors, his heart pounding like a bass drum. His arms still ached, his pride even more so. The week had been a humiliating blur of misfires, stubbed toes, and pratfalls. Gayle hovered beside him like an overly patient driving instructor.

"You ready?" she asked.

"Nope," he muttered.

"Too bad." She grinned, knocked once, and the double doors swung open without a sound.

The chamber inside stretched farther than any courtroom he'd ever seen—like a cross between a Roman senate hall and a cosmic opera house. Vaulted walls shimmered faintly, with no windows in sight. No chairs. No inconspicuous exits.

Seven figures sat at a long table on a raised platform. Their robes drifted slightly, as if stirred by an unseen breeze. At the center sat The Boss, more luminous than the rest, his silver-trimmed robe pulsing subtly with light.

Ron gulped. *So, this is it. Judgment day. And I'm in golf shorts.*

He noticed Gayle's strained smile. Despite their constant bickering, he sensed she might be warming up to him—just a little. *She's probably still annoyed that I don't do things her way.* He knew she had done her part, and now The Boss would have to decide his fate. *I'll sink or swim on this mission. Right?* He waited, resigned to his outcome.

Ron felt The Boss's dark eyes pierce into him like lasers.

"Go talk to him, Ron. You can do it," Gayle said, helping him levitate and nudging him toward the table. He could almost hear her worry that he'd make her look bad. She gave him a little push, but as if a supporting air current vanished, he fell onto the long table. Papers, a pitcher of water, and The Boss's sports bottle went flying. Ron's leg remained submerged while the rest of him sprawled on the tabletop, like a fish flopping on a boat deck. Gayle slipped back into the crowd.

The ghost on The Boss's right quickly cleaned up the mess. A voice boomed, "Please remove yourself from my table, sir!"

Ron twisted and wriggled, but to no avail. "I'm trying my best."

"Oh, for the love of Pete." The Boss waved his hand, and Ron stood upright before the group.

"Now, then. I see you have been here a week and are still having trouble with your coordination. Gayle has never let me down, but I expected better."

Ron held his temper, but the frustrations of the week had wound him up like a steel spring. *That's it. I don't care what they think.* He seethed, his voice rising. "Why am I here, anyway? Flying around and dragging stupid chains? I managed eighty-ton airplanes, so a million people landed safely. I'm an expert kite flyer. Hell, I excel at everything but these damn tests!"

The Boss glared at him, though a grin curled at his lips. "Don't know why you're here? Not lounging on a puffy cloud somewhere? Stand by." The Boss pressed a button on his console. "Joey, would you roll the footage of Ronald Richardson's last day on Earth, please?" He stared at Ron while speaking into the intercom. "Just skip to the good parts."

In the Control Room, Joey snapped to attention at the voice of authority. "Coming right up, Boss." In a flurry of keystrokes, he directed the media file to the Evaluation Room.

Ron stood, feeling a bit queasy as Joey's voice crackled through the speaker.

A soft hum vibrated through the chamber as a towering hologram shimmered into clarity, rising to the ceiling. Ron heard someone whisper, "Where's the popcorn?"

There he was. First, on his way to work, cursing and gesturing rudely at construction workers and flagmen. Then in the tower, berating a pilot for asking him to repeat an instruction and insulting a co-worker. Cutting off a driver on the way to the beach. Drinking a beer and tossing the can in the sand next to a trash bin. Next, a twenty-foot-tall close-up of the disgusted scowl he gave a little boy feeding seagulls, followed by the boy's hurt reaction.

Silence. Then laughter. Even The Boss shook his head, chuckling. Ron heard a disapproving 'boo.' The highlight reel closed with him preening on top of a boulder, attacked by his own fancy sport kite, and falling to his death. Ron's exchanges with Edward and Gayle upon his arrival in Ghostland rolled behind the credits.

Ron blanched at his image, his history of arrogance and denial caught in his throat. *Am I that obnoxious? If it were anyone else, I'd say he deserved what he got. Who am I kidding? I deserved it. What a jerk.* He hung his head.

"Ron, you've had a week to get used to being dead. But I think you need more proof to believe in yourself. We can't have you doubting ghosts now, can we?" The Boss paused, letting that sink in.

"So, you'll remain on probation while you gain more practical experience. I'm hoping it will adjust your attitude and teach you how to give and receive help. I am sending you on a mission to assist some people in need. But you are not prepared to do it alone, so I am sending your mentor as well to train you further."

"No!" Everyone turned to Gayle, who hovered, aghast, at the back of the room. "I mean, no. Please. Sir." Ron saw the panic on her face and felt even worse. She looked at The Boss as if begging him to reconsider.

The Boss's voice carried to Gayle at the rear of the chamber. "He is still your responsibility. You'll need to see him through this if you want your wings. Trust me, Gayle. There is a lot riding on this one. You're an excellent operative, and I expect your best. Take Ron to Records and pick up your assignment." He motioned Ron away from the table. "Good luck, Ron. I think you're going to need it." He chuckled, turning to his aides. "Now, what's next?"

The crowd parted, creating a path as Ron and Gayle left the room. Many murmured their support. Gayle escorted Ron silently down a long hallway with many turns to an office door simply marked Records.

File cabinets and tables stacked with folders lined the walls. More folders were piled on the floor in various stages of organization.

A soldering iron smoldered on a workbench littered with green circuit boards, meters, and assorted electronic components. Gayle approached a ghost in a plaid sport shirt and khakis, who swiveled from the bench to a desk piled so high that only the white hair on his head was visible. Gayle introduced herself and said, "This is Ron; we're here to pick up his assignment."

The ghost stood up and extended his hand. "Albert Cunningham. I've been waiting to meet you both. Ron, before I give you the file, may I have a word?"

Ron shook his hand and looked at Gayle, then back at the ghost. "Sure, what's on your mind?"

Gayle frowned, tapping her foot but curious. Albert continued. "Needless to say, I know what's in the folder and who you'll be helping. But I could use your help, too. I've been here a little over a year, and I can't seem to get closure."

Ron nodded. "Okay, but I'm just a rookie ghost on probation."

"When you read the file, you'll discover that Mrs. Miller died when she was struck by a vehicle. Both she and the driver died instantly." Albert cleared his throat, blinking.

Ron noticed. "Let me guess. Were you the driver?"

The ghost looked at him and nodded. "Driving to pick up some ice cream, my heart stopped. I lost control of the car. I didn't even know I died. I wound up here, and here I stayed." Albert's broad shoulders sagged. "Please, if you could check on my wife, Rosie. See if she's all right? Of course, the family of the poor woman I killed comes first..."

"But what can I do?" *Geez, I can barely help myself. Maybe that's the point.* Albert looked at him with hopeful eyes, and Ron felt a stirring of something unfamiliar—empathy.

Realizing this role required compassion and understanding—traits he'd often ignored in life—Ron felt a wave of doubt. *What do I know about helping anyone?* Memories of choosing ambition over connection nagged at him.

He looked away, searching for confidence but finding only uncertainty. Hiding behind work had always been easier than facing the vulnerability of real connection. Now, as a ghost, there was no escaping his motives, and the stakes were far higher.

With a resigned sigh, Ron understood. To succeed, he had to confront his past and grow beyond it. This mission wasn't just about helping others—it was about his own redemption.

"I'm sure we could check on her at some point. Right, Gayle? We'll make sure she's okay. But I'm not sure how long our mission will take, Albert."

"I understand. When you see Mr. Miller and his child, you'll only be a few blocks away. I wanted to help that family any way I could." He placed his hands on a stack of folders, representing other cases, other lives. "I've done a fair bit of research on their file. You'll find it's up to date."

Gayle stepped in. "Albert? We would love to help you. I see now this mission has consequences beyond just our training assignment. Right, Ron?"

Ron nodded, mumbling his agreement.

"Thank you both; it means a great deal to me," Albert said.

Reaching across the desk, he handed Ron the folder. "The father, Nick Miller, is the widower. He and his young daughter, Claire, have had difficulty adjusting." He paused, "As have I, since their loss is partly due to my fondness for pistachio."

Ron took the file. "I'm beginning to understand how random dying can be. I'm here partly because of cheese puffs." He looked at Gayle. "Am I ready for this?"

"Not quite, but believe it or not, I have faith in you. The Boss said there's a lot riding on this job, and he knows what he's doing. It'll probably affect more people than we know. So, let's study the case file. I haven't been in the field for a while, and we need a plan."

C H A P T E R

FOUR

She's too young to be so sad for so long. Nick watched his daughter through the kitchen window. *I know how you feel, sweetheart. I just don't know how to fix it.* They lived in a town bordered by the Sierra Bonita Mountains, about ten miles south of Provo. Memories of sledding, ice skating, snow angels, and laughter with his girls now felt like gray shadows of the past. He hadn't even taken the sleds out of the garage this winter. Fourteen months ago, Claire lost her mom, and Nick lost the love of his life.

He couldn't bring himself to do those things anymore. *I can't even take Claire skating without the emptiness overtaking me. It's not fair to my daughter.* He recalled falling on the ice while skating, trying to stand only to be piled on by his girls until they were all in a heap. Ann laughed until tears ran down her cheeks. On the sled, Ann had tickled Claire from behind, causing her to lose control and tumble into the snow. She created fond memories from the simplest moments.

Claire sat in the backyard swing, shuffling her feet in the dirt. Nick joined her, giving her a few pushes, but his mind was elsewhere. He asked about her day at school. She replied, 'fine,' and offered little more. After dinner,

3 5

Claire took her dish to the sink and walked to the couch, unzipping her backpack to find her notebook.

Claire stood in front of him, waiting. Nick looked up from a remodeling bid he was working on. "Can you listen to my spelling words, Daddy?" She handed him the list and recited all ten words correctly.

"Good job, honey," he said, gently squeezing her arm. He knew Claire's mother would have given her a hug and a tickle, but he didn't seem to have it in him. He returned to calculating the bid, which was due tomorrow morning.

After her bath, Nick sat on her bed to say goodnight. *She looks even more like her mother. Her hair is curlier and lighter, but her eyes have lost their sparkle.* A dull pain settled in his chest as he smiled. He brushed his hand over her hair and kissed her head, fragrant with baby shampoo, then turned off the light and left, leaving her door ajar.

Outside her door, Nick heard Claire climb out of bed and kneel on the floor. He peeked in as she clasped her hands together and prayed. "Please God, tell Mommy I miss her, and if you can, please make Daddy feel good again. I don't know how to make him happy anymore. Thank you and goodnight." She crawled back into bed, pulling the covers up to her chin as Nick quietly walked down the hall, his heart aching.

Downstairs, Nick started the dishwasher and wiped down the counters. He turned on the TV and flipped through the channels, not caring which one, just needing a distraction. *It's been too long. Why can't I get past this? I'm letting all of us down.*

His head rested on the armrest as the screen faded to a blur. He relived the day for the umpteenth time. *Such a pointless accident. The man's poor wife sent him to the grocery store. He was dead before he hit Ann. The last time we saw our spouses alive.* Unspoken guilt jabbed at his heart, as usual.

I'll never resolve arguing with her that morning. It was only a weekend. Work could have waited. Damn my pride.

She had been his rock and conscience in balancing husband, father, and provider. Now he felt adrift, merely surviving—paying the bills, saving for someday. No longer a husband, he was lacking as a father.

Ann's eyes had brightened as she planned their mountain getaway, then darkened when his boss called with an urgent job for the weekend. He had to disappoint someone.

Nick's mind drifted, sinking into the armrest. Pictures flashed in his mind, teetering on the edge of sleep.

Surprise kisses. Twirling her around and embracing her. Fresh flowers on the table I made. Conspiring to build Claire's dollhouse in secret; her birthday surprise.

A noise pulled him awake, and for an instant, he saw Ann between him and the television, watching a DIY channel while pressing their clothes. Her hair was in a ponytail, with strays curling on her cheek. She blew them back from the side of her mouth. He could almost touch her cream-colored sweater. Her presence felt so real, yet...

Claire's cries jolted him fully awake. He ran up the stairs to her bedroom. She sat up in bed, hugging her knees and crying. Nick gathered her in his arms, rocking her as he smoothed her hair.

"I want Mommy," she cried.

Nick held her tighter. Containing his tears, he whispered, "So do I, honey, so do I." He rocked her until she fell back asleep and tucked her under the Dora the Explorer blanket. He watched until her breath deepened and her face relaxed. She looked so small and vulnerable. *How long will this go on? My little girl needs me now. And where's God in all this? A little help here?*

Nick lingered, watching her small, peaceful face. The weight of his role as her sole guardian pressed heavily on him. He was practical—always had been—with responsibilities aligned in neat columns of figures and diagrams. But the emotional geometry of single parenthood eluded him. What more could he do to fill the void? Where was the divine whisper of guidance when he needed it most?

He didn't expect answers, but he quietly vowed to be everything Claire needed, despite the deep chasm of their loss.

CHAPTER
FIVE

"**A**ll right, class. Take your seats." Maggie Sanderson settled her second-grade class and smiled. A vibrant twenty-eight-year-old with reddish-brown hair and alert brown eyes, she wore a knee-length chocolate brown flared skirt with an ecru sweater today. A chunky brown necklace accented her outfit. She tried to set a good example for the girls. She loved her job, and life was good. What more could she ask for?

The students took their seats, and she took attendance. Calling Claire Miller's name and hearing no answer, she looked up to find her chair empty. Marking an X after her name, she continued the roll call.

Just as Maggie sat at her desk, the classroom door creaked open. She glanced up as Claire entered the room and quietly hung her coat in the cloakroom. Dressed in pink corduroys and a flowered T-shirt, Claire appeared both sullen and colorful. She walked toward Maggie's desk and handed her a note from Nick that read, 'Claire overslept.'

Throughout the day, Maggie kept an eye on her. Soft-spoken but attentive, Claire sat with her head down, silent and withdrawn. That troubled Maggie. She knew Claire's history and had watched her steady progress throughout the school year, often engaging in class and playing with two other girls at recess. But not recently.

Before class was dismissed for the day, she gave Claire a note for her father, wanting to schedule a parent-teacher conference.

After school, Maggie drove to her childhood home, where she'd lived with her mother, Jenny, for several years. When her father, Tom, died, she moved back in, sharing their mutual grief and settling affairs. Even while Tom was sick, he would call Maggie, asking her to invite her mother for a day trip hiking, horseback riding, or water skiing. He knew how much Jenny loved the outdoors and didn't want her stuck at home all the time.

Maggie recalled a particular hike they took with friends near Maple Lake, a few months after her father's passing. She remembered Jenny photographing birds, flowers, and random compositions that caught her eye. Maggie watched her mother, pleased that Jenny had agreed to step out of her house-bound grief for a walk in the forest. She turned as Jenny gasped excitedly, whispering as she set up a rare shot of a horned owl in the dappled light. Maggie saw the danger and screamed as Jenny stepped too close to the edge of the trail, lost her balance, and tumbled forty feet down the side. Rocks and fallen trees slowed her descent, but the fall shattered her legs and pelvic bones in several places. Maggie's mother lay unconscious, with internal injuries and a severe concussion.

Horrified, Maggie and their friends scrambled down the hill to keep her comfortable as they waited for Search and Rescue. Jenny regained consciousness several times, murmuring about her dear Tom.

When stabilized, she befriended the team that hoisted her out of the gully, laughing and joking through a haze of heavy-duty pain meds. Weeks in the hospital and months of physical therapy helped her regain a limited amount of strength and balance. But her hips were badly damaged, and she could only stand for short periods. Maggie watched her mother challenge her trauma and recovery as she did any other endeavor—with stubborn optimism.

She installed an electric lift on her SUV for the wheelchair so she could take Jenny to enjoy the local outdoors, like watching hot air balloons or having simple picnics in the mountains.

Opening the door, Maggie called out, "Lucy, I'm home!" That was a joke between them. She tossed her keys on the hall table. The aromas wafting into the foyer teased of something baked and delicious. She stepped into the well-used and accessible kitchen, where her mother rolled to the oven, checking the roast. Two pies cooled on racks.

"Hello, dear. Fabulous day?" Jenny Sanderson, a vibrant woman in her mid-fifties, greeted her daughter with a bright smile and a pat on Maggie's waist. Flour dusted her short brown hair, and her dark eyes crinkled when she smiled. In charcoal slacks and a red blouse, Maggie chuckled at the skunk slippers on her feet.

Leaning over to kiss her cheek, Maggie said, "Better now. I'm starving. Skunks today? What's the occasion?"

"It started out as a stinky day because my toothbrush batteries died. It was horrible, Maggie. But maybe tomorrow it'll be ducks."

Her limited mobility never dampened her outlook on life. She often wore earrings and a necklace around the house, sometimes even lipstick. "The chair just saves wear and tear on my shoes. Think of the money I'm saving," she once said. Maggie loved her company and spent as much time with her as possible.

As Maggie washed her hands and peeled potatoes, she told Jenny about Claire. "I don't know, Mom; it tears me up to see her so sad. She lost her mom over a year ago, but I thought she had healed more. It must still be hard on her."

"Poor darling, so young to lose her mother," Jenny replied. Maggie rinsed and quartered the potatoes, tossing them into a pot of salted water before turning on the gas.

"Well, don't get in *too* deep. You know how you are. You sometimes go overboard. Maybe she just needs more time to heal."

"What do you mean, 'overboard'?" Her voice rose an octave. "Just because I take an interest in my students ..."

"No need to get huffy, dear. I'm just stating the facts."

Maggie softened her tone. "I guess it is getting to me. I want to help her."

"I know. Just chill."

Maggie raised an eyebrow. "Listen to you, 'chill.' Where do you pick up this slang? Have you been watching kid's shows again?" She wiped the cutting board and selected a wooden salad bowl. "What would I do without you, Mom?"

"Go out on dates, maybe? Find a nice young man to, you know, chill with?"

"Don't start." She smiled, pretending to check the potatoes.

"I don't need a babysitter, dear. I do just fine rocking and rolling my way around."

"I know, Mom. I just like staying home with you, and I have papers to grade and lesson plans to make ..."

"And hiding in the house? Whatever happened to that Daniel fellow? He seemed nice. How did you scare him off?"

"I did not scare him off." She turned and sighed, holding a tomato. "We just sort of fizzled out. We didn't have much in common."

"Have you heard that opposites attract?" Jenny grinned.

"Do they, now? Okay, Mom. I'll make a salad."

"Did Daniel like salad?"

"Mom!" Both laughed as Maggie opened the refrigerator door and found fresh spinach and a red bell pepper.

They finished preparing the meal and ate at the kitchen table. During dinner, Maggie spoke more about her students.

"It's wonderful how you care for the children, sweetheart. I know their welfare is your prime concern," Jenny said.

"It is. Now tell me what you did today. Did you hang out in the backyard?"

"Of course! I love to listen to the birds and bugs. I take my Kindle to read, but I forget when I'm with all God's creatures."

"I admire you, Mom. After what life has thrown at you, you still enjoy the pleasures of nature."

"Why wouldn't I? Nature didn't throw me off that trail; I wasn't careful and paid the price." Jenny's eyes grew distant for a moment before she shook it off with a soft laugh. "Oh, I even ventured to the front door and talked to Henry, the mailman. The tales he tells about his route! He made me laugh about a ferocious dog that threatened him. I asked what kind of dog it was. He said, 'A Taco Bell dog.' Can you imagine? A cute little Chihuahua? I guess they can be snippy. One of those pies is for him and his family."

Later that evening, Jenny and Maggie sat in their parlor enjoying berry pie with tea. Maggie related how a student asked her, "What do you get if you're kissed by a bird?" She tucked her feet under her on the loveseat, grateful for their gentle companionship.

"I said, 'I don't know, what do you get if you're kissed by a bird?' And he said, 'A peck on the cheek.' Then he hugged my neck and kissed me on the cheek. I almost cried; it was so cute."

"You'll make a great mother one day, dear." She added in a stage whisper, "Hopefully sooner rather than later."

Standing, Maggie passed by her mother and kissed her cheek. "Good night, *Mother*."

"Humph." Jenny sighed.

CHAPTER
SIX

The school bus dropped Claire off in front of her house at 3:00 p.m., with Nick due home from work by 3:30. She waved at the bus driver, who always waited for her to enter the house before continuing his route. Her dad didn't like leaving her alone, even for half an hour, but he trusted her to lock the door after going inside.

She reached for the key in her backpack, easily finding it on a chain with a little plastic Elsa from one of her favorite movies. She unlocked the door, stepped inside, and locked it behind her. After placing the key back in the special compartment of her bag, she took off her jacket, hung it carefully on the back of her chair, and began her homework. Daddy didn't allow TV until after dinner.

Halfway through a page of arithmetic, she daydreamed. *The house is always quiet now. Mommy used to have cookies ready for me when I came home. Her smile was so pretty. Even the little lines around her eyes were lovely. I wonder if she still smiles that way now that she's in Heaven.* She sighed and finished the remaining problems just as she heard the key in the door.

Nick walked in and tossed his keys into the dish by the front door—he sometimes misplaces them. "Hi," he said, watching her for a moment before placing his hand on her shoulder as he walked by to hang up his jacket.

"Hi." Claire barely looked up from her homework, hoping for something more—a hug, maybe a kiss. Mommy always greeted her that way. *Why doesn't Daddy kiss me hello?* Then she remembered the note. "Daddy, Miss Sanderson wrote you a note."

"Why would your teacher send me a note? Did you turn in your homework? Did something happen in class today?" His tone was sharp as he rubbed his forehead.

"No, sir." She replied, her voice small as she reached into her backpack and handed him the note without meeting his gaze.

Nick unfolded the note and read it silently, frowning. "Well, something must have happened." He sighed, frustration evident. "I'll have to meet with her. It's hard for me to take off work right now. It'll have to wait."

"But Daddy ..."

"Claire, I need to make arrangements to meet her after work. You'll have to stay after school that day."

Claire noticed he wasn't too upset as he looked down and lowered his voice. "I'm sorry, honey girl. I didn't mean to be cross with you." He sat at the table across from her, taking her hand. "Claire, I'm very busy at work." She nodded. "I'll plan to see Miss..."

"Sanderson."

"Sanderson," he repeated. "Do you know why she wants to see me?"

"No, I gave her your note right away, and I behaved during school, honest."

"I believe you, sweetie. We'll see what she wants. Don't worry. After I check your homework, we'll start dinner, okay?"

With a tentative smile, she replied, "Okay, Daddy."

CHAPTER
SEVEN

Nick sat at his desk, reviewing the bottlenecks that slowed his current project. The paperwork and revisions demanded all his attention today, and he'd need to take it home again. He pinched the bridge of his nose, longing to be in the shop, where commercial woodworking equipment sprawled over three thousand square feet—a space he preferred over the office.

The office always felt stifling. While he kept things professional with the women who worked there, he sensed their glances lingering on him when they thought he wasn't looking. At least, that's what he suspected whenever their conversations quieted as he passed. He brushed the thought aside, focusing on the phone as he dialed Claire's school.

Later that evening, Nick struggled with his work at the dining table, the familiar weight of his responsibilities pressing down on him. His phone buzzed, pulling him from the page. Maggie introduced herself briskly when he answered, her tone professional yet warm.

After a terse exchange, they agreed to meet the next day at 3:30. "I'll arrange for Claire to stay in the activity room," Maggie said.

Nick barely heard her next words, too focused on the stack of paperwork awaiting him. Still, he managed a polite response before hanging up.

-»※«-

The next afternoon, Nick showed his ID, and after affixing the visitor's pass to his shirt, proceeded down the hall to locate Claire's classroom. He tapped on the doorjamb and entered; Maggie stood behind her desk and reached out her hand.

"Good afternoon, Mr. Miller. Thank you for coming. Please have a seat." She gestured toward the small chairs in the front row.

He raised an eyebrow at the tiny seats, shook her hand, and remained standing, feeling uncomfortable. "May I ask what Claire has done?"

Maggie sat across from him, her posture straight and hands folded on the desk. She studied him for a moment before speaking.

With a grimace, he finally folded himself into a chair, stretching his legs into the aisle. "Why else would you want to see me?"

"Mr. Miller, I think you may have gotten the wrong idea. Claire hasn't done anything wrong, but I am concerned about her."

"If she hasn't done anything wrong, why are you so concerned? Isn't that my job?" A gauge in his head signaled his rising anger.

"Of course, but she spends much of her day with me. As her teacher, part of my responsibility is to notice changes in my students' behavior. That's why I wanted to speak with you."

"To evaluate my parenting skills?" He squirmed in the child-sized chair. *Don't try to push me around, lady.*

She paused, and Nick tensed, assuming she was about to criticize him. *She must think I'm being defensive. But she doesn't know how hard I work. Don't I get any credit for that?*

"First, let me express my condolences about the loss of your wife," Maggie began, her voice gentle yet direct. "I can only imagine how difficult this must be for both of you. I realize there is no timetable for healing or grief, but I have observed Claire throughout the school year. Lately, she has become more withdrawn and doesn't participate in class. Has something changed at home?" She fixed her calm gaze on him.

Worry and guilt hit him simultaneously. He clenched his teeth as her words struck a nerve, sending a current to his temples. He couldn't admit that he felt lost in how to help her. If he acknowledged his weakness, he might dissolve into a blubbering mess. Instead, like a cornered animal, he growled, "My daughter lost her mother. Are you saying she should be over it by now?"

"No, of course not. Please, I'm trying to help. Have you noticed any behavioral changes? Can you explain why she overslept the other night?"

Nick rubbed his face, her voice barely breaking through the buzzing in his ears. "She had a nightmare and couldn't fall back to sleep." *Neither did I— and I still have three hours of work to do.*

"I see. Mr. Miller, did Claire receive any professional counseling after your wife died?"

"No. She didn't need it then, and I don't believe she needs it now. We'll handle it together." *That's it. I'm not going to sit here and be interrogated.* He attempted to rise from the tiny chair with the ease and grace of a man in control but struggled. Scowling, he got to his feet.

"Mr. Miller, it's my job to observe and report when a child may be in crisis. Frankly, your demeanor raises some concern."

Heat rushed to his neck, his head pounding. "This meeting is over."

Maggie stood as well. "Please, I only want what's best for Claire."

"So do I," he barked, walking out and forgetting to turn in his pass at the school office.

Nick got in his car and slammed the door, fuming. *Who does she think she is? She probably doesn't even have kids of her own.* His hands tightened around the steering wheel. Then it hit him... Claire! After his outburst, he'd forgotten to pick her up. *Way to go, Miller. You're in the running for father-of-the-year now.* He rushed back into the school, slamming the car door behind him. Maggie stood outside her classroom, tight-lipped, keys in hand.

Great. Now she thinks I'm a flake, too. Or worse. He couldn't meet her eyes. "Where is Claire?"

Maggie turned without a word and walked down the hall. He followed her into another classroom where several giggling children played checkers, worked puzzles, colored in books, and laughed, like kids should. Claire sat by herself, solemnly watching the others. It shocked him. She looked so alone, so... forlorn.

Nick's heart sank. *Could she be that lonely? She never brought friends to the house anymore. I guess that's my fault, too. Ann used to handle that, calling the other parents, setting up playdates, having juice and cookies ready. Another thing I've messed up.*

Nick stood next to Claire as she watched the other children, seemingly wanting to join the fun but remaining still. He touched her shoulder, and she looked up with a small smile. Gathering her backpack, she started for the door.

Maggie observed them with narrowed eyes. Claire glanced at her, then down at the floor. Nick wondered if Claire's teacher was right. *This is a crisis.* He also felt a chill wash over him, like a bucket of ice water, in the stuffy classroom.

CHAPTER
EIGHT

Gayle grabbed Ron's arm just before he floated straight through Nick. "Watch it, Wrong Way. You almost blew your cover."

Ron muttered, waving his arms to stabilize himself near the ceiling. "Just because I've had to correct a few turns doesn't mean I deserve that name." Feigning confidence, he added, "A pilot's flight path requires constant adjustment. It's never a straight line from A to B. And I never caused an accident on the job..."

"Easy, Fella," Gayle interrupted, her voice calm but firm. "Let's just stay on our toes and get down to business. The kid looks like she really needs a friend. Can you handle that?"

"Sure. I can handle that." After a moment, he asked, "How do I handle that? I haven't been around many kids, and the ones I met, I didn't care for much."

Gayle sighed. "Right." They floated out of the classroom. "First, observe. Try to understand how she feels. Use what you learn to comfort her and help her feel less alone. But for Heaven's sake, don't scare her."

"Okay." *Understand. Comfort. Don't scare. I have no idea what to do.* "What will you be working on?"

"The adults are going to be a problem, especially Nick. He's in bad shape, and I think the teacher can help him see that. But they don't like each other much right now." The ghosts watched as Maggie crossed her arms while Claire hurried to keep up with Nick's long strides.

"That's the job, Ron. It will amaze you if you keep your head in the game. Ready, Freddy?"

"Not at all, Coach."

"Oh, knock it off." She giggled, circling him in the air.

"I've never been the comforting type, Gayle. You know my history—I'm not exactly Mr. Empathy."

"No, but you have heart in there, somewhere beneath all that bravado. You need to listen to her. Really listen. Grief doesn't require solving, Ron. It needs understanding—and sometimes, just company."

"Well, I'm here, anyway. That counts for something, right?

"More than you realize. Human emotions may weave a tangled web, but the threads are strong. They connect us, holding people together even when they're unraveling. We'll get there, step by step."

"Even if I need a course correction?"

"We'll keep you on course." Gayle laughed. "After all, it's the journey, not the destination, that teaches us the most."

They flew alongside Nick's car as he drove home. Twice, the wind knocked Ron off his flight path, and Gayle flanked him to help guide him back. *So, that's what she meant,* he thought.

Ron concentrated on maintaining his steadiness, despite the occasional gusts throwing him off balance. He found it ironic—he had learned so much about flight in life but had been too afraid to actually try flying. *Funny, the things you think about after you die. Earth was easy compared to this.*

Nick and Claire entered the house, each falling into their routines. At the kitchen table, Claire arranged her books. Her binder slipped off the table and fell to the floor. Bending to retrieve it, she lifted her gaze and noticed something on the ceiling. Clouds and shadows swirled in the air, then shaped into figures. One resembled a blonde lady in a long white gown, though she appeared slightly blurry; the other was a man in regular clothes, like her dad wore on weekends.

Not at all afraid, she smiled and mouthed 'hello.' She had always imagined things vividly in her mind. When she felt hungry and thought about hamburgers, they looked so delicious that her hunger intensified.

But this was different; it wasn't like drawing a picture or reading a story and envisioning castles, beanstalks, and princesses. She stole another glance to confirm they were still there—and they were. The man started to fall, waving his arms around with wide eyes. Claire giggled at the sight but quickly covered her mouth to stifle her laughter.

"I can see you!" she whispered. Claire followed Ron with her eyes, her happy smile brightening the room. The man almost dropped to the floor, but the blurry lady blew a puff of air to keep him steady. She heard him ask the lady, "Is that supposed to happen?"

Claire looked up at them, put her finger to her lips, and pretended to zip her mouth shut. Throughout homework and dinner, she watched them closely. She didn't let on to Nick but waved at them when he wasn't looking, wiggling in her chair, itching to know why they were in her house.

Finally, after her bath, Nick kissed Claire goodnight and went downstairs. She lay still in her bed, wondering where her new friends were. They must be friends because she could see them, they could fly, and they seemed very friendly.

Not feeling sleepy, Claire knelt next to her bed. "God bless Mommy in Heaven, and bless Daddy. Sorry I didn't tell him about the people floating around the living room. Oh, and God? Please bless my teacher, the other kids in my class, and the man on my ceiling. Thank you and goodnight." She crawled back under the blankets, snuggling deeper. "Hello."

Ron directed his landing to the lower left corner of the bed. "Hi," he said.

Her eyes widened, and she smiled through gapped teeth. "Are you a ghost?"

"Yes, I am. Um, don't be afraid. I'm a good ghost. I won't try to scare you or anything."

She laughed lightly. "You're not very scary, so I'm not afraid. Why are you and that lady following Daddy and me? Is she a ghost too? I can see her kinda blurry but can't hear her."

"Yes, she's a ghost too. I'm glad you can see and hear me. You must be a lucky girl, Claire. This is only my first assignment, but I don't think many people can talk to ghosts."

"I'm not very lucky," she said. "My mommy died and went to live in Heaven as an angel. But I can't see her."

Claire thought Ron looked like Daddy did when he was deep in thought.

"I'm sure your mommy is happy in Heaven," Ron said gently. "She probably has a good job and is watching over you and your daddy every day, wanting you to be happy, too. That's kind of why I'm here."

Claire sat up in bed with a start. "You know my mommy?"

Ron hesitated. "No," he admitted, "but I know she wouldn't want you to be sad. That makes her sad, too."

Claire fell back onto her pillow. "She was hardly ever sad when we all lived together. She laughed all the time. But once, she cried when she broke a dish."

"If she cried over a broken dish, how do you think she feels when she sees you so sad?"

"I don't know." She smoothed her blanket.

"Think about it." He smiled a little.

After a moment, she said, "I guess it makes her sad, too."

"That's right, and we don't want her to be sad, do we?"

"No. But I don't know how to make her happy," Claire said, her eyes downcast.

"I think she will be happy if you're happy. I'm supposed to help, too. But I have a problem."

She looked up, curious. "What?"

"I wasn't very cheerful when I was alive, so I don't know many jokes or anything. But I'll try. Would that be okay?"

"I guess so, especially if it would please Mommy."

"Great. I think it would be good for your dad, too. Now, get some sleep, and I'll see you tomorrow. We can both work on being happy."

Claire settled on her pillow, pulling the blanket up to her chin. "How long will you stay here?"

"I don't know yet. But, um, hang in there. Goodnight, Claire."

"Goodnight ... you know my name. What's yours?"

"It's Ron. You can call me Ron."

"Goodnight, Ron."

After Claire fell asleep, Ron hovered near the top of the stairs, thinking, *What a beautiful child. I hope I can help her.* Hazy memories of that age came to him, and he quickly pushed them aside. They weren't happy thoughts, and he needed to be happy. Without wondering if he could, he tried floating through the bathroom door. This time, he succeeded.

He imagined his life and what might have been: love, family. But he had never experienced those, only the dull routine of solitude and a jaded distrust of an imperfect world. *With so few friends and lovers*, he thought... *Hey, snap out of it! This isn't about you; just listen and try to make her feel better. You can do it.*

Downstairs, Nick turned on the TV out of habit, replaying the day's events in his mind. Claire's teacher's words still gnawed at him. *She was persistent and held her ground better than I did. I hate to admit it, but she might see things I've missed. Work has kept me busy... too busy. Oh, stop it. I've been wallowing in my own pity party.*

He exhaled sharply, frustration bubbling up. *But damn it, Claire's hair is always brushed, her clothes are clean, I feed her, and I help her with her homework. Doesn't that count for something?*

He got up to check the thermostat. A draft in the house gave him pause; the day had been mild. The thermostat setting at 72 should have been warm enough, so he left it but pulled a sweater from the closet, recalling the sudden chill at Claire's school.

The slate gray cable-knit sweater, one of several holiday gifts from Ann, brought back a flood of memories. She loved him in sweaters, even though he never particularly liked wearing them, except with her. This was the last present she had given him before she died. He remembered cuddling on the couch with her, watching TV or just talking. He wouldn't admit it, but he felt warm, safe, and even loved when he wore it. A man wasn't supposed to get all gooey inside, but the sweater helped. He was meant to be strong and responsible, yet also supportive and attentive, and he didn't feel like he was doing a very good job.

His thoughts slowed and softened, stored for later reflection, as his body relaxed from the stresses of the day, and he fell asleep on the sofa.

-»※«-

Ron joined Gayle at the top of the stairs. "How's Nick?" he asked.

"He's hurting, but he has to push through this—for himself and his daughter."

"I think I made some progress with Claire," he said.

"Oh, good," she said, concealing that she had overheard the conversation between the girl and the ghost. *Not too bad, Ron. A little rough around the edges, but we kind of expected that. Stay the course, Casper. You might do okay.*

With hours to kill while their charges slept, they decided to scout the area separately. Before she left, Gayle hovered over Nick, thinking, *Gird your loins, mister. You're in for the ride of your life.*

CHAPTER
NINE

In the Sandersons' parlor, wood trim and a 100-year-old walnut credenza rescued from a yard sale glowed with the subtle aroma of lemon oil. Maggie and Jenny sat in matching burgundy club chairs, discussing death, while the empty wheelchair beside Jenny lent an eerie symbolism to the conversation.

"It took us both a while to come to terms with your father's death, and we were able to comfort each other. Claire's father can't cry on her shoulder; he has to show strength by holding in his emotions."

"You're right, Mom. But we sure got off on the wrong foot today. He's not an easy person to talk to." She frowned, dipping a strawberry into freshly whipped cream.

Jenny wiped figurines and replied with a knowing grin. "Remember, a lot of men have only a few emotions at their disposal: happy, sad, mad, hungry, and... uh, frisky. And stubborn, of course, if that counts as an emotion."

Maggie burst out laughing, covering her mouthful of strawberry. "Close enough. Frisky, huh?" She sighed. "But what about Claire? If she withdraws any more, it'll be even harder to reach her."

"How did he respond when you asked him about counseling for the girl?"

"He practically bit my head off. He flat-out refused, saying they'll 'handle it together.'" She made air quotes with her fingers. "The jerk doesn't see that it's not weak for him to talk to someone. Ugh, he was no fun to talk to." She reached for another berry.

"Jerk, huh? Well, you gave it your best shot, dear." She replaced a figurine on the side table.

"Oh, no, I'm not giving up yet. I don't care how mad he gets. Claire needs help, and I'm going to make sure she gets it."

Jenny asked, "What does Mr. Miller look like?"

"These are delicious, Mom." She swallowed. "What does that matter?"

"I don't know. Just curious."

"He's kinda tall with dark hair. I remember that. He has a little scar on his eyebrow. I enjoyed watching him sit on a kid's chair." She looked up with a grin.

"Hmm." Jenny innocently raised her eyebrows.

"What's 'hmm' supposed to mean?" Maggie tilted her head, squinting.

"Nothing, dear." She shrugged. "Nothing at all."

Days passed, and Maggie noticed a shift in Claire's behavior. She would catch her smiling and talking to herself. At first, Maggie thought the girl seemed happier, but the whispering and mumbling unsettled her. *Maybe she's created an imaginary friend,* Maggie thought. *An only child might need someone to play with or confide in. But this...this borders on fantasy.* Even more concerning was the question: *What is she trying to escape from?*

Ron floated above Claire's desk, hovering indecisively before plopping down as if he were exhausted. Claire smothered a giggle behind her hand, glancing at the teacher before whispering, "You're funny. You're all grown up, and you still do silly things."

Ron grinned and leaned forward. "Pay attention to your teacher, Claire. It's important that you learn. I know you're smart, but there's always more to learn."

"Okay," she whispered back.

Over the next few days, Maggie kept a closer eye on Claire. The girl's mood seemed to brighten—she smiled more and even laughed. But she still talked to herself, fully engaged with someone or something only she could see. One afternoon at recess, Maggie saw her sitting alone, chattering away and gesturing animatedly, as if having a lively conversation. Maggie frowned, the sight gnawing at her. *Okay, now I'm more than concerned. Looks like I'll have to consult her charming father again. Swell.*

CHAPTER
TEN

omething's not right. Nick noticed Claire in conversation with someone he couldn't see, but he didn't know what, if anything, he should do about it. Then there was the problem of the cold—certain spots in the house felt drafty, though they'd never had issues before. He checked the weatherstripping and the windows. Nothing. Even at work, he felt phantom breezes, as if something unseen brushed past. *No wonder I've been so edgy. What the hell's going on?*

Gayle nudged Ron with a surge of ghost energy. "First, we need to get him to pay attention to his surroundings. He's stepping out of his comfort zone, which is a good sign. We're going to see some action soon." She puffed a cool breath toward Nick as a reminder.

The house phone rang. Nick sprang off the sofa. "Hello?" He half-expected ominous static and a shadow in the window. He held the phone to his shoulder, his hand resting on his chilly neck.

"It's Maggie Sanderson. Sorry to disturb you at home, Mr. Miller, but I think we should have another meeting."

He didn't argue. "When?"

"Is tomorrow after school convenient? Same arrangements for Claire?"

"I'll be there. Thanks." He hung up.

At Maggie's house, she slowly replaced the handset in its cradle and turned to her mother, who was reading her Kindle at the kitchen table. "Well, that's a switch. He sounded concerned."

Without looking up, Jenny muttered, "Who's concerned, dear? Make it snappy. I think I've discovered the killer."

Maggie smirked, but Jenny remained focused on her novel. "Mr. Miller and I have another meeting tomorrow."

Jenny finally glanced up. "Are you still badgering the poor man?"

"I'm not badgering. He seemed a little tense, though. Maybe he's coming to grips with Claire's problem." Maggie watched her mother's eyes return to her book, scanning rapidly.

"Coming to grips, yes." Jenny mumbled, then gasped, "Oh no, it can't be. Not her!"

Maggie chuckled. "I'll leave you to your story, Mom."

"Mmm, hmm."

⸻ ❋ ⸻

The following afternoon, Nick signed in for a visitor's pass and walked down the hall to Maggie's classroom, passing colorful artwork and smiling faces in the class photos. He adjusted the neatly cuffed sleeves of his blue oxford shirt and loosened the tie he'd worn to meet a client earlier. At the door, he knocked lightly on the frame.

"Come in."

Maggie sat behind her desk in a light pink sweater, which he complimented, and she returned the gesture with a nod toward his shirt. He settled into a small desk chair in the front row.

She smiled in amusement and got to the point. "Mr. Miller, have you noticed any changes in Claire lately?"

Nick hesitated. "Like what?"

You're not getting off the hook that easily, pal. She said, "Anything unusual?"

"She seems more relaxed, even a little happier," he said. "We're working through it."

Yeah, right. "Have you noticed anything else?"

Maggie thought she saw him shiver as he adjusted his collar. "She, uh, she's been talking to herself."

Now we're getting somewhere. "Does she do that often?"

"I walked past her room a couple of times, and she was having quite a conversation."

"Mr. Miller, I've seen it too, here at school. I think Claire may have an imaginary friend. That's not uncommon for an only child; it can serve as a playmate or someone with whom she can relate."

"Is that a bad thing?"

"Not really; it's usually just a phase at her age. But it could indicate something else."

He sat quietly, waiting.

She took a breath. "A child might withdraw from reality after experiencing trauma or ongoing stress they can't process. We know about the trauma of losing her mother. Is it possible that something has triggered her recent behavior?"

He shifted in his chair, his eyes flaring before settling on the desktop. He sighed, his turmoil etched on his face.

"Maybe she's lonely and doesn't feel like she can talk to me. I've done my best to ensure she's clean, well-fed, and does her homework." He stood, clearly uncomfortable sitting any longer.

She began to rise, but he gestured for her to stay seated. "Please, I'm not leaving in a huff. She doesn't have her friends over like she did when my wife was alive, and my work has made playdates difficult. Maybe that's it." He flicked a glance at her.

Moved but not fully convinced, she took a different approach. "Has she mentioned the school picnic?"

"No, when is that?"

"The school holds one at this time of year. It's this Saturday, starting around eleven and lasting most of the day. Some of her friends might be there." She handed him a flyer.

"I wonder why she didn't tell me?"

"Maybe it slipped her mind," Maggie said, thinking, *or maybe she doesn't want to go.*

"I'll clear my schedule that day. I'll talk to her and see if she wants to go."

She stood. Nick brushed off his slacks and started for the door. He hesitated, looking back at her. "Thanks. I'm not always a monster, you know."

Maggie smiled, caught off guard by the comment. "I hope we see you at the picnic."

As Nick left, she reflected on the moment, her gaze drifting to the child-sized desk chairs. *Maybe I should scrounge a grown-up chair for my desk,* she mused. *Nah.*

C H A P T E R

ELEVEN

On the way to the school soccer field, Nick and Claire stopped at KFC to order their favorites—his crispy, hers original. After paying for the food, Nick answered a call from work.

Bright and sunny, Claire thought it was a perfect day for a picnic. She leaned out the window and whispered to Ron, "Are you going with us?"

He hovered just outside. "Wouldn't miss it for the world. Are you excited?"

"I'm happy you're coming. You're my best friend."

Ron hesitated. "Thank you, Claire. But you should still have other friends your age—real ones you can play games with."

"I play games with you."

"Ah, but we can't jump rope or play catch, can we?"

"No," she giggled quietly. "The ball goes right through you. And it looks silly."

Her dad ended his call. "Becky and her family always come. She used to be my best friend, too. Maybe I'll see her."

"I hope so, sweet pea." Nick patted her hand as Ron smiled and flew away.

Ron and Gayle drifted between groups of people, visible only to Claire. "Did you hear that, Gayle? She said I'm her best friend. I don't know what to do with that," Ron said.

"It's a new one for me, too. You should—" Gayle paused, "You should do what you think is right for the mission. Try not to dispense too much of your questionable wisdom." She grinned. "I'm going to see what I can do with the adults."

Ron tilted his head and hovered close. "Hey, did you just tell me to do what I think is right? Okay!" He puffed up a little. "I'll catch up with you later."

When they arrived, Claire saw families setting up their lunches on the soccer field. A softball game was in progress on an adjoining diamond. The crack of the bat and cheers from parents drifted across the field. Booths were set up for games: darts and balloons, milk cans, a ball toss, even a dunking booth. Kids ran and laughed, carrying balloons and eating cotton candy.

On the grass, Frisbees flew, kites soared, and dogs tugged at their leashes, eager to join the fun. Claire scanned the field but didn't see Becky. Her shoulders slumped slightly, but she kept her disappointment to herself.

Claire watched Gayle fly left and Ron fly to the right, right through Vice Principal Haney, who hunched his shoulders and shivered, glancing around for the source of his chill.

Claire laughed.

Nick looked around. "What's so funny?"

"R—Oh, nobody, Daddy. I'm just glad we're here." Her eyes drooped for a moment. *I wish I could tell him.*

Nick didn't press. "I'm glad you're glad. Where do you want to start?"

"Games!" She hopped in place. "And I want to find Becky and Miss Sanderson."

They spread the blanket on the grass and ate, making father-daughter small talk until Claire asked, "Can we go now?"

"Sure." They tossed the remnants of their lunch in a nearby trash can and walked toward the booths. Nick's eyes widened as a large, excited labrador barreled toward Claire, chasing a wayward frisbee. Nick grabbed her by the waist, lifted her in the air, twirled her around, and set her, wide-eyed, on his shoulders. The dog rushed by, oblivious to the chaos it left in its wake. Claire peered over his head.

"Are you okay?" Nick asked.

"Yes, Daddy. Wow, you're like a superhero!" She raised her arms, feeling taller than everyone else.

Nick chuckled. "As long as you're alright." He set her back on the ground.

"I am, Daddy. Thank you."

Claire looked up at her dad and took his hand. *I know Daddy would protect me from anything. He's my hero.* A warm glow filled her chest.

From above, Gayle observed Claire and Nick and glanced at Ron. "Maybe you are doing something right after all. She looks happy."

"That was her dad's doing, but I'm trying."

"Well, look at you. Giving someone else credit." She teased him with a smile.

"Yeah, yeah," he grumbled.

Claire watched the two ghosts swoop toward Maggie's booth. Ron tried to impress her by doing somersaults in the air but failed miserably, careening through a cotton candy machine. He emerged tinted pink, and Claire barely held in a laugh.

"Hi, Miss Sanderson," Claire smiled.

"Hello, Claire. Having fun?"

"Yes," she bounced on her toes. "We had KFC for lunch on a blanket, just like a picnic, and now we're walking around. But you know what?"

Maggie smiled. "No, what?"

"Daddy rescued me from a dog, and he made me fly—just like, um, just like an angel!"

"Is that so?" Maggie smiled.

"Yeah, he's my superhero."

Maggie looked at Nick, eyes twinkling. "It must be nice to have a superhero dad."

Nick's face flushed. Shrugging, he grinned.

Claire piped up. "What are you guys doing?"

"My mom and I are in charge of making buttons. Would you or your dad like one?" she asked, glancing at Nick.

"Hi," he said. "Sure, you can make her a button. I'll pay for it. Right?" He cleared his throat.

"You bet you'll pay for it. It's for a good cause." Jenny smiled, rolling over to Nick.

"Hello." Stretching her arm over the folding table, she shook Nick's hand.

"I'm Jenny Sanderson, Maggie's mother. It's so nice to meet you." Looking at Claire, she extended her hand. "You must be Claire. How do you do, young lady?"

"Fine, thank you. Are you helping Miss Sanderson?"

"I sure am, but we need all the help we can get. Would you like to help, too?"

Claire smiled and looked up at Nick. "Can I, Daddy?"

"If it's okay with Miss Sanderson and her mom, I guess it's okay with me."

Ron hovered over the neighboring booth, still pink, with threads of cotton candy drifting in the light breeze. He gave Claire a thumbs up and said, 'Go for it!'

In her enthusiasm, she blurted, "I will! Watch me!" and joined Jenny in the booth.

Jenny let it pass, showing Claire the machine and how to assemble the buttons. "What would you like on your button, Claire?"

"I don't know." She bit her lip, worried she might have messed up. She kept her eyes on the buttons.

Jenny smiled warmly. "Think about what makes you happy."

Claire's face lit up. "My friend!" She clapped her hands and pointed but stopped when she saw Maggie and Nick look at each other, confused.

"Who's your friend, dear?" Jenny asked. "Is it a friend from school?" She glanced at Maggie, who shrugged.

"No," Claire murmured, feeling sad and afraid the adults wouldn't believe her and would think she was a weirdo. Her dad and her teacher moved closer, and she felt like everyone was looking at her.

Claire spun around, searching for Ron. She didn't know what to say, and she didn't want to lie. Ron darted around them and spotted a dog trotting by their booth with a ball in its mouth. Claire watched him swoop closer, trying to guide the dog into their midst.

Ron stuck out his tongue and copied the dog, panting and sniffing. Then he patted it on the nose and meowed like a cat. The dog dropped the ball, cocked its head in confusion, and then followed the ball that Ron rolled toward Nick and Maggie with a puff of air. Ron stood up and did a little dance, which the dog mimicked by rearing up on its hind legs, barking, and then trotting off with the ball.

Claire pressed her lips together, trying not to laugh, but when Ron started flapping his arms and hovering like a frantic bird over the button-making table, she couldn't hold it in. Laughter bubbled out of her, unstoppable.

Gayle joined Ron in the air, but he kept flapping while she wagged her finger at him. They came to rest just above Maggie's head, perched cross-legged like genies on a magic carpet. Claire laughed so hard she couldn't catch her breath. She pointed over Maggie's head, tears streaming down her face, and sat on the grass, picking up fallen buttons.

Nick, Maggie, and Jenny stared at her for a moment. Then Nick ducked into the booth and crouched next to Claire. "Can you let us in on the joke?" He touched her arm. She settled into a few giggles.

"It's like she had some kind of fit," Nick said to no one in particular.

Jenny said, "The girl's just having a good laugh, maybe at our expense, but she's alright." But Claire thought she looked different. Maggie crouched next to Nick and quietly asked, "Claire?"

Catching her breath, Claire hiccupped. She calmed down and looked up at her teacher. "Yes, Miss Sanderson?"

"I'm glad you're having such a good time. I didn't think the buttons were that funny, though. Can you tell us so we can laugh, too?"

"I can't."

Nick opened his mouth, but Maggie shook her head and continued. "Why can't you, sweetheart? Is it a secret?"

"Kinda." Claire couldn't look at the grownups and kept her eyes on the ground.

Maggie continued, "Well, if it's a secret, then we'll understand if you can't tell us."

Nick said, "I didn't think we had secrets between us, Claire."

Claire realized she had become the center of attention. "I didn't do anything wrong, Daddy." Looking at Nick and Miss Sanderson, she sighed. "Am I in trouble?"

"No, honey, you're not in trouble. But can you tell me who you share your secret with?" Claire looked at Ron and Gayle, wanting either of them to tell her what to say, but they were flying around arguing with each other and didn't notice her.

"It's my new friend, Daddy."

Maggie held her breath as Nick asked, "Is your friend, the one you've been talking to, with you by yourself?"

With her head down, Claire nodded, "Yes."

Rising, Nick absently offered his hand to help Maggie stand. She took it, and they exchanged glances with Claire before looking at each other. "Okay," he said.

Claire turned to Jenny, who explained how the buttons were made. Claire wondered why Ron's friend Gayle floated between her dad and her teacher. She giggled when Jenny gave her a little squeeze; it tickled.

Satisfied that his daughter was occupied, Nick turned to Maggie. "Walk with me?"

She nodded and said to Jenny, "Hold down the fort for a few minutes, Mom?"

"Take your time," Jenny replied. "We've got this. Right, Claire?"

Claire bobbed her head, smiling.

Nick and Maggie left the booth, moving out of earshot. "Okay, before you say, 'I told you so,' what do you think is going on with her?"

"I'm not sure, Mr. Miller. I'm concerned about this 'friend' she's created. She seems to actually see it—or him—like a hallucination."

"I'm worried, too. I don't like it one bit!" Nick growled, catching himself before his tone sharpened. He took a breath, forcing himself to stay calm.

"I have an idea, if you don't bite my head off."

He shook his head, contrite. "I won't bite your head off. I love my daughter, and I'm... kind of scared. Sorry if that came out angry. What's your idea?" He made eye contact.

"I have a good friend who is a child psychologist. Hear me out. She might help. I could have her over to my house, and maybe you two could come, too. It would give Janet time to observe her." She paused, waiting for his response.

"I don't know. I never thought she'd need therapy."

"We don't know if she will or not. It could be very informal—maybe a barbecue. Claire doesn't have to know she's being observed. Janet might have some insights."

"That's a tough one. I'm used to handling my own problems."

"I get it." She crossed her arms, grinning. "How's that working out for you?"

Nick shot her a look and sighed. "Yeah, I guess you're right. And since we're in this together, call me Nick."

"Thank you, Nick. I'm Maggie. I really think this will help." She started to touch his arm but caught herself.

As they walked back to the booth, Nick watched his daughter working and chatting with Jenny. "When?" he asked.

"I'll talk to Janet and set it up. How about next Saturday if you're both free?"

"Sure, that works for me."

They reached the booth, and Maggie said, "I'll call you."

Floating overhead, Gayle punched her fist in the air. "See, Ron, that's how it's done. No dog tricks necessary."

"Yeah, yeah. That was a stunt, not a trick." He twisted a grin as she rolled her eyes.

Claire and Jenny finished making several buttons. She gave one to her father that read, "World's Greatest Dad" with a heart, one for Maggie that said "World's Greatest Teacher," and another for Jenny that said "Rock and Roller," Jenny's idea. The one for herself simply said "Claire."

"That's good work, Claire—I'm impressed." Maggie smiled. She sly-eyed Nick and announced in a very business-like voice, "That will be $4.00, please."

"Highway robbery," he said, digging into his pocket to pay the lady.

As they left, Nick offered to shake hands with Maggie. Just as her hand reached for his, she had second thoughts and gave a little wave and a smile instead, turning to talk to her mother.

Claire eagerly skipped to the game booths, even enjoying some cotton candy with her dad. She learned how to have fun with Ron and Gayle without making the adults ask her a lot of questions. That wasn't fun, and she didn't want to lie. But she thought it was okay not to tell them, as she didn't want her dad and her teacher to worry about her special friends, the ghosts.

She and Nick entered a three-legged race, and Claire thought Ron had helped when a cool breeze pushed them over the finish line to win by a nose. Her daddy laughed, and Claire beamed, glancing at Ron, who floated nearby. He looked like he was having as much fun as she was.

On the way to their car, they people-watched while Gayle floated above, watching them. Claire eyed Ron playing with a dog catching Frisbees. When a dog leaped, Ron pushed the flying disc a few inches away, causing the dog to snap at thin air with a bewildered look on its face. She fell asleep in their car, clutching her blue ribbon. It had been a fun day.

CHAPTER

TWELVE

Maggie called Nick, and after some hesitation, he agreed to bring Claire to the barbecue. That morning, Nick paced and talked to himself as strange things happened around the house. First, there were drafts. Then, he nearly dropped the coffeepot when a cat appeared at his kitchen window, hissed, and darted from the backyard.

Now, his keys had vanished from the dish on the table by the front door. He searched everywhere, only to find them in the freezer. He muttered, casting a look at Claire, who simply shrugged.

Ron whispered to Claire, "That was Gayle's prank. Grownups sometimes think too much, and she thought a little puzzle would loosen him up."

Keys in the ignition, Nick exhaled deeply, looked at his daughter, and smiled. "Okay. We have the keys."

"Check," she said.

"We're dressed."

"Check." She nodded.

"Got the cookies?"

"Check." She raised the plastic-wrapped plate from her lap.

"I think we're ready to go." He started the car.

"Ready to go. Check, Daddy-o." She giggled, making him laugh.

Backing out of their driveway, he stopped. *Wait, did I turn the oven off? Yes, I did. I need to get a grip—or I might wind up in therapy.*

When they arrived, Nick paused on the walkway to admire the Sandersons' home. It stood tall on a grassy lot—a Victorian house with gingerbread trim in two shades of green and dark red trim around the shutters.

"It's like the dollhouse you made for me, Daddy, except mine is yellow with white trim. It's so pretty," Claire smiled at Nick.

He let Claire press the doorbell, and Maggie ushered them from the foyer toward the kitchen, where Nick took in the polished wooden staircase that curved to the upper floor. A maple hall table held a vase with fresh flowers from their garden. They walked past the staircase and the parlor on their left, with its tasteful mix of vintage and casual furniture.

The order and simplicity put Nick at ease. Claire handed the plate of cookies to Maggie and proudly announced she had sprinkled the raisins and stirred the batter. Maggie thanked her for helping and led them through the house to the back door. They passed through the kitchen, where Nick couldn't help but study another craftsman's work—a mix of period design and modern conveniences adapted to Jenny's mobility. They walked down the ramp to the backyard, where mellow acoustic rock thrummed from a speaker on the deck.

Jenny sat at the grill, flipping hamburgers and rolling hot dogs. Pitchers of lemonade and iced tea were set next to paper plates, napkins, and plasticware. Maggie placed the cookies at the end of the table next to the sliced watermelon. Near Jenny stood a slender woman with shiny black hair that hung straight past her shoulders. She wore jeans and a T-shirt like Maggie, but Nick's eyes lingered on Maggie's attire.

Maggie introduced Janet Hill as her friend. Nick shook her hand, and Claire craned her neck to look up. She leaned against her dad's legs and announced, "Hello, my name is Claire."

Janet smiled and crouched to Claire's eye level to shake her hand. "I'm very glad to meet you, Claire. Did I hear something about you baking cookies?"

Claire giggled. "I just helped. I put the raisins in and stirred the batter around."

After some small talk, Claire took her father's hand and led him to the hot dogs and watermelon. Maggie mumbled that she couldn't find the mustard, and Janet's eyes followed her friend's return to the kitchen.

Alone, Janet wandered into Jenny's garden, pondering her journey into child psychology, which began during her undergraduate years after a summer spent volunteering at a community center. There, she met Lucas, a quiet boy whose story changed her life.

One afternoon, she found him alone, sketching intricate, imaginary worlds. His mother had passed away earlier that year, and through his drawings, Lucas expressed emotions he couldn't yet articulate. Janet encouraged him to share his creations, gently guiding him to open up. Their bond became a quiet rhythm of trust—a summer-long conversation where words and art worked together to help him heal.

That experience stayed with her, planting a purpose she hadn't fully understood until then. It showed her how powerful compassion and connection could be, how even small acts of care could transform pain into resilience. Years later, Lucas—now a college student studying in a related field—sent her a Christmas message, a heartfelt reminder of how far that summer had carried them both.

In that moment, Janet was reminded of why she chose this path: to help children navigate their grief, not just with her training, but with the kind of presence and understanding she'd learned from Lucas. It wasn't just about their healing; it was about rediscovering hope together.

Her thoughts returning to the task at hand, Janet observed Claire covertly communicating with someone while munching on a hot dog. She couldn't see Gayle flitting about the backyard, misplacing items to prompt Nick into helping Maggie search for them. Nor could she spot Ron hovering close to Claire.

From his elevated perspective, Ron studied the dark-haired woman and the scene before him. Watching Janet engage Claire with humor and kindness, he realized that she genuinely cared and grew confident that she could help the girl.

Ron also observed Gayle guiding Nick and Maggie together in their search for mustard, which they eventually found in a drawer alongside stray cords and AAA batteries, as well as the melon baller, which Gayle had cleverly hidden in a vase of flowers near the sink.

"Thank you, Nick," Maggie said. "I don't know why I'm so absent-minded today."

"No problem. I wish someone had been with me this morning to help find my keys. How they ended up in the freezer, I'll never know." Nick's face brightened as Maggie laughed easily. They walked outside.

Ron caught Gayle's eye. Impressed, he gave her a thumbs-up.

Jenny, having finished her duties at the grill, sipped her lemonade while watching the tentative interactions between Nick and Maggie. She loved her daughter dearly and wanted her to find romance, with all its treasures and trials, rather than spending all her time at home with her. Yet, she knew better than to get ahead of herself. Patience had never been her strong suit.

C H A P T E R

THIRTEEN

After Nick and Claire waved their goodbyes, Maggie and Janet sat at the kitchen table, swapping their iced tea for glasses of Moscato. Janet expressed her concern and recommended Claire for an assessment. "Talking to oneself or to an imaginary friend isn't all that bad. Heck, I do it myself. What worries me are the bursts of laughter and her focus on a point in space as if someone is there."

Maggie sipped the sweet wine. "Talking about it might help Claire accept reality, right? Is she avoiding her feelings about her mother's death? Is this how a seven-year-old might process loss?"

"Good questions—to be determined. I'd prefer to see her again rather than sending her to someone new who might make her feel like she has a problem. We hit it off pretty well, and she seemed comfortable with me."

Maggie smiled. "I was hoping you'd say that. How should we go about it?"

Janet patted her hand on the table. "You're always diving into the thick of it, aren't you, Maggie? Like that time we swore we'd never speak of again?"

"Which one? Oh, *that* one." She looked off into a distant memory. "Gosh, that was so long ago; we were just kids ourselves." They laughed together. Jenny called from the other room.

"I'm coming in. Hide whatever you don't want your mama to see."

"Maybe we can meet here again, where she's comfortable," Janet suggested.

"Sure," Maggie agreed.

"Great." Taking a sip of her wine, Janet looked into her friend's eyes. "Claire's father seemed like an okay guy, just struggling to raise his daughter alone. What's your take on him?"

Maggie smiled. "He was a real schmuck at our first meeting. But to give him credit, he's realizing there's a problem. He just doesn't know how to deal with it."

"That's half the battle. Sometimes parents can't accept that their child might benefit from outside help. So, what devious and convoluted plan should we contrive this time?"

Jenny rolled in, pouring herself a glass of wine. "Remember the time you two tried to set up Tony and Toni and kept mixing them up? You were not exactly the matchmaking masterminds you presumed to be."

Maggie laughed. "Yeah, or when we planned that surprise party for what's-his-name? That didn't go as planned, either. No surprise there."

"It's a wonder everyone survived our well-intentioned schemes and went on to live reasonably happy and productive lives." Janet clinked their glasses.

Jenny said, "Hear, hear. But seriously, what about the Millers?"

Maggie chuckled. "What do you suggest, Mom?"

"How about a movie?" Jenny proposed. "Keep it simple. We know what can happen when you two put your heads together."

Janet said, "A movie's not a bad idea. I'd like to see how she interacts with a fictional world on screen."

Jenny suggested, "I happen to have a couple of Harry Potter films on DVD. We'll need popcorn. And Raisinets. To mix in the popcorn." She looked at her daughter and Janet, noticing the expressions on their faces reminded her of the pair as willowy teens a decade ago. "What? It's delicious."

"Well, that settles it," Janet chuckled, rising from the table. "Mama Jen is in charge of the convoluted plan. Probably better for all concerned. Keep me posted." Janet kissed Jenny's forehead and hugged Maggie. They agreed to touch base in a few days.

Maggie called Nick the next evening to share their plan.

Nick offered, "Why not show the movie at our house? You bring the DVD, and I'll supply the popcorn."

"I think that's a great idea," Maggie agreed. "Janet can assess Claire's behavior and invite her to talk further at her office or suggest tools for you to help her through this phase. Are you sure?"

"Sure, I'm sure. Janet can see Claire in her own surroundings. Your mother is welcome too; my house is on ground level."

"Thank you, I'll let her know."

The following Saturday afternoon, Maggie and Janet arrived at the Miller home in the newer section of town. The two-story traditional-style house was beige with stone veneers and dark blue shutters—slightly drafty inside. The décor showed a woman's touch, with toss pillows, family pictures on the walls, and curtains on the windows.

Claire was shy at first but quickly warmed to her teacher and her nice friend. As hostess, she took the DVD from Maggie and laid it on the coffee table. Noticing the handsome piece of furniture, Maggie smoothed her hand over the surface. "Is this cherry? It has such a beautiful sheen; it feels like it's been hand-rubbed."

"Daddy made it. He makes lots of things, that's what he does."

Maggie said, "Nick, it's gorgeous. It's a work of art. I love the drawers and the nooks and crannies. There's a place for everything. I'm impressed."

Nick shrugged. "Thanks, it's my job. I enjoy creating anything out of wood. Your mother couldn't join us?"

"No, she stayed home to tend the garden before it rained."

Janet looked around to see what else Nick had built. Claire grabbed her hand. "Come see my room, Miss Janet. I have a dollhouse Daddy made for me." She looked at Maggie. "It kinda looks like your house."

"I'll be right there, okay? I'm going to help your dad for a minute," Maggie answered.

"Okay," she replied. "Daddy bought soda and popcorn. Do you like microwave popcorn?"

"Of course, that's the best kind," Janet said.

"Come on," Claire pulled Janet's hand. "Let's go upstairs." She'd spent all morning cleaning her room.

Maggie assisted Nick in setting up while reassuring him of their intentions. Ron and Gayle watched from the banister as she climbed the stairs.

The ladies complimented Claire's bedroom. Sunny yellow gingham curtains hung from a large window, with afternoon sunlight illuminating a padded window seat just right for reading or daydreaming. A small vanity and chair awaited a young lady to brush her hair and someday apply makeup. A glossy white dresser and nightstand completed the look. The bedspread matched the curtains, and a dozen stuffed animals crowded the bed—her mother's influence, designed for a daughter with lots of love.

The dollhouse stood in the corner like a relic of a previous generation, waiting to be discovered. Its miniature shingles and hand-carved window trim told a story of patience and care—details unnoticed by most, but not by Maggie. She ran her fingers along the roof's edge, her gaze softening. The craftsmanship was not just impressive; it was tender. Nick had built this for Claire. Not bought. Built. A quiet gift from a man who struggled to show his heart yet somehow managed to express it in cedar and glue.

Maggie marveled at the intricate workmanship, skill, and patience involved. Tiny rooms, doors, even light fixtures. She imagined Claire spending hours moving the furniture and playing house.

She turned as Claire covered her mouth to suppress giggles. Unbeknownst to the adults, Claire spotted Ron's head poking out from between her stuffed monkey and a giraffe. Her eyes darted to Gayle, who hovered above the headboard, arms crossed like a teacher silently scolding an unruly student. Maggie and Janet exchanged glances as Claire's eyes moved from a spot on the bed to directly above it and back. She clearly saw something they did not.

Downstairs, Nick stared at the collection of bowls in the cabinet. "Which ones should I use for popcorn, Claire?" he whispered aloud, his thoughts drifting. *What am I doing? I don't care what Maggie thinks of my bowls. Do I?* He tugged at the collar of his golf shirt. *Do I care what she thinks of my outfit?*

When Maggie and Janet descended the stairs, Nick called out, "Is everybody ready for popcorn?" Claire jumped down the last two steps and skipped to her father.

"Can I put the popcorn in the microwave, Daddy?"

"Sure," he said, as Claire positioned a step stool and stood on it.

Unwrapping the package, she asked, "What numbers do I use?"

Maggie joined her. "Can you find the number on the bag that matches the one on the microwave? Then press the button with the same number to 'Quick Start.'"

Claire grinned when the microwave started. Listening intently, she waited for the popping to slow, counting two or three seconds between pops. Maggie removed the hot bag as Nick swung Claire off the stool, pushing it out of the way with his foot. He took the bag from Maggie, and their fingers brushed against each other. Claire took Maggie's hand and led her to the TV.

Realizing he still held the hot bag of popcorn, Nick shook his head, chuckling to himself. He opened the bag, shook some into individual bowls, and carried them into the living room.

Ron hovered over the couch. Claire giggled when he offered her a 'high five.' She nonchalantly slapped through his hand and plopped onto the end cushion.

"What's so funny, Claire?" Nick asked.

"Nothing, Daddy." She smiled at him.

Nick turned to Maggie and raised his eyebrows in question as he distributed the colorful bowls heaped with popcorn.

"I like these bowls, Nick," Maggie said with a wry smile. She inserted the disk and sat on the middle cushion next to Claire.

Janet moved to sit next to Maggie but suddenly pivoted, as if nudged, to accept a bowl of popcorn from Nick. Maggie noted the surprise on her face as her friend settled into the armchair. That left only one place for Nick to sit, next to Maggie. Their knees brushed, sending a tingle up her spine. He leaned a little closer and whispered, "Thank you for this," smiling as he did. She knew he could smell her hair. It was a place she hadn't visited in a long time—the space between possibility and consequence.

Maggie's neck flushed with warmth. *Okay, calm down. The last thing I need is to get mixed up with one of my student's parents. That would be ridiculous... wouldn't it?* She lingered a moment and leaned forward. "Oh! I almost forgot." She reached for her purse. "Raisinets! For the popcorn—my mother's special recipe." She shook some into their bowls and her own.

Nick adjusted his position on the couch, seeming to avoid brushing their legs again. Maggie shifted slightly, her focus fixed on the screen, though her neck flushed pink. Hovering near the banister, Gayle gave Ron a thumbs-up.

After the movie, Claire gushed about how cool it was that Harry could fly, holding out her arms as she swerved to the kitchen for a broom. Ron followed her path from the ceiling. "You don't even need a broom!" Claire exclaimed, looking up at him.

Maggie heard her but didn't engage. A cool draft brushed past her, and she turned to Janet, her eyes widening slightly. While Claire played in the kitchen, Janet conferred with Nick.

As they were leaving, she bent down to speak to Claire. "Would you like to see where I work? I take an elevator to my office on the fifth floor. I keep some neat things to play with that a young girl like you would enjoy."

Claire answered, "Yes, I would. Can my daddy come too?"

"He can, but I think it might be more fun if it's just us girls." Maggie saw the wheels turning in Claire's head and noticed that Janet wanted her to decide on her own. Janet waited.

"Okay," Claire said, looking at Nick and solemnly adding, "You can't come, Daddy. It's just us girls."

Nick gasped, playing along. "Where can't I come?"

Claire hesitated, gazing at a point on the ceiling, then at Janet. The psychologist said, "Claire and I are going to have a girls' party. Very exclusive. Right, Claire?"

Maggie stepped in, sensing Claire's confusion. "In this case, 'exclusive' means only for you girls. How exciting! I wish I could be there, but I'll probably be working anyway."

"It's okay, Miss Sanderson. Maybe next time you can come. Thank you for the movie and Raisinets in my popcorn. That was great! Right, Daddy?"

Maggie saw the concern on Nick's face, sending a pang to her heart. He asked, "Are you sure you want to go?"

Claire nodded.

C H A P T E R

FOURTEEN

The building's architecture and weathered brick revealed it had stood in downtown Provo for nearly one hundred years. Nick picked up Claire at home, and they drove to Janet's office building. He knew this was a step in the right direction but felt out of his depth. He promised Claire burgers and fries when she finished with her party.

Janet met them in the lobby, smiling warmly. "We'll see you in about half an hour," she said to Nick. He stooped to kiss Claire on the head. She looked surprised, patting her hair as she smiled shyly. Nick gave her a little wave and crossed the street for a cup of coffee.

In the elevator, Janet crouched to Claire's level. "Do you want to press the button for floor five?" she asked. Claire nodded eagerly, reaching for the button and counting the floors aloud as the elevator rose.

Inside her office, a short, bright red table and colored chairs occupied part of the room. Claire touched each one as she walked around the table, singing 'yellow, blue, green, and purple.' Colorful boxes and pillows of different sizes were scattered on the floor, creating the look of a big playhouse, and she liked it.

Janet watched her explore the room with wide-eyed curiosity. When Claire paused, her gaze lingering on the corner, her expression briefly shifted to something like concern. Janet tilted her head but said nothing, allowing the girl to process on her own.

After a moment, they settled on the rug with toys and stuffed animals, Janet folding her legs to the side. After building rapport with comforting small talk, Janet eased into her first question. "What do you miss most about your mom?"

Claire brushed her hair away from her face. "When she laughed, her eyes almost closed, and little lines came out from the corners." Holding her fingers to her own eyes, she showed Janet what she meant. "When she hugged me, I could smell her, too."

"What did she smell like?" Janet smiled.

"Soap—and flowers."

"Did you like that?"

"Yes, it made me happy."

"Are you still happy, Claire?"

Claire bobbed her knee. "Not always. I'm kinda sad sometimes."

"Why are you sad sometimes?"

Claire studied the corner of the room, where Ron sat quietly. She picked up a stuffed bunny, holding it close to her chest.

Janet asked, "What are you looking at, Claire? Do you see something over there?"

Ron shrugged as if to say, 'it's up to you, kiddo.'

She sighed, making eye contact. "I'm not as sad as I used to be. Is that bad? Will it hurt Mommy's feelings?"

Janet held her gaze. "Is that how you feel, Claire? That you should stay sad because she's gone?"

She nodded. "Daddy's still sad."

"How do you feel about your dad being sad?"

"I'm lonely when he's sad. Because I can't talk to him or make him feel better."

"I understand. Is there anyone else you can talk to?"

Claire's eyes moistened as she glanced at Ron. She took a deep breath and whispered, "I have a friend."

"Can you tell me about your friend? Is it a girl from school?"

She giggled. "He's not a girl."

"Oh. What's your friend's name?"

Claire turned towards him and smiled. "Ron."

"Does Ron have a last name?"

"I don't know," Claire frowned.

"That's okay. Do you see him all the time?"

"Mostly."

Placing her hand on Claire's twisting fingers, Janet asked, "Is Ron here now?"

"Yes." Nodding, she bit her lip.

"Where?"

She pointed to Ron, sitting cross-legged on a purple cushion.

"Would you like to tell me more about him?"

"Will I get in trouble?"

A soft smile. "No."

"Well, he's silly and does things to make me laugh, and that makes me feel good inside."

"That sounds nice. I can't see Ron. Can anyone else see him?"

"I don't think so. He said his job is to make me happy because Mommy doesn't want me to stay sad."

"Okay. Can you tell me what he looks like?" Janet observed her scanning the corner.

"He looks like a regular grown-up. Sometimes he wears a shirt like my dad's, and sometimes he doesn't wear clothes."

Claire saw Ron visibly flinch, his mouth falling open as he looked from Claire to Janet. Claire giggled at his reaction.

Janet spoke evenly, "He doesn't wear any clothes?"

"He's wearing a long white nightgown today. Like a bathrobe."

"All right, what else can you tell me about him?"

"He's funny and does tricks, too, but not very well." She giggled and spoke to him. "I'm sorry, but you try really hard, and you still make me laugh." She turned back to Janet, her face animated. "He is learning how to fly but needs a lot of practice."

Janet watched Claire closely, quietly organizing what she'd observed so far. *Talk therapy to address grief. Tools to help establish social boundaries, but what about the hallucinations...*

Janet stood and told Claire, "It's almost time for your dad to pick you up, but I would love to hear more about Ron. Maybe you could draw a picture of him for me because I can't see him. Would you like to do that?"

"Okay. Do I have to tell Daddy about Ron?"

"Do you want to?"

"I thought our party was ex...excloo... just between us girls, and I don't think he would understand, and I don't want to make him sad."

"Why do you think he'd be sad, Claire?"

"I don't know, I just do."

"All right. Let's keep it exclusive, then. Just between us. Would you like to come see me again?"

Ron floated up from his cushion and nodded. Claire said, "Ron thinks it's okay, so I guess so. I like talking to you about Ron. Just us girls. Ex-cloo-sive." She giggled, and Janet took Claire's trust to heart.

Janet held Claire's hand as they walked to meet her father in the lobby. She replayed the session in her mind, already jotting down notes for their next meeting. This was just the beginning, but it was clear—there was more to explore than she'd initially thought.

CHAPTER
FIFTEEN

Three weeks and six visits later, with updates from her therapist, Nick drove Claire to her 'exclusive Tuesday girl party.' He didn't know all the specifics of her therapy, but Janet had explained it focused on helping Claire process the trauma of losing her mother and navigate social integration, both real and imagined. He remembered how proud Claire had been when she showed him a drawing of her imaginary friend. Their pediatrician's recent reassurance that Claire was healthy and developing normally eased some of his lingering worries.

Claire talked with him more often and even teased him now and then. Sometimes they went to the park, where she interacted with other kids. Her confidence in making new friends and healthy curiosity reassured him like a pat on the back. *She's opened up more since we started. Janet says she's progressing. Maggie says her grades are still good, and she's more engaged in class. I should be optimistic, right?*

Crossing the street from Janet's office, he thought, *Maggie has been the driving force behind Claire's progress, persisting even when I resisted.* He owed her more than a thank-you. She was an ally, a friend, even...

something more? Laughing at his own feelings, he pressed her number on his weathered work phone.

Jenny answered, teasing him before calling for her daughter. "Maggie—it's for yooou," she sang, her tone full of playful mischief. Maggie rose from the dining room table, having been reading an article on elementary education. Distracted, she answered the phone, twirling the spiraled cord around her finger.

A deep and sultry voice came through the line. "Hello."

Taken aback, she blurted, "Who is this?" before hearing a soft laugh on the other end.

"Sorry, it's Nick. Did I catch you at a bad time?"

"No, it's fine. What can I do for you, Nick?" *What can I do for you?* She hoped her mom hadn't heard.

"I just wanted to thank you for all your help with Claire."

"Oh. Well, it's my pleasure. She's a special girl, and she seems happier at school. She's doing well, as always, with her lessons." I told him the same thing last week. She crossed her legs, wiggled in the chair, then uncrossed them.

Maggie hesitated. *Should I tell him she still giggles with her imaginary friend at school?*

On the other end, Nick wondered, *Should I tell her how I still hear her talking after I put her to bed?*

"How are you?" they both said at the same time, chuckling at the awkward overlap.

Nick said, "I guess that's it, then. I'll let you get back to what you were doing. Thank you, Maggie. I couldn't have done it..." He stopped as emotion crept into his voice.

Touched, Maggie realized she didn't want him to hang up.

"Nick?"

"Yeah?"

"Would you like to get together to talk about Claire?"

"You mean another parent-teacher conference? I think the lady at the school office is getting a crush on me."

"Or she wants to feed you milk and cookies. Mrs. Jackson? She's old enough to be your grandma." She pictured him smiling.

"Well, it's never too late, and I do like cookies. I just dropped Claire off at Janet's office, and I'll be at the coffee joint across the street for another hour. Or I'll be here at the same time on Thursday."

"You're at The Coop now?" Suddenly, she craved something sweet and a cup of coffee.

"Yeah, that's the one."

She looked at her watch. "Tell you what, if you split one of their giant double-fudge chocolate chip cookies with me, I can be there in fifteen minutes."

"It's a deal. See you here."

Singing drifted from the kitchen. Maggie's eyes narrowed as she called out, "Mom, what's gotten into you?"

Jenny's voice came back, light and full of humor, "Oh, just happy to be alive, dear."

Gayle and Ron watched from the kitchen window, hooking arms in a do-si-do and laughing silently.

CHAPTER
SIXTEEN

The Coop was slow that afternoon. Only a few students hunched over their phones and an older couple sat by the door. Maggie walked in with a smile and a current of fresh air as the door jingled and a server called out 'Welcome to The Coop.' Nick stood and waved her to the corner booth, where two coffees, sugar, and half-and-half awaited. He touched her arm in greeting.

"I ordered you a coffee. As you can see plainly in front of you."

A freckled redhead delivered the chocolate indulgence, giving Nick a once-over and asking, "Anything else you need, hon?"

"No, this will do, thanks," he said. She turned on her heels to bus a table.

"Do you get that a lot?" Maggie grinned.

"Get what a lot?"

"You know." She nodded toward the waitress.

Nick chuckled. "No. I don't know, maybe."

Maggie's gaze lingered on the waitress retreating to another table. "She was ogling you," she said, her tone teasing but firm.

Nick leaned back on the vinyl bench seat. "Ogling, huh?"

"Oh, never mind," she said, smiling as she folded her napkin into an origami shape. "What would you like to talk about?"

"Anything you like."

Maggie began with a familiar but not always safe topic. "Claire seems happier these days." At Nick's nod, she continued, "Janet seems to help her a lot."

"Mmm, hmm." He waited, breaking the cookie in half and taking a bite.

She looked into his green eyes and gathered her thoughts. "I'm still concerned about her imaginary friend, if that's what it is. At recess today, she went off by herself and had a chat with him." She broke off a piece of cookie and hummed as she chased the bite with lightened coffee.

Nick watched her fidget with the mug in her hands, noticing her nails—short, clear, and shiny. "She's still talking to herself at home, too. Janet told me not to worry." He sighed. "Maggie, sometimes she looks at him, or off into space, before answering a question. I'm glad she's opening up more, but sometimes I feel like there are three of us in the car."

"I'm concerned the other kids might label or pick on her. It hasn't happened yet, but..." She looked away, as if remembering something.

Nick glanced up at her, then back at his empty cup. "I'd hate for that to happen. Let's both talk to Janet, and afterwards, maybe we could meet and get some answers from Claire."

"Of course, Nick. I'll call her."

The waitress came back and smiled at Nick, filling his mug. She glanced at Maggie like an afterthought and topped off hers as well. Maggie laughed, shaking her head. Now Nick fidgeted, but he liked the sound of her laugh—a lot.

Maggie tilted her head, watching him stir his coffee. "Can I ask you a personal question?"

Nick met her gaze. "Given how we met, and you're involved in the most important part of my life, I guess it's personal already. Go ahead, shoot."

She steadied her breath. "How did you meet your wife?"

Her eyes shone light brown, full of genuine interest. Taking a sip of his coffee, he began.

"We met at my college basketball game. She came in late with a group of girls, laughing and joking around. From the colors they wore, I knew they were there to root for the away team.

"The game was in full swing, and they didn't want to cross the court, so they sat in the bleachers on our side. She was cute, with a high ponytail and bundled up, and I razzed her when she cheered for her team. She didn't care they were sitting on our side. So, I would boo her when they scored, and then when I cheered for us, she'd sneak a look at me and boo.

"Their team won, and I walked over to congratulate her. I asked if she'd like to go for pizza. Her girlfriends teased her, and she said yes, but only if her friends came along. We went in separate cars. I thought she was smart to figure there was safety in numbers."

"We ate, had a good time. I asked if I could drive her home, and she talked to her friends. I gave them my phone number and license plate, and they decided I was okay. She let me drive her home, and we listened to the radio, talked, then we were at her place. I didn't want the night to end but wasn't sure if I should ask her out again.

"It turned out she lived in Salt Lake City but stayed with her grandparents a few times a year. When I walked her to the door, a sweet old guy opened it before I even thought of kissing her and invited me in. They asked me about myself—my major and what I wanted to do when I graduated. I couldn't ask her out then and there, but I had her phone number and figured I'd call her later."

Chuckling, he remembered that night with her grandparents. "I was so nervous. Part of me must have known my life would change forever that night." He checked his phone and looked outside. It would be time to pick up Claire soon.

"I went home and texted her to ask if I could call. We talked for a while, and I asked if I could see her again. She said she'd like that, and so it began. We spent the entire summer together, never tiring of each other's company. I'll always remember our first kiss."

Nick stopped himself. "Ah, you don't want to hear all this. I got caught up in the memories."

"No, it's fine, Nick. Thank you for sharing."

"Anyway, I made many long trips to the city after that. We dated for over a year before I asked her to marry me. It's funny, but the night I proposed, she knew before I did—she even knew how I was going to ask. I hadn't planned anything special, yet she just knew. It seemed I could never surprise her. I never gave that much thought until now. It was uncanny, almost supernatural. Do you think...?" He frowned, considering the implication but decided it was a conversation for another time.

"I got a job in Salt Lake as an apprentice woodworker but never finished my degree. We rented a small apartment and were happy. When we got pregnant, we used our savings and worked hard to buy the house down here.

"She had worked at a scrapbooking store but was also an artist. She wanted to stay home with Claire, and I wanted that too. They always shared a unique bond as Claire grew. I fell in with a company that did high-end custom woodwork. Back then, I could set everything aside to spend time with my family. Now, as the company has grown, that's becoming much harder. I'm not making excuses, though. I need to do better with Claire."

As Nick spoke, Maggie listened intently, wondering how good people handled such a raw deal. She waited for him to finish before adding softly, "Claire wasn't in my class last year, but the whole faculty knew of the accident."

He looked at her as though he'd forgotten she sat across from him. Staring down at his cold coffee, he lowered his voice to a monotone. "She was hit by a car at the grocery store. The man had a heart attack, and they both died instantly. No one's fault, no one to blame. Just like that." He snapped his fingers, startling her. "Two lives gone, two families picking up the pieces."

She hesitated before speaking. "At least when my father died, my mother and I had each other to lean on as adults. He was young, in his 50s, and the love of Jenny's life. We struggled but got through it." Maggie placed her hand over his larger, calloused one. "I'm so sorry, Nick."

He nodded, his voice quieter. "You're a good listener. I know we're not the only ones to survive a loss, but it's been difficult for Claire. I can't seem to fill the void her mother left."

Maggie paused, looking at their hands. "You're still hurting as well. I'm sure you two have your own special bond. I know how much I loved my dad."

Nick turned his hand over and entwined his fingers with hers, taking silent comfort in their connection. "Ann will always have a special place in my heart, but I accept she's gone, and Claire and I have to move on. I feel in my heart that's what she would have wanted."

Nick smiled, releasing her hand. "Your eyes changed from dark to light. Like walnut to hickory, if you will. When you're calm, the brown is a lighter shade. When we first met, they were pretty dark. Pretty, though."

Maggie blinked in surprise. "Hmm, I wonder why. Well, thank you," she laughed softly, turning her wrist to check the time. "Claire must be finished by now."

"What's your favorite color?" he blurted.

She raised her eyebrows. "What?"

"Here I've been going on about myself, and I don't know enough about you, except that you're an exceptional teacher."

"Aww, thanks. My favorite color is green, like your eyes." *Oh, my gosh, I'm flirting.* She blinked rapidly, a saucy grin forming as the waitress approached with the check. *Ha.*

Nick winked at her as he stood and tossed some bills on the table. "Now, don't forget to talk to Janet, and then we can get together at my place."

Maggie did a double-take. *Did he just wink at me? No, he must have had something in his eye.*

He helped her with her jacket, his arm lingering around her shoulders as he inhaled the scent of her hair. *Flowers? Maybe strawberries.* As they left the coffee shop, Nick slipped his hand into hers. The waitress watched them leave, a wistful expression crossing her face as she cleared their table.

He walked Maggie to her car and opened the door. When she slipped in, he caught another whiff of her hair. *Strawberries, I think.*

CHAPTER
SEVENTEEN

Nick listened as Janet explained why she didn't want to push Claire too hard, too soon. Claire held a consistent belief in her imaginary friend, Ron. Exploring the attachment could expose or rule out a traumatic event they may not be aware of. A trauma could cause a withdrawal into an imagined safer place. She suggested he attend the next meeting to see if Claire was ready to confide in him.

Nick called Maggie the next night to tell her how the meeting had gone. Claire slept soundly upstairs, and he had been trying to fix—or at least diagnose—the heating issue. "It's nice to talk with you. This furnace is driving me nuts. I can't find anything wrong with it, but the house is still so drafty. I need a break."

He filled her in on his conversation with Janet and heard the concern in her voice when she said, "I'm going to call her now."

⁂

En route to her next session, Claire asked, "How come you're coming with me today, Daddy? I thought this was for girls only?"

"I'd like to see how my little girl is enjoying herself. You like coming here, don't you?"

"Yes, I like Miss Janet. She talks to me like I'm a grown-up," she replied.

"I think the last time I checked you were only 7 years old. Did you grow up when I wasn't looking?"

"Daddy, don't be silly."

"I didn't think I could be silly."

Nick's heart warmed when Claire took his hand and said, in a very grown-up voice, "I'm still your little girl, but when I talk to Miss Janet, she listens to me differently."

Nick forced a smile, a pang of guilt pricking his thoughts. "I listen to you."

"Yes, Daddy. But sometimes, you just grunt."

"Grunt? You mean like this?" He grabbed her around the waist, tickling her and grunting like an ape.

Claire laughed and squirmed in his arms. "I love you, Daddy. You're my big superhero gorilla." She threw her arms around his neck.

Nick stopped tickling and hugged her tightly, feeling more hopeful. He whispered, "Daddy loves you too, sweet pea," and grunted.

Nick sat in the child-size purple chair in Janet's office. Claire told Janet how she felt about her progress in naming her feelings. Janet acknowledged her and turned the conversation to her special friend, Ron. When Janet asked if her dad knew about him, Claire hesitated. Janet said it was her choice to make but suggested she ask him if he wanted to know.

Meet her imaginary friend? Here we go. Nick held his breath and waited.

Later that evening, he called Maggie. "She told me about her friend. His name is Ron." Nick grimaced at the name, his voice thick with frustration. "I can't help feeling I must be doing something wrong. Why does she need this guy? Okay, he can fly—I guess he's a better superhero than me, but I wanted to say 'stop! You don't need him. I'm here.'" He paced in his kitchen, stirring a pot of macaroni and cheese.

Maggie's voice softened on the line. "We'll sort this out, Nick. Trust her." She stood by her phone, gazing at a seascape painting on the wall.

"I do, but geez. My little girl."

"I know."

Nick groaned. "You and Janet know her better than I do, it seems. Why didn't I pay better attention to her? I feel like such a jerk."

"Nick, you're not a jerk. A little stubborn maybe, some macho superhero delusions..."

"All right, I get the picture."

Laughing, she said, "Seriously, that was a lot to take in yesterday, and it's out of your experience. Mine too, and I spend my days with a room full of seven-year-olds." She paused. "Do you believe Claire?"

"It's so real to her. I believe *she* believes it. But I'm not sure what I believe. She talked about how funny he is and how he makes her laugh. He was there at the picnic and when we watched the movie. I must be dense or in denial."

"Take it easy, Miller. Give yourself a break. She's in excellent hands with Janet, and they're figuring things out."

"I know, and I'm grateful for you both. I haven't given her much reason to confide in me. Okay, I'm done with my pity party." In an upbeat tone, he said, "What are you up to this evening, Miss Sanderson?"

"Mom and I just finished a rousing game of Rummy. She's a formidable opponent and hates to lose."

"And did she?"

"Nope, she kicked my butt. Hands down."

"I guess we all have our limitations. You two seem to have a great relationship."

"We do, except she's always trying to..."

"Trying to what? Fix you up?"

"Sort of. How did you know?" He couldn't see her blush but could tell she did.

"I've seen her in action. She has this certain look whenever I come over."

Maggie snorted, not knowing what to say. "Yeah, right."

Maybe I'm onto something. "What, no snappy comeback?" He smiled. "I like Jenny a lot. She makes me feel like a contender, not some stubborn, clueless bum with superhero delusions."

"You're not a bum, anyway."

"That's more like it." They laughed and talked about mothers and daughters for a while longer until the conversation began to wind down. "Dinner's almost ready. That girl could have mac and cheese every night if I let her."

Maggie pictured Nick and Claire eating dinner alone and wondered if Nick would continue to confide in her after Claire outgrew her imaginary friend. Concerned she might cross a professional line, she offered an invitation before she could back out. "Nick, would you and Claire like to have dinner with us tomorrow night? I'm sure my mother would love to whip something up; she's been asking about Claire."

"Sure, Maggie. That's very thoughtful of you. We'd like that."

"Great! See you around six?"

"We'll be there."

-»»※««-

Things were progressing between Nick and Maggie; they were hitting it off. Gayle thought that boosted the mission. Dr. Janet talked to Claire about her 'imaginary friend,' Ron, but no one else was aware that they were ghosts. Gayle wanted to wrap things up and make her case for getting her wings and advancing in her afterlife. She called The Boss with her pitch.

"Yes, sir, the mission has exceeded our expectations. No, sir, Ron's going to need more practical experience. He has entertained the girl, but I'm sure he'll improve on his next mission. I, myself, have brought Nick and Maggie together most effectively. Love is in the air, as they say. I feel ready and able to take on those wings, sir. I could use a change of scenery."

The Boss replied, "I'm sorry, Gayle. The job is not done. Remember, I told you this mission has far-reaching consequences. I need you to see it through. Carry on."

Gayle met Ron at the Sanderson house, her energy sparking with impatience. "Blast it, anyway. Not finished?" She crossed her arms. "You need to speed things up with Claire and, for goodness' sake, work on your flight patterns." Her sigh lingered as she drifted toward the ceiling, her longing for freedom unmistakable.

Ron hovered silently for a moment, her words ringing in his thoughts. He had little experience with children but had grown attached to Claire. Making her laugh was his greatest joy, but he knew the risks of her being labeled a weirdo if others discovered she spoke to ghosts. He didn't want to go back until he knew she'd be okay. "Be patient, Gayle. Maybe this is a teachable moment for you." He met her scowl with a cheerful grin.

Gayle looked skyward and whispered, 'Why me?' before turning her attention to the task at hand. Nick and Claire had arrived, and dinner was about to be served.

Maggie caught her breath when Nick presented her with flowers. *I didn't expect that.* His smile lifted her spirits. Claire squealed and launched into a hug.

Maggie laughed. A little flustered, she said, "I think Mom is in the kitchen. I've been grading papers, and…" She took a red pen from behind her ear. Regaining her composure, she waved them inside, thanking him for the flowers and Claire for the hug. When Jenny arrived, she invited Claire to come outside with her. "I've set up a lovely tea party just for us. Would you like to see it?" She winked at Nick.

Claire looked at her dad. "An exclusive girls' tea party!" Her voice rose in pitch. "Is it okay, Daddy? I really, really want to!"

Nick smiled at Jenny. "Sure, honey, go on and have fun."

The dining room table was set for two, a bottle of wine breathing on the side. A roast brisket rested on the cutting board in the kitchen. Nick stepped closer to Maggie and placed his hands on her shoulders. "The table looks really nice. One might think Jenny had a plan."

A new intensity lit Nick's eyes. He lifted his hand from her shoulder to caress her cheek, first with a gentle stroke of his thumb. Locking her gaze, he slid his hand to her neck and lowered his head. His mouth brushed against her soft lips, and his heart swelled. Maggie leaned into him, swept up in the sensations of their first kiss, his arms warm and solid around her.

"Wow," she murmured, her lips still lingering against his.

"Yeah, wow," he breathed, touching his forehead to hers.

They stood in each other's arms, exploring their feelings. He looked down and chuckled, reminding her to put the flowers in water before they crushed them. Blinking, she pulled away and headed into the kitchen, where the aroma of the roast lingered. She found a vase and ruffled the flowers while walking to the dining room.

Nick carved slices of beef. Roasted vegetables, warm from the oven, and a fresh tomato vinaigrette completed their plates. They gazed at each other across the table, bowed their heads, held hands, said a few words of gratitude, and began to eat. Dinner satisfied their hunger, but not their desire. Afterwards, sitting on the loveseat in the parlor, Nick stretched his arm around her shoulder, and they sat together. Content, but not for long, he tasted her lips once again but stopped.

"Is that your mom?" Nick asked, frowning.

Maggie, a little dazed, replied, "Is what my mom?"

"I could swear I heard someone giggling. But it didn't sound like Claire or Jenny."

"It wasn't me, either." She pulled his head down for another kiss.

Feeling a shift of air on his neck, he looked up, thinking Claire and Jenny had opened the door to come inside. But they were still alone.

Claire fell asleep on the drive home, and Nick thought about Maggie. He didn't believe he would ever feel this way again. With a twinge in his heart, he hoped Ann understood and wanted them to be happy again. He believed she would.

Maggie kissed her mom goodnight and thanked her, bounding upstairs to her room. She flopped down on her bed. Wow! Her feelings for Nick had grown like ivy, surprising her as if discovered on a forgotten wall. She changed into yoga pants and a tank top, slipped into bed, and fell asleep, dreaming of a lush courtyard and muffled laughter.

The next day, Gayle decided to present the recent kissing evidence to The Boss. *That will convince him.* She flew in circles, eager to go. If she could've stomped her foot, she would have. *I want my wings, and I'm going to get them. He must accept that.* "I'm done!" she said aloud. "I'm so outta here." She disappeared.

Ron and Claire played cards in her room when he felt the emptiness. He couldn't put his finger on it but knew something was missing. He looked around and listened. *Gayle. I don't feel her presence. She's gone! Panic! No, don't panic. I can do this. I know I can.*

Claire shuffled the deck and started dealing. "What's the matter, Ron?"

He looked at her and said, "Gayle is gone."

"Gone where?"

"Back to where we came from, I think."

"Does that mean you're going too? I hope not." She stopped dealing and waited for his answer.

"I don't think so." *I've become so attached to her; I can't leave now.*

"What are you going to do, Ron?" She didn't want him to leave and held back her tears.

"I'll tell them I'm not going until you're ready." *Can I do that?*

Claire let out her breath and dealt the cards. "Good."

While Claire was taking her bath, Ron flew by Rosie Cunningham's house. It was still early, and he needed time to think. He flew around the neighborhood and around the block, practicing his right turns. He found Rosie sitting in a rocking chair on her front porch. She looked up from a crossword puzzle to watch the children playing catch under the streetlamp.

Ron hovered over the porch, observing the neat but slightly overgrown yard. Rosie's petite frame appeared healthy, but there was something about her posture—a quiet loneliness in the slump of her shoulders—that moved him.

A gray cat leapt onto the porch and twined around her ankles. She bent to pet it, a soft smile gracing her face as she murmured to the animal. It jumped onto her lap.

The cat turned its head, looked straight at Ron, hissed, and growled. *Oh, that's not good,* he thought.

The cat leapt off Rosie's lap and ran down the stairs. She frowned, rubbing the scratch the cat left on her leg. Ron watched as Rosie stood on unsteady legs, stretched with a groan, and reached for her cane.

Ron wanted to help her. He could report to Albert that he checked in on his widow, but he had an idea. He wasn't sure it would work. The mission came first, but he needed to make some decisions, especially now that Gayle was gone.

Rosie limped to the door, pulling the handle, which held fast to the latch. Ron swooped in with a puff of breath to free it. She stopped and turned, as if she felt his presence. Shaking her head, she opened the screen door and went inside.

C H A P T E R

EIGHTEEN

Nick wanted to see Maggie alone, but he wasn't sure how to arrange it. Kissing her had awakened long-dormant feelings, and he craved more. He hoped she would join him and help nourish the flame between them.

He had never left Claire with a sitter and didn't know one. The problem solved itself when he received a call from Jenny. Surprised, he feared something had happened to Maggie. "What's wrong? Is Maggie okay?"

"Yes, Nick, she's fine. I called for a different reason." The line fell silent.

Nick took a breath to steady his heart, the unsettling images fading away. "Hi Jenny, how are you?"

"I'm well, thanks. But I've been craving tea and your daughter's company. I thought we might set up another tea party."

"Oh, umm." He glanced at his watch, unsure why.

Jenny's voice held a playful edge. "Nick, wouldn't you like to go on a proper date with Maggie?"

He hesitated, caught off guard. "Yeah, of course, but..."

Jenny laughed, her amusement bubbling through the receiver. "Come on, Nick, don't think I'm interfering—though I am. You and my daughter get along so well; you both deserve some quality time. Alone."

"When you put it that way," he chuckled, "I've been wondering how to arrange that, but I don't... I've never left Claire with a sitter."

"I hope you trust me to look after her, Nick."

"Of course, I do."

"Don't worry. Claire knows me, and we get along wonderfully. So, what do you say, handsome? Is it a date for Claire and me?"

"Sure! That'd be terrific, Jenny. Claire will be thrilled. Maybe I should ask Maggie first. For a date, I mean. Geez, I sound like a kid."

Jenny chuckled. "Why don't you call her tonight and ask?"

"Why didn't I think of that?" he said, his fondness for her growing. "Thanks, Jenny. You're a sweetheart."

"Back at ya, mister."

Nick didn't know where to take Maggie on their first proper date. Dinner and a movie sounded so predictable. *Predictable is good, right?* He knew little about local museums or if Maggie even liked them. The amusement park in Farmington was an hour's drive. *Oh hell, I'll just ask her.*

Maggie answered the phone that night. "I'd like to take you out on a proper date," Nick said.

"Um, sure, I'd love to, but what about Claire? Do you have a sitter?" The indecision was clear in her voice.

"It's all been arranged. What do you say? Is Friday at 7:00 okay? So, it's not a school night?"

"That sounds great! Thank you, see you then." Maggie smiled but also frowned. *This is really happening. I hope we're doing the right thing.*

"I'm looking forward to seeing you, Maggie," he said.

"Me, too." *It'll be okay.* Excitement and hope churned in her belly. Maggie hung up and squealed, whirling with her arms wide. She danced into the kitchen, where Jenny held two dessert plates of cheesecake topped with fresh blueberries and handed one to Maggie.

"Land's sake, girl! What's gotten into you?" Jenny raised an eyebrow.

"Nick asked me out on a date!"

Jenny's face lit up. "That's awesome, honey. Are you surprised? You like him, right?"

Maggie's cheeks flushed. "I really do, Mom. I know I griped about him at first, but he's not like that. He's kinda sweet, and I think he really likes me, too." She grinned. "He even found a babysitter."

Jenny chuckled. "I'm sure he's taken care of things. Now, what are you going to wear?"

"Oh, my gosh, I didn't even ask him what we'll be doing. What am I going to wear?" Maggie giggled with her mom, like only mothers and daughters do.

When Friday evening *finally* arrived, Claire couldn't wait to spend time with Jenny. She fussed with her hair and laid her clothes on her bed, thinking Jenny would be a super cool grandma for someone. She didn't really know her grandparents. Mommy's parents lived far away, and she hardly saw them anymore. Her Daddy's mom died before she was born, and his dad lived somewhere where people helped take care of him.

Nick came home from work with a hamburger for Claire, explaining he would eat later with Miss Sanderson. Claire didn't mind. All her new friends saw each other often—Miss Sanderson, Miss Jenny, Miss Janet, Daddy, Ron, Gayle, and me. *Wow! That's a lot of friends.*

When they arrived at the Sanderson's house, Nick rang the doorbell. Maggie answered, glancing at Nick, clearly confused when she saw Claire in a church dress, white socks with ruffles, black patent leather Mary Janes, and white gloves.

Huh, Maggie thought. She complimented Claire's outfit and turned to Nick. "Did you have trouble finding a sitter?"

Jenny rolled up behind her. "Come in. I've been waiting for you."

Maggie stepped back, allowing Nick and Claire to enter. She narrowed her eyes as he walked by, smiling.

"Hi, Miss Jenny!" Claire said. "I dressed up for our tea party." She twirled and hugged Jenny's neck.

"You look so pretty, Claire. Now come help me with the tea service."

Maggie looked at her mother, Jenny looked at Nick, and Nick grinned at Maggie. Maggie shook her head, getting the picture. "You are too much, Mama."

Jenny took Claire's hand and said, "I know, right?" over her shoulder. They glided down the hall into the kitchen.

Nick took Maggie's hand. "Is this okay?"

"I don't think I want to know about your secret plans with my mom, but it's definitely okay. Let's go."

"Let me say goodbye to Claire first—if she even remembers I'm here."

Nick and Maggie peeked into the kitchen to catch Jenny and Claire setting the table with cucumber sandwiches, cheese, nuts, and strawberries, artfully arranged on a three-tiered crystal server. Mom's special teapot and teacups were displayed on a table covered with a Battenburg lace tablecloth. They were both so engrossed in their task that Nick put his finger to his lips, took Maggie's hand, and quietly led her back into the hall to grab her jacket. Together, they tiptoed out the front door, exchanging amused glances before bursting into laughter.

"You're not mad?"

"Nah, that's just Mom being Mom."

Nick opened the car door for her and slid into his seat. As he closed his door, he leaned toward her, pressing a kiss to her lips. She responded without hesitation, her fingers sliding into his hair. A warm tingle spread down his spine.

He pulled back, his breathing uneven. Maggie smiled, smoothing her dress. "So... where are we going? I forgot to ask—and didn't know what to wear."

"You look beautiful. I thought we'd go to a movie, but you'll have to choose because I don't know what you like."

"Thank you. I wasn't fishing for a compliment," she laughed, flattered. "I'm pretty flexible; I like action, comedy, even westerns, but I draw the line at horror movies."

"Good to know. How about dinner? Do you like Mexican food?"

"Love it! Good choice."

"I don't want to take you out for Thai or Chinese and find out you hate it."

"Not much food I hate. But for the record, Thai—nah, Chinese—meh."

Nick laughed and backed out of the driveway. After chips and salsa came fajitas, chiles rellenos, and a couple of margaritas. They relaxed and sipped their drinks.

"It is delicious, but I'm stopping at one. Have another if you'd like."

"One is fine. I don't want to lose *all* my inhibitions."

Nick grinned, unable to come up with a snappy comeback, which amused them both.

Maggie relaxed as they talked easily about his work and her teaching, their likes and dislikes, skiing and music, and even football. She was a fan of the Utes, while he preferred Utah Jazz basketball. Nick reached across the table and took Maggie's hand, interlocking their fingers, and she felt his sincerity. "I could learn to like college football if I didn't have to watch it alone. So, maybe there's hope for us after all?"

Leaning forward, she said, "To quote the Magic 8 Ball, 'The odds are in your favor.'"

"I think I saw that in a fortune cookie."

"Or a horoscope."

After an easy laugh, Nick looked into her eyes. "Maggie, I don't want to rush into things. But I didn't anticipate feeling this way so soon."

"What way is that, Nick?" Her eyes sparkled in the soft light as her stomach tingled.

"Stubborn, with macho superhero delusions." With a teasing grin, she pulled her hand away, but he gripped it tighter.

"Just kidding. It's been a long time since I dated. With you, I feel I can be myself, and I know how you are with Claire. I see us doing things together. We all seem to fit, right? Maybe your matchmaker mom is onto something."

She laughed. "You think so, huh?

Nick's voice softened. "I really like you and want to see where this goes. I hope I'm not scaring you off."

Maggie's heart raced as she met his steady green eyes. "You're not scaring me off, Nick Miller. Not by a long shot."

He smiled, relief evident on his face. They finished their drinks, and he paid the bill before offering her his hand. She took it, the warmth of his touch grounding her as they left the restaurant together.

They chose an action movie starring Dwayne Johnson, one of Maggie's favorite actors. During the show, Nick kept his arm around Maggie's shoulders until it felt numb. He caught her looking at him, and she saw him watching her, but he didn't try to kiss her during the movie.

Back in the car, Nick expressed his affection for her. Their breath fogged the windows, but when they came up for air, something felt wrong.

"Maggie, you make me feel like a randy teenager. I don't want to offend you, but I'd like to take this further."

"It's not that I don't want to, but Nick," she pleaded, her eyes desperate. "I'm afraid. You are the parent of one of my students."

"What are you saying?"

Maggie grappled with her choices. She wanted to date Nick, maybe more, but feared for her job. Her heart sank. *I can't risk it.* "I have to think about it. But not while we're making out."

She sensed the tension in his voice. "What's to think about? We're adults who enjoy each other's company. Why shouldn't we see each other?"

Torn, the words spilled out. "I don't know! Nick, I'm not trying to lead you on or hurt your feelings, but I need some space. It's a small school in a small town. People judge. Please, let's not spoil a wonderful evening." Maggie glanced out the window into the night, resting her head against the cool glass, deflated. *I knew this would happen. It never works out. I can't get close to anyone.*

"Okay." Nick started the car and, without another word, drove her back home. She exited before he could open her door.

Jenny sat in the parlor, while Claire slept on the loveseat, still wearing her dainty white gloves smudged with chocolate.

"How was your date, dear?" Jenny asked, still dressed for the tea party, enjoying a glass of iced tea.

"We had a very nice time, Mom. But if you'll excuse me, I'm very tired." Turning to Nick, she added, "Thank you for a lovely evening, Nick. Goodnight." She hurried upstairs.

Jenny watched her go, then turned to Nick. "What just happened? Didn't it go well?"

Nick sighed. "Dinner went well, we talked. The movie was fine. But Maggie had second thoughts about dating a student's parent. That put the kibosh on everything."

"Oh, fiddlesticks, that's rubbish. This is not the 1950s. What's her problem?" She rocked back and forth in her wheelchair.

"We had fun, and then when we were, uh, we were..."

"Kissing, dear. When you were kissing," Jenny interjected.

"Yeah, that's it." He looked at her with a crooked grin. "I told her how I felt, and she started backpedaling." He held his hands out at his sides, dismayed.

"She'll come around, Nick. I'll talk to her. Not to change her mind—that's your job—but to let her vent. I know she likes you. Just where did she think this would lead, for Heaven's sake?" She spun a 360 in her chair, ending in a wheelie before bringing the front wheels down with a thud on the hardwood floor. "Sorry, got a little worked up there. Here's Claire's stuff. Get some rest, buddy."

Jenny's bluntness offered him hope, but not a plan. Still, she was an ally, and he was running short of those. He lifted Claire from the loveseat and held her close. Jenny opened the door for him, expressing how much she enjoyed having Claire over for tea. He thanked her and walked out, touching her shoulder with his free hand.

He settled Claire in the back seat and glanced back at the house. Jenny stood in the entryway and waved goodbye. Nick waved back and looked up at Maggie's bedroom window, but he didn't see her.

Back at The Boss's office, Gayle was fit to be tied—or chained, or whatever would restrain her from flying around in frustration. She hovered over his exotic executive desk, papers fluttering in the air current she created. "What do you mean, 'incomplete?' I failed? They were getting on like a house afire! It's not my fault she lost her nerve. I got them together—that was my job!"

The Boss scowled. "First of all, cool your jets and *sit the hell down!* Secondly, the mission parameters are still to stabilize Nick and his daughter while training and managing Ron. Claire's teacher plays an important role, but the objective is not just fixing them up on a date." He rose from his desk.

Gayle stopped short, fuming. "I don't belong down there. I have waited so long and done everything I was asked. I want to go to Heaven." She slumped in her chair. *All the training, the teaching, the putting up with. There must be a better plane of existence.*

"Gayle, all the best operatives have been where you are. Frankly, I think you've lost the plot. You're so eager to get your way that you're getting in your own way! How do you think this will play out with the Bureau of Angels? Are you just going to stomp your little feet and want your way to Heaven? You have got to get Ron and your human assignments through this chapter of their lives." He conjured a scene of the drama in Mapleton, complete with three-dimensional characters and set pieces on top of his desk. She grunted, impressed.

"Now settle down and let's figure this out. Start by connecting the dots in your mission. What problems do they need to solve, and what tools do they need to resolve their conflicts? Maggie—job or Nick, conflict. Nick and his daughter's 'imaginary friend,' conflict. Jenny and even Janet have big decisions to make, and so forth. I'll give you a hint." He poked her forehead with his finger.

"Hey," she protested.

"It's all in there. Your fears, your desires. What do you need to resolve?" He was a reasonable man, but a leader had obligations. "Look for clues. How do their problems relate to your own? Next clue. You and Ron— even you and me?"

She squirmed. "Conflict. Humph."

⁕

Saturday morning, Jenny heard Maggie clump down the stairs to the breakfast table. Sleepy and bedraggled, she trudged to the coffeemaker. Jenny waited her out. Maggie sat down with her coffee, stirred in a teaspoon of sugar, and took a sip. She looked at her mother, put the cup down, and started crying.

Jenny wrapped her arm around her daughter. "Ah, honey, what's wrong?"

"I messed up, Mom!" She blew her nose on a napkin. "I'm pretty sure I told Nick I couldn't see him."

"What happened, dear?"

"He's a great guy, but... I'm scared." More tears followed.

"Okay, pull yourself together, Margaret Ann, and tell me what you did."

With a very unladylike sniff, more like a snort, Maggie hiccupped and grabbed a dozen napkins from the lazy Susan. She blew her nose, wiped her eyes, and told her mother about the wonderful date, the things they talked about, and the movie. Leaving out the R-rated stuff from the car, she got to the crux of her concerns: she worried about reprimands, damaging her reputation, or even losing her job for dating a student's parent.

Jenny asked, "What about the by-laws or school constitution—Is that even a thing? Does the policy state that it's forbidden to date a parent of a student?"

Maggie admitted she didn't know, but she would talk to her principal on Monday. "I never had to deal with this problem."

"Of course not. It's not like last semester when you were moonlighting as an exotic dancer."

Maggie sprayed a mouthful of coffee, laughing. "Mother!"

Jenny rolled to the sink and tossed her a dish towel. "Gotcha. Now clean up your messes, young lady. The table and your love life. I'd hate for you to lose Nick before you even caught him."

CHAPTER
NINETEEN

After seeing Nick and Maggie moping around Saturday morning, Gayle threw a supernatural hissy fit, darting around the Millers' kitchen like a large, angry hummingbird.

Ron's patience frayed with every sharp turn. "Will you please stop flying around like that? You're gonna make a mess. What's gotten into you?"

Gayle whipped around to face him, her tone sharp. "What's gotten into me? Here you were all googly-eyed over Claire and her talks with Janet. Her dad is actually paying attention to her, holding her hand, kissing her head. Well, whoop-de-doo. For a novice you're doing fine. Clumsy, a menace in the air, but... argh! Here I am, an experienced ghost, and I have apparently overestimated my skills. I can't even keep two people together that really like each other!"

"Gayle, they're adults, and Maggie has to decide how much Nick means to her, and if it means putting her job in jeopardy." Ron pleaded.

"Oh, is that all? She won't risk her job. She loves teaching! That, and her mother are her entire world. Now, I have to use all my powers to make sure they not only get back together but stay together." She huffed and flew straight up as if she were a helicopter on takeoff.

Fed up, Ron barked. "Enough with the tantrum, you big baby! Do something helpful! This isn't just about you getting your way! "

She zoomed, and stopped in mid-air, her trail whirling like a dust devil. "What did you say?"

Ron blanched. *Uh oh.*

⇥❋⇤

Of course it's raining, it's Monday. The dismal weather matched Maggie's mood. She usually looked forward to a new week, asking her students what they did over the weekend, and refining her lesson plan to engage them as much as possible. Today, she needed an appointment with Principal Gates, and worried about what she would learn.

When she checked in at the school office that morning, Maggie made her appointment with Mrs. Jackson, recalling Nick's joke about the crush he suspected she had on him. All business, the school secretary, in her mid-70s, glanced at Maggie with what she perceived as disapproval—tight lips and a creased brow. *Is that a stink-eye? Oh no, she suspects something about Nick's visits.* The older woman checked the principal's calendar, and they agreed on 12:15.

Gayle followed Maggie all morning, trailing her through the halls, the teachers' lounge, and even the ladies' room. She needed to get inside Maggie's head and convince her that Nick was the guy. But Ron's comments nagged at her, and she hovered over Maggie's shoulder as she arrived for her appointment.

Mrs. Gates, a compact woman with tight gray curls, met Maggie's eyes with little expression. Her professional uniform of dark slacks and a jacket only added to her no-nonsense demeanor. A knot tightened in Maggie's stomach as she explained her situation, aware of the principal's strict adherence to rules.

"I find it unprofessional to date a single parent of one of your students," Mrs. Gates began, her tone cool but not unkind. "However, I wouldn't fire you unless the relationship disrupted your classroom..." She paused, looking out her window.

"That happened to a teacher once before, when a jilted lover accused her of flunking his son because she broke up with him. He complained to the school board and made quite a scene; it was the kind of scandal I won't tolerate. If I were you, I'd use extreme caution. If I find any preferential treatment or public drama on school grounds, I will have to take action." She stood and circled her desk to where Maggie sat. "Consider this a warning."

"On a more personal note, Maggie, you are one of our best teachers. Your class loves you. You're bright and dedicated, and this profession can be lonely work. Choose wisely, and you'll have a satisfying career."

Gayle listened in, recalling her own rebellious teens. This wasn't her first—or fifth—time in a principal's office. *Maybe I can still fix this.* She had to ensure Nick and Maggie stayed together. *Don't they see I'm right?*

Chastised by The Boss, Gayle couldn't shake Ron's words. Maybe she was being selfish and manipulative. She scowled, trying to push the thought aside. *Nah. I'll sit back, let things fall apart, and they'll beg me to fix it.* But her conscience, like a nagging puppy, yapped in her ear. *Do something helpful,* it said. *Look for clues.* She groaned, torn between pride and purpose.

On the way out, she couldn't resist gliding past Mrs. Gates, who clutched her collar and swiveled her head in search of the chill. After ending the meeting, Maggie thanked her for her time, left the office, and struggled through her afternoon lessons. At least she knew she probably wouldn't be fired unless Nick barged into her class and made a scene. *Would he? Was it worth the risk? What if it didn't work out? What if...*

That night, when Nick called, Maggie was in a dark mood and told him she couldn't talk; she had a lot on her mind.

Jenny overheard Maggie's tense voice and took her hand. "What's going on, Maggie? Why are you so upset with Nick?"

Maggie shook her head, unable to meet her mother's gaze. "I'm fine, Mom. Just... tired," she mumbled before retreating upstairs.

In her room, Maggie collapsed onto her bed, only to sit up moments later. She paced the floor, her thoughts circling endlessly. *Why did I push him away? Why does this feel so impossible?*

No answers came—just the familiar weight of sadness and guilt. A murky memory lingered at the edges of her mind, leaving her feeling more lost than ever.

Nick stared at his phone, feeling the sting of Maggie's brusque response. *Why won't she just tell me what's wrong so I can fix it?* He huffed. *Right, because I'm such a genius at fixing things.*

Claire sat on the couch, whispering to herself—or maybe to Ron. Nick watched her for a moment, debating whether to interrupt. *She looks happy enough,* he thought. *I shouldn't pump her for information, but...*

He walked over and sat beside her—on top of Ron. He jumped up to grab the sweater he kept on the banister, since he needed it so often, then sat down again. Ron had moved to the other side, watching Nick. Claire looked at her dad with big eyes and sidled closer.

Nick brushed her cheek with his finger. "Honey, how was your day at school?"

"Oh." Relieved, she said, "It was okay."

"Did anything unusual happen?"

"No."

"Did Miss Sanderson come in today?”

"Yes," she thought for a moment. "But she seemed kind of sad."

“Why do you say that?" He put his hand on her knee.

“She didn't smile like usual and wouldn’t call on me when I raised my hand."

“Do you think maybe she didn't feel well?"

"Maybe." She looked at Ron, but he said nothing. “She didn’t talk to you on the phone just now. Do you think she doesn't like us anymore?”

“Oh, sweet pea, I'm sure that's not the reason. I'll call her later and ask how she's feeling.”

Claire smiled and nodded, “That's a good idea, Daddy.”

"Sometimes, even daddies get good ideas." He tickled her ear, laughter lifting both their spirits.

CHAPTER

TWENTY

Maggie sat in a chair by the phone, her mind wandering as she tried to focus on a student's homework. When the phone rang, she startled.

"Hello?"

"Hi." The voice on the other end was hesitant, quiet.

Maggie sat up straighter, her heartbeat quickening. "Nick?"

"Yes, it's me. Don't put me off again, please." He paused, the weight of his words hanging in the air. "What's going on, Maggie? Claire asked me if you don't like us anymore. She doesn't understand, and frankly, neither do I."

Maggie closed her eyes, guilt tightening her throat. "Oh no. I'm sorry..."

"Why would she say that? Whatever is going on—or not going on—with us, please don't take it out on her."

Aghast, Maggie hissed. "I would never!" She pictured him yelling, banging on her classroom door. *Is this how it starts?*

"I wouldn't think so." His tone softened. "So why the cold shoulder?"

Maggie opened her mouth, but no words came. She swallowed. "Oh, Nick. It's a mess."

Nick waited. "Maggie, are you okay? Talk to me, honey."

His sweetness broke her resolve. "I still don't know what to do." She reached for a tissue, sniffling.

"About us? Please talk to me, Mags. Let's try to work it out."

She heard the pain in his voice. "We need to talk, but not on the phone. Can we meet somewhere neutral?"

"I can't leave Claire," Nick said tightly.

"Oh, of course."

Silence.

"Can't you tell me anything? Maybe I can help."

She cried and laughed at the same time. "No, you can't; you're the problem."

"What have I done?"

She pictured him pacing as far as the corded phone would allow. "Nothing; you've done nothing wrong."

"Then...what?"

Reclaiming her composure, she told Nick about her meeting with Mrs. Gates. He stayed quiet while she recounted the story about favoritism in the classroom and the consequences of another teacher dating a parent who made a scene at the school. "Our dating could be a scandal!"

On the other end of the line, Nick pinched the bridge of his nose. His voice rose. "How archaic! So what if you're my daughter's teacher? Who does she think she is? I'd like to give her a piece of my..." Nick paused.

Maggie heard a scratchy sound in her ear, imagining it to be the stubble on his chin.

Calmer, Nick continued. "Okay. Geez, I see where she's coming from. I wasn't always such a hothead. I wonder if you bring it out in me." He spoke dramatically. "So, we're dating, huh?"

Maggie leaned back in her chair, tension easing. "Well, we have had coffee and margaritas together. You even kissed me a couple of times."

"Ah, I remember. It seems so long ago now. Well, you can take me out anytime. I like Italian food. I might even let you kiss me. Seriously, we can work this out, Maggie. Don't give up on us. I promise I'll never show up at your school angry. Uh, again." Maggie recalled their first meeting and how far they'd come.

Nick said, "I'm so sorry you have to make this choice, but I'll respect it, whatever you decide. Just know that you mean a lot to me and Claire. Will you let her know you still like her, and even her dad?" He swallowed hard. "Please?"

"Of course, Nick," she whispered. "What am I going to do with you?"

His voice dropped to a husky whisper. "Do you really want me to tell you? On the phone? With Claire here and your mom there?" Maggie hugged herself. Yes, I kinda would.

"Maggie?"

"I'm here. Please let me think about this, Nick. My heart wants to be with you, but this is my career, my life. Jobs like mine are hard to find around here—especially if there are improprieties on your record." There are things he doesn't know, but I'll have to tell him eventually. "Give me time, Nick. I'll talk to Claire, and I'll call you."

At Nick's house, Gayle hovered in the living room, observing his side of the phone call. Discouraged, she paced in the air.

"Nick's on board," she muttered to Ron. "But Maggie's going to be a challenge."

Ron, perched on the back of the couch, tapped his chin thoughtfully. "What if she had examples? You know, other teachers who made it work with parents?"

Gayle stopped mid-air, arms crossed. "That's not the worst idea you've ever had. What's gotten into you, Wrong Way?"

Ron bristled at the nickname but shrugged. "Nothing. I pay attention."

"Now you'll have to do some investigating."

"Me?" He hesitated. "Okay, I'll do it. I'll follow Maggie to school in the morning and see if I can find some records."

"Make sure you…" She caught herself. "Do what you think is right." In the back of her mind, she mulled over a backup plan involving small-town intrigue and finessing a rebellion against the school policy with signs and chanting. Nick and Maggie would live happily ever after thanks to Gayle, who would be immortalized…

"Gayle," Ron waited. "Gayle, I'm leaving."

She snapped out of her reverie. "All right, Ron. Good luck."

Ron noted the shift in her attitude with a hint of suspicion. The next morning, he hurried to the elementary school where Maggie taught. In the school office, Principal Gates chatted with Mrs. Jackson before most of the children and faculty arrived, discussing the day's agenda. Ron perched on the copy machine.

Mrs. Gates leaned over the counter, her voice low as she spoke to Mrs. Jackson. "Anything noteworthy in the visitor log for Maggie Sanderson?"

Mrs. Jackson flipped through the pages, her brows knitting together. "Nick Miller—Claire Miller's father—visited Miss Sanderson's class twice. You remember him, right? His wife passed last year."

"I do." Gates tapped her pen against the counter, her face unreadable. "Let me know if he visits again."

Across the room, Maggie entered to sign in, oblivious to the conversation as she pondered her lesson plan. No one spoke for a moment.

Principal Gates said, "Good morning, Miss Sanderson. May I speak with you?"

"Sure, Mrs. Gates." They walked to her office, with Ron following. Principal Gates closed the door.

"Maggie," she said, "I've been thinking about our meeting the other day. First, I wanted to thank you for speaking with me about it. That took some courage, and I admire you for it."

"Thank you."

"It won't surprise you that I get regular updates on visitors, and sometimes I just glance at them. But I noticed that Nick Miller had two meetings with you recently. Of course, his daughter Claire is in your class, and we all know about the terrible tragedy of her mother's passing."

Ron observed Maggie's discomfort as she gripped her purse. *Where is Gates going with this?*

"I'm pleased that you took time to have a conference with her father. I'm sure it has been difficult for both of them. We thought the world of Ann."

Maggie started to speak, but Mrs. Gates raised her finger to signal 'wait a moment.'

"I'm getting to the point, which is that I know you and your mother help to chaperone the Sophomore dance at Wilson High this weekend. There is someone I think you should meet there, another chaperone. His name is Mark Minsky. He's a biology teacher and an old friend. Look him up and say hello for me, would you? And please give your mother my regards. That's all I wanted to say. Have a wonderful day!" She smiled, standing.

"I will, thank you." Maggie left for her classroom, and Ron thought she looked as curious as he was.

Ron considered this his best lead. He hurried to the high school. *Mrs. Gates would know about the Millers, but who is this Minsky guy?*

Ron found him in the teachers' lounge at the high school. Just an average-looking guy teaching biology. In his classroom, he spoke about cell division. *What was Principal Gates up to?*

Following him home, Ron watched him kiss his wife and greet a young man in his late teens, who snacked at the refrigerator.

With little else to investigate, he returned to the Miller home, figuring he'd learn more at the dance.

Later that evening, Ron found comfort in the simple pleasure of sipping pretend tea with Claire. She served with her plastic teapot and cups, just as she had done with Jenny. Ron couldn't hold the cup, but they raised their pinkies in the air like rich ladies.

"You really like Miss Jenny, don't you, Claire?" he asked, his voice warm.

"Yes. She has a funny smile she said was 'just for me.' I like the way she smells too—like baby powder. We talk about lots of things, except you. I wish I could. And her chocolate-covered raisin and coconut macaroon cookies are delicious too." She stirred her cup with an imaginary spoon, and her smile faded. She looked up at Ron with sad eyes.

"Do you know why my Daddy is so sad? If he knew about you, maybe it could make him happy too."

"I think we should wait until Miss Janet says it's okay. I know it's hard to keep a secret like that, but you're doing great! Just remember, never keep secrets about people if they hurt you or make you feel bad, like your teacher says."

Seeing the frown on Claire's face, Ron continued. "Your dad and Miss Sanderson have to figure out some things they don't think are fair, and they want to make them better. You didn't do anything wrong."

"Gosh, I hope they can be friends. I really like Miss Sanderson, and I know she likes me because Daddy said so. She just can't show parshi...part...partiality. Daddy said that means she has to like everyone in our class the same." She smiled, proud she could say that big word.

Ron pretended to sip his tea. "That's exactly right, Claire."

C H A P T E R

TWENTY-ONE

Maggie and Jenny arrived early for the dance, around 7:00. Decorations in the school colors, crimson and silver, adorned the gym. Folding tables held refreshments. Their task was simple: let the kids have fun without spiking the punch, fighting, or dancing too closely.

Overhead, Gayle and Ron floated, watching the scene unfold below. "Think this Mark guy will give her the advice she needs?" Ron asked.

"She's got a good head on her shoulders, but she needs a push in the right direction." "If he doesn't, I will," Gayle muttered, her gaze darting toward Maggie.

"Let's hope it doesn't come to that," Ron teased.

Gayle ignored him. "Let's split up for a while; I'll catch up with you later."

Two other chaperones stood at the double doors, greeting the kids as they entered. They were a good-looking couple in their mid-40s. He had wavy brown hair, wore a dark blue shirt and tie, filled out a bit in the middle, and had a friendly smile. She was a striking brunette in a sleeveless red dress that fell just below her knees. Gayle flew over her shoulder and hovered there for a few seconds, listening.

The woman told the man she was chilly. "I think I'll get my wrap, Mark. I'll be right back."

Gayle rose higher. *Oops. Got a little too close.*

"Honey, I'll get it for you."

"That's okay. I also need to use the ladies' room. I'll get someone to take my place while I'm gone."

"Okay," he said, smiling at three girls entering the gym in their finery.

The woman spotted Jenny on her way to the ladies' room and swerved towards her, laughing. "Jenny! So glad to see you again!" She bent to hug her. "And who is this lovely young lady?"

"Amy, you haven't met my daughter, Maggie. Maggie, this is Amy Tanner." Turning to Maggie while they greeted each other, "We met at a support group after your father passed." She turned to Amy. "Has it been that long?"

"It's been too long, Jenny. It's actually Amy Minsky now—well, Tanner-Minsky. I've remarried. That's Mark, he's the cute one guarding the doors. But let's talk later. I know you're staff tonight. Can you cover for me? I really have to, you know."

"Of course," Jenny said. "Maggie, you join Mark. I'll guard the punch bowl."

Aha, Gayle thought, *I think I know where this is going.* She followed Maggie.

Maggie threaded through the students on her way to the doors. Gayle thought she looked curious but wary as she approached the man.

"Hey, you must be Mark. I'm Maggie Sanderson, your wife's temporary relief."

"Oh, good." He met her direct eye contact. "There's going to be a throng soon. Can you be a bouncer in that dress too?" They smiled, and she watched his eyes follow Amy. "You look terrific, but you also look like you want to ask me something."

Maggie nodded, visibly calmer. "I do, Mark."

"Sorry, Maggie, I'm taken." He gave her a sly grin.

"Really? I hadn't noticed that goofy grin when you looked at Amy." She relaxed a bit more.

"That obvious, huh?"

Maggie laughed softly. "A little. But seriously, Mrs. Gates suggested I talk to you about... well, you know, dating as a teacher."

Mark leaned against the doorframe, his expression turning thoughtful. "Ah, the old 'appearance of impropriety' meeting. Let me guess—you've got your eye on a parent of one of your students?"

"Now, I get it. So, I'm not the first lonely heart to seek your wisdom? We just started dating, but Mrs. Gates cautioned me—warned me, really. Now let me guess. My mother, over by the punch bowl, knew Amy as Tanner, and she said she remarried. Was she a parent of your student?"

Mark waved two couples into the gym and turned to Maggie. "You got it. Maddie and I go back a ways. I knew what happened to her, and she helped me through a rough patch or two. Not that the townsfolk ever came after us with torches and pitchforks. But 'this isn't the big city; everybody knows everybody.' Yada yada."

"Long story short: Amy lost her husband a few years ago, and their son got into some trouble in my class, so I called a conference. We hit it off and have been together ever since."

"I sense there's more to the story," Maggie said.

Good girl, Gayle hovered near the doors, eavesdropping. *There's gotta be more.*

"Yeah, when we started dating, I worried about it. I had a long talk with our principal and my brother-in-law, the lawyer. We checked the rules and didn't find any grounds for dismissal. By then, we were almost in love and decided to stick it out discreetly. We dated privately and went out to dinner, sometimes even the three of us. People from school saw us, but so what?

"I got razzed by the kids a couple of times, but most of the faculty attended the wedding. It can be done, Maggie. We're just regular folks living our lives, not the high court where just the 'appearance of impropriety' is enough to ruin you. If you really like this guy, and he's not psycho, I say go for it. I've never been happier. You can tell Maddie I said so."

"I will," she thought about what he said. "Wait, you mentioned 'what happened to her.'"

"Did she tell you about the teacher who nearly lost everything because of a jilted lover?" Mark asked, tilting his head with a grin.

Maggie's eyes widened. "No! Do you mean...?"

"Yes. It was her," Mark chuckled. "The guy caused a scandal, but she handled it with grace. It wasn't easy, but she came through stronger on the other side. She knows what it's like to be in your shoes, Maggie."

Bingo, Gayle thought. *That ought to settle her down.*

Gayle saw it in Maggie's face: a smile of relief. "That's good to know, Mark."

Amy came up behind them. Mark kissed her forehead and took her hand. "Hey, sweetheart."

Maggie said, "Thanks for the encouragement, Mark. I'd better get back to Mom before she gets on the dance floor. Bye, Amy."

Amy asked him, "What's that about?"

"Just some friendly advice about dating civilians, dear."

"Ah, another referral." She took his arm.

"Where's your wrap? Are you warm enough?"

"Funny, I wasn't cold anymore."

Gayle flew a couple of loops near the ceiling and sped off to find Ron.

Maggie drove home, lost in her thoughts. In bed, she tossed and turned, tangling the sheets. She stretched, reflecting on her college days. *I was such a nerd; my roommate always teased me about studying all the time and not going out with boys. To me, that's what they were: immature boys, wanting to drink and party all the time. I wanted to be a teacher, so I studied hard, researched, and took on extra credit. I dated a few guys, from class or through friends. The dates were all right—the usual dinner and a movie—but nothing special, like canoeing or a hot air balloon ride. No one seemed to click.*

She rolled over, her mind drifting back to the darker corners of her past. Though she didn't want to think about it, the memory surfaced unbidden, as vivid as if it were yesterday.

She'd been optimistic and focused on her studies. He seemed like a nice guy—until he wasn't. The date had started innocently, with casual conversation and dinner. But when he crossed a line, she pushed him away, feeling disgusted and betrayed.

The aftermath had been worse: rumors, harassment, and a roommate who chose his side. Maggie squeezed her eyes shut, willing the memory to fade.

She came home on a break and shared the incident with her father. She'd always been able to talk frankly with him. The experience affected her so deeply that she swore she wouldn't date until after she got her teaching credentials.

Clearing that hurdle, she celebrated at a local bar with her soon-to-be teacher friends. A man singled her out and bought her a drink. He was good-looking, and she was feeling feisty; one thing led to another. Another disaster. Another reason she vowed not to date anyone else until she learned why she attracted such horrible losers. Maybe it was her fault. She had her dear friend Janet to thank for helping her through it.

Her father died that year. Her career had just begun, and she lived with her mother through their profound grief, supporting one another. Months later, when Jenny joined her and some friends on a hike in Rock Canyon and fell, Maggie stayed with her through her long recovery. She learned about resilience, optimism, and how to love life again—but not how to trust, really trust another man.

Now she'd found someone. She saw Nick in his strength and vulnerability, his loyalty and persistence. Sure, he could be stubborn, resistant, and even quick-tempered, but these weren't deal breakers. *Were they? I can't believe he would endanger my career.* Could she look past all that and see the man?

A small voice in her head reminded her of her father. 'Finding a good man is like finding a decent parking space at the mall. You gotta get past the speed bumps and maybe wait for someone to leave. But you find one eventually.' Her eyes welled with the memory of that adage, delivered at their kitchen table one morning so long ago.

Clarity came to her as she dabbed her eyes, chuckling. *Get it together, girl. You're an adult now, and so is Nick. He's not like those jerks. Janet would urge you to acknowledge your past but not keep replaying the tapes, or something like that.*

Have I finally found someone I can trust, someone to love and be loved by? I'll need to trust myself first. Let my past stay in the past; I'm moving forward.

Maggie lay in bed, staring at the ceiling as fragments of her past swirled in her mind. The faces of the ghosts of those days mingled with Nick's warm smile. Was she brave enough to let him in?

Her father's voice echoed in her memory, offering wisdom wrapped in humor. "You'll find the right one, Mags. Just don't park in the wrong space too long."

She chuckled softly, tears welling in her eyes. Maybe, just maybe, Nick wasn't the wrong space. Maybe he was the one she'd been waiting for.

As she drifted into sleep, hope wrapped around her like a warm embrace, filling the cracks of her uncertainty.

CHAPTER

TWENTY-TWO

Sunday morning sunlight streamed through her window. Maggie woke up with thoughts of Nick and Claire. Should she call him? Should she wait for him to call her? Stretching her arms above her head and feeling optimistic about their relationship, she pushed off the covers and hopped out of bed. She had to do this. If it could work, she'd make it work.

Standing under the shower spray, she rehearsed. Hi, I'm ready to continue dating now. *Hey Nick, how's it going? Oh, by the way, I'd enjoy kissing you again. Oh brother, am I a scriptwriter or what?*

Dressed for the day and light on her feet, Maggie swooped into the kitchen, making a beeline for the coffee. Jenny sat at the stove, turning French toast in a buttered skillet and humming along with the oldies station on the radio.

"Morning, Mom. Oh, my favorite. It smells delicious." Cinnamon and vanilla wafted through the kitchen as she kissed her mother's cheek.

"Morning, dear. You're in fine fettle." Jenny smiled.

"I hope my fettle is fine after I talk to Nick." She sipped, her eyes twinkling.

"Are you expecting a call from him today?" Jenny asked, tending the pan.

"Nope, I'm going to call him. Maybe I'll even visit him today; what do you think of that?"

"I think it's a bitchin' idea."

"Bitchin', Mom? Really?"

"Hey, I'm an oldie too. I think you should finish your coffee, forfeit your breakfast, and get over there right now."

"Forfeit my breakfast? That's whack."

"Whack? I'll give you a whack," she brandished her spatula menacingly. "Do you want to see them or not? You're burnin' daylight."

"Chill, dude. It's like, eight o'clock." She recoiled in mock horror. "Whose side are you on anyway?"

"Always yours, Margaret. Of course, Nick's and Claire's too. All three of you, really."

"May I at least have one slice of your fabulous French toast?" she asked.

Jenny plated a slice with a dusting of powdered sugar and a dozen mixed berries. "Eat, drink, and go forth."

"Bossy."

"Loving."

Knocking on Nick's door, Maggie had second thoughts. She'd never been one to act first and think later. Her stomach fluttered with butterflies. Before she could change her mind, Nick opened the door.

His mouth dropped open. "Maggie! Hi. Hello. We were just—I'm glad you're here. "His eyes scanned the silky brown hair falling around her shoulders with tiny sparkles that reflected the morning sun. Her lemon-yellow dress highlighted the curves of her legs. She could tell he wanted to touch her; his hands moved hesitantly.

"May I come in?" Her eyes met his. Her voice sounded far away.

"Of course." He brushed his jacket with his hand. "Please, come in." He opened the door wider.

Smiling at his awkward yet kind reception, she moved past him into the foyer. Nick sighed as she drifted by, captivated by her unique scent of shampoo, lotion, and exotic oil. *Oh, yeah. That's the reaction I was going for.*

Claire bounded down the stairs. "Hi, Miss Sanderson! Did you come to go to church with us?" Before Nick could respond, Maggie noticed how nice they both looked in their Sunday clothes—Nick in a charcoal gray suit and greenish tie. Wow, he looked handsome. Claire wore a cute white dress adorned with pink and green flowers, and she was glad she had chosen a dress.

"I'd like that very much, Claire, but I'm not sure of your dad's plans." She turned to Nick.

He looked at his watch and then back at her. "We have about 20 minutes to spare, if that's okay." Grinning, he added, "You don't have to go if you don't want to."

Maggie relaxed her shoulders, swiveling her head between the man and his daughter. Claire's hopeful eyes stirred butterflies in Nick's stomach again.

"I'd love to go to church with two of my favorite people." She glanced shyly at Nick.

Nick released the breath he'd been holding, and Claire jumped up and down, singing an impromptu "Yaaay! We're going to church to-_geth-_er." She grabbed Maggie's hand and smiled at Nick. "Let's go, Daddy-o." She giggled.

"Hold your horses, sweet pea. We have a few minutes. Did you make your bed?"

"Yes, sir!" She saluted. "I sure did, and Ron even helped." Her smile faded.

The adults let it slide. Nick chuckled, "Tell him thanks for me."

They walked into church with Claire between them, holding hands like a young family. In her excitement, Claire would have skipped to the pew if they hadn't slowed her down.

Maggie noticed the looks they received as they entered—curious, not nosy or judgmental. Nick hadn't brought a woman to church since Ann, but she felt welcomed and listened peacefully to the sermon.

The pastor spoke of love—patient and kind. *All right, God, you have my attention. I'll be patient.* She glanced at Claire and then at Nick, who was to her left. *Thanks for giving us a chance.*

After the service, several parishioners greeted them. Nick introduced Maggie simply as Maggie, not as his girlfriend or Claire's teacher. That was fine with her.

Nick drove with Maggie by his side and Claire in the back seat. He suggested they stop for lunch, and Claire bounced in her seat, yelling, "Hamburgers!"

Nick laughed. "I think we can do better than hamburgers, sweetie. Don't you?"

Maggie suggested an Italian restaurant, slyly recalling Nick's comment about wanting Italian food. Claire chimed in, saying that meatballs were just as good as hamburgers.

The restaurant's casual ambiance put them at ease. A candle flickered in a Chianti bottle on the red, white, and green tablecloth. Maggie and Nick's eyes met. *So far, so good.*

A dapper waiter with black curly hair and a handlebar mustache approached their table. Claire ordered spaghetti and meatballs, Nick chose lasagna primavera, and Maggie opted for antipasto—hold the anchovy.

They chatted about current events, including Claire in their conversation. Maggie could tell Nick was being cautious. *Poor guy, I've confused him, running hot and cold like that. He looks at me like I'll disappear any minute.*

She reached over and covered his hand with hers. "I'm sorry."

Nick smiled. "I'm just glad you're here."

Claire tilted her head and asked, "What are you sorry for, Miss Sanderson?"

Nick gently admonished her. "Don't be impolite, honey."

Maggie looked at Claire. "I think I got mixed up about being friends with your dad. If I hurt his feelings or yours, I didn't mean to, and it's good manners to say I'm sorry."

"Okay, and I'm sorry I was impolite." She looked at the two adults. "Do I have good manners, too?"

Nick patted her hand, smiling. "Yes, you do, young lady."

When the food arrived, Maggie thought she had ordered wrong upon seeing the huge platter of cheeses, meats, and more in front of her.

"I thought this would be the lunch salad."

The waiter smiled. "It is the luncheon salad."

"It looks scrumptious, but I won't do it justice. You two are going to have to help me eat it."

Nick raised his eyebrows. "I'm concentrating on my lasagna."

Claire chimed in, "I'm eating my meatballs." She kissed her fingertips and flung them open. "Mmm, mmm, good."

Maggie laughed. "Thanks for nothing, guys."

They did their best and still ended up with three takeout boxes—a satisfying lunch, indeed. They passed, with some regret, on the spumoni and tiramisu.

Driving home, Nick asked Maggie if she could stay a while. "I'd like that," she said, smiling to confirm it.

Once inside, Maggie asked, "Can I use your house phone to check in with my mom?" Nick nodded, and she added, "I really think it's time I trade in my cell phone or my plan. My reception is so bad at home, I hardly use it."

"Yeah, I've been thinking about that, myself."

Claire gasped excitedly. "Do I get one, too?"

"Not yet, Claire, but when I get mine, I'll let you call someone. How's that?"

"But I don't know who to call," she said, her eyes downcast.

"You could call my mother and talk about your tea party," Maggie suggested.

"Yeah, that would be fun. When, Daddy? When will you get a new cell phone?"

"Not so fast. I'll have to see which one is the best," Nick replied.

"But that'll take foreverrr," she whined.

"Claire Elizabeth, does someone need a nap?"

"I don't think so. I'm not sleepy. Do you need a nap, Daddy?"

Maggie hid her grin.

"I'm okay, thank you." Nick tousled her hair. "Honey, please sit on the couch for a little while. You can watch TV if you want."

She complied.

Maggie made her call, and Jenny told her to stay as long as she liked. She hung up, shaking her head.

"What's so funny?" Nick asked.

"My mother, need I say more?"

"No, I think she's on my side."

With a raised eyebrow, Maggie replied, "Oh really?"

"Well, she must be right. She's older and wiser. Just sayin'." He winked.

They decided to play cards. Claire bounded upstairs to get her deck of Old Maid cards and skipped down the stairs. They quickly got into it. Soon, the friendly competition turned comical, with cards slapping down and teasing all around. By the end of the game, Claire stood on her chair with arms raised, proclaiming, "I am the champion!"

Nick rose to get iced tea from the refrigerator. Maggie moved behind him to reach for the glasses. When Nick turned, their faces were inches apart, and she felt an undeniable connection. He looked at her lips, and she put her hand on his chest...

"Are we having iced tea, or what, Daddy?" Claire interjected, still basking in her victory, breaking their moment.

"Coming right up, my champion."

Nick took Maggie's shoulders and guided her toward the correct cabinet for the glasses. They filled the glasses and returned to the battleground.

They switched to War and then back to Old Maid. Maggie taught Claire how to play Rummy, and so the afternoon went. Near dinner time, Claire announced she was hungry.

Nick said he'd enjoyed himself so much that he lost track of time. He pulled Claire close and kissed her forehead.

Maggie said, "I can whip up something for dinner if you don't mind."

He looked at her, clearly touched. "That would be great, Maggie. Whatever's in the fridge. We'll save the Italian for tomorrow."

She moved gracefully around the kitchen, preparing a simple meal of grilled cheese sandwiches, green salad, and, to Claire's obvious delight, tomato soup. While the cards were cleared, Nick and Claire set the table. They talked about simple pleasures and scooped butter pecan ice cream for dessert.

"It's been a wonderful day, guys, but I need to prepare for school tomorrow." As darkness fell, Maggie needed to go. Nick ushered Claire to the tub and returned to have a few moments alone with her. He walked her to the front door, put his hands on her waist, and drew her close. Maggie slipped her arms around his shoulders, put one hand behind his head, pulled him forward, and met his kiss.

When their lips touched, Maggie felt as if an old movie projector had whirred to life. Alone with the man she'd been waiting for, she caught her breath as scenes of their future played in her mind: meals, birthdays, family outings. She hummed softly. In response, Nick brushed his lips from hers to her cheek, then to the soft spot between her neck and shoulder. Her past worries melted in the warmth of his embrace. Her thoughts receded, dissolving into trust. She was no longer an observer and willingly shared her heart, allowing him to lead.

Nick kissed her, also imagining their future together: leisurely breakfasts, coming home to her after work, and sharing their day. He envisioned catching an expression on her face he believed was only his to decode. His hand moved up her back and down to her waist, almost sliding further before he stopped himself. Pressing his forehead to hers, he thought, *there will be time.*

"Woman, you drive me crazy."

"That's a compliment, right?" Her cheek rested on his chest as she breathed in his scent.

"I never thought I would find someone like you, Mags. Today showed me what we could be together."

His fingers raked through her hair, his thumb stroking her ear; she had forgotten how good that felt. "Mmm. You drive me crazy, too. Man."

Nick laughed. "So, what now? I don't know about you, but I need a cold shower."

"Well, I do have to go. Maybe we can arrange another tea party with my mother," she grinned. "A late one, where Claire might have to sleep over." Her eyes sparkled with promise.

"You're clever, aren't you?" He kissed her again.

"Hmm," she licked her lips, her words a breathy whisper. "I'll have Jenny call Claire and invite her. How's her schedule?"

"I'll clear her calendar. You're sure about this?"

"I'm sure, Nick. I want to level up. But promise me I won't drive you so crazy that you run around my school like a lunatic, throwing rocks at my window and screaming my name, okay?" She smirked and kissed him.

"I promise—to try really hard. One more kiss, and then I'll let you go."

One kiss led to two, and finally, Maggie pulled away with a crooked smile. "See you later... Man."

"Wait." He called upstairs, "Claire, I'm going to walk Miss Maggie to her car. Are you okay?"

"Yes, Daddy. I'm almost done."

Nick walked her to her car and closed the door. He rubbed his face as she drove away, filled with gratitude for the woman who had entered their lives. At first, he hadn't wanted anything to do with her, but now he couldn't imagine life without her—especially when he and Claire needed her most. As he gazed up at the stars on his way back inside, he felt as though someone up there was watching over them.

C H A P T E R

TWENTY-THREE

In their cozy dining room, Jenny nodded, her fingers wrapped around a steaming cup of tea. "It's about time you found happiness, Maggie. How's Claire doing? And her 'special friend'?"

Maggie smiled, settling into the cushioned chair opposite her mother. "Janet's been great with Claire. She's teaching her that imaginary friends are okay while encouraging her to make real ones too. Having her over is a big help. Claire adores your tea parties."

Jenny leaned back, a soft chuckle escaping her lips. "I adore that little girl. Honestly, she's like the granddaughter I never had."

"Okay, Mom. Are we going there already?" Maggie warned, but her eyes sparkled. She fussed with a drooping flower in the vase, her gaze distant. Then she blinked and looked at Jenny as if struck by a revelation. "Oh...oh, my."

Jenny arched an eyebrow, a hint of teasing in her tone. "What's that look about?"

"Mom," Maggie whispered, leaning closer as if sharing a secret meant only for them. "I love her, too. And I love being with them. I think I..."

1 6 5

"You love him." Jenny's voice was gentle, her smile knowing.

Maggie's eyes filled with surprise and delight. She took a breath, her voice growing steadier. "I do. I really do love him!"

Jenny set her cup aside and squeezed Maggie's hand. "I've seen it in your eyes when you say his name, even when you were sulking around here. And I know you care deeply about Claire too. The three of you together seems more than just chance. Maybe Ann is looking down, grateful that Nick stumbled into your life. Some would say it's fate, but I call it a blessing."

Gayle floated with Ron above them. "They're always thanking Him, but we play our part, too." She turned to him and sighed. "I have to admit, Ron, you did good work at the dance. That guy made an impact on her." *There, that wasn't so hard.*

"Why, thank you, Gayle. Just doing my job," he drawled.

"Don't push it, mister."

⁕

The next evening, Nick smiled as he answered the phone. "Why yes, she's right here." He handed Claire the receiver. "You have a phone call."

"Huh? No one's ever called me before. Who is it, Daddy?"

"You'll need to answer the phone to find out, sweetheart."

She put the receiver to her ear. "Hello?"

"Hi, Claire, it's Miss Jenny. How are you, dear?"

Claire brightened and looked at her dad. "It's Miss Jenny." He smiled and motioned for her to keep talking.

"Hi, Miss Jenny. I'm fine, thank you. How are you?"

He heard Jenny chuckle on the line. "I'm also fine, thank you. I called because I would love to have you over for an exclusive girl's tea party. Would you like that? I enjoyed our last one, but I'm afraid it will have to be later in the day. You might want to stay overnight. Would that be all right with you and your dad?"

Claire nodded with wide eyes, bouncing on her toes. Nick smiled. "She can't see you, honey. What's up?"

"She wants me to come over for another exclusive girl's tea party and spend the night. Can I, Daddy? Can I?"

"Well, let me think about this." He put a hand to his mouth as if deep in thought, hiding his grin. "Spend the night, huh? Would you have to take your nightie and toothbrush?"

"Yes, of course," she giggled. "Can I, Dad?"

Nick almost laughed out loud as his daughter assumed a serious tone, scrunching her face in contemplation. *Oh my, she has me wrapped around her finger.*

"I really learn a lot about manners from Miss Jenny, and that's important."

Relenting, Nick teased, "Well, manners *are* important. If you're sure..."

Remembering Jenny was still on the line, Claire put the receiver to her ear. "Yes, I can, Miss Jenny! Daddy said it's okay, and I can bring my toothbrush too."

"Why, I'm so glad you can come, dear. You just made an old lady very happy."

"Are you very old, Miss Jenny?"

"Ah, dear, you are such a sweetheart. Let's just say I'm old enough to be your grandma."

"You would be an awesome grandma, Miss Jenny."

"Thank you, dear. Now, let me talk to your daddy, and we'll set up the date, okay?"

"See ya later, alligator." She handed the phone to Nick and skipped up the stairs to her room.

As Nick and Jenny made the arrangements, Claire danced around her room and saw Ron and Gayle. She couldn't hear or really talk with Gayle; she just knew she was there. "I'm going to have another tea party, Ron. Isn't that great? I have to make sure my gloves are clean; I got chocolate on them last time. Oh, what should I wear?"

Gayle floated restlessly, feeling a twinge of insecurity. She hoped Nick and Maggie would stay together—not just for their sake, but for her own success and the mission's progress. She grudgingly admitted that Ron's recent idea had worked out fine—maybe better than her original plan. It felt strange, but for once, she didn't mind letting him take the lead.

Ron and Claire searched her closet for a proper tea party outfit, making little progress. Gayle hovered closer, peering into the closet as Claire held up the yellow dress she wore last time. Ron glanced at Gayle, waiting for her input. She hesitated, her head tilting slightly as if battling her own thoughts. *I just want her to look nice—because she deserves it. But she should choose for herself, shouldn't she? Ugh, what's wrong with me?*

"What do you think, Ron? Should I wear this one again?" Claire asked.

"Um, I think so?" Gayle tugged at Ron's sleeve. "Oh, wait a minute, Claire. Gayle has an idea."

Gayle sighed, searching for words. "Ron, this is just an idea... you don't have to, and neither does she. But if you mention that one," she pointed, "it needs a little work, but I could help." She forced a smile. "One shouldn't wear the same dress twice to a proper tea party, if there's an alternative."

Ron gave Gayle a side-eye, grunting. He grinned at her and turned to Claire. "What about this one, the white with purple flowers? Gayle wants to see."

"She does? Cool! She's..." Claire faced Ron's mentor with the dress. "You're so pretty, Miss Gayle. But this dress is kinda messed up and wrinkly. It has a little rip."

Ron nodded at Gayle and turned to Claire. "She said she can fix it if you want."

"Yes, please!" As she spoke, the dress whirled in the air, and Claire watched in delight as a needle and thread appeared, mending the sleeve and ruffle, while a puff of air smoothed the wrinkles. She jumped and clapped when the dress, good as new, hung itself on a hanger in her closet.

"Thank you, Miss Gayle! You're awesome!"

Ron chuckled. "She said, 'you're welcome. It will look beautiful on you for the tea party.'"

Downstairs, Nick laughed, thanking Jenny for making Claire's day. Although grateful for her help, a twinge of awkwardness crept in as he thought about his motives.

Jenny's voice softened. "I may be old, but I remember." She paused, then added, "Be careful with my daughter's heart, young fella."

Nick's tone was steady. "Always."

Claire wanted to know if her party was that night. Every day that week, Nick finally got out the calendar and had her draw a big red circle on Friday. He told her to mark every night before she went to bed, and she would be one day closer to Friday. That satisfied her, but it was only Monday.

Friday finally arrived. Nick pretended not to notice when Claire looked at the calendar on the kitchen wall and raised her fist, punching the air. "Yes!"

When Nick arrived home from work, Claire bounded over to him, giggling. "That was the longest day of school, *ever!*"

"Are you excited?" he asked, giving her a hug as they walked to the kitchen.

"Yes, I love, love, love going to Miss Jenny's for our parties."

"I'm kind of excited too," he smiled, opening a bottle of water and handing Claire an apple.

"Why are you excited, Daddy? Are you and Miss Sanderson having a tea party too?"

Nick coughed a little on his drink. "I suppose you could say that."

"Does that mean yes?" She bounced playfully on her toes.

"Yes, sweet pea, it means yes."

"Good, then we're both going to be happy. Isn't that great?" She smiled and took a bite of her apple.

"It sure is. I think we deserve it, don't you?"

Nodding, she said, "Absolutely! Ron tells me that all the time."

"Do you know what you're going to wear? We should leave soon."

"Yes, Daddy. Gayle even fixed my dress!" Her eyes flew open, and she stopped chewing.

Nick lowered his bottle and studied his daughter's worried face. "Gayle?"

Claire looked down at her apple and closed her mouth.

"Claire?" No answer. "Claire, look at me."

No response.

Nick squatted next to Claire and lifted her chin to look at him. "Claire, talk to me. Who is Gayle?"

She squeezed her eyes shut and shook her head. "Mmm, mmm." She shook her head back and forth, her lips tight. Clearly, she didn't want to talk about it.

He frowned. The pressure in his head rose a notch, then another. Steadying his voice, he asked, "Honey, is that one of your friends from school?" Claire shook her head no.

Guilt hit him in a wave of nausea. He'd failed his daughter. Then the fear of losing her to some unseen force he could not defend against weakened his knees. Anger simmered with no definable target. He set his jaw and whispered, "Is she a friend of Ron's?" Slowly, she nodded.

Panic surged through him, a visceral urge to grab Claire and run. Memories of Ann's loss swirled in his mind, leaving him feeling helpless once again. The fragile progress Claire had made seemed to splinter under the weight of this new threat. "Focus," he told himself, though his thoughts felt like shattered glass. As calmly as he could manage, he said, "All right, Claire, go up to your room and pack your pajamas and things." When he heard her bedroom door open, he picked up the phone.

Janet was tidying her office, preparing to close for the weekend, when her phone rang. Nick explained what Claire had admitted, dread in his voice. "I thought we were getting somewhere. Now she's getting worse! Am I going to lose her, too? *What is happening to my little girl? What am I doing so* wrong?"

Her voice tempered his crisis. She spoke to him with kind firmness, understanding his feelings of helplessness and unresolved pain. Directing him not to alarm Claire, she instructed him to bring her to the office when he could focus on driving.

Nick agreed, though he had settled on a plan. *That's it. That's all I can do. I can't have any distractions if I hope to save my daughter.*

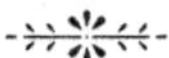

Maggie fussed with her hair, organized her medicine cabinet, then her linen closet. Her mind had drifted during class, and it seemed to her that Claire had the same problem. *She must be looking forward to her tea party as much as I am.*

When Nick called, she was initially glad to hear his voice but soon sensed the distress in it. He sounded worried yet determined. He said he needed to cancel their date, but it felt like more than that. She asked what had changed his mind. He explained that he needed to spend more time with Claire and that he'd gotten his priorities mixed up, but now he knew what he had to do.

"How can I help?" Maggie asked, part of her dreading the answer.

His voice quavered as he broke the silence. "Maggie, no, I can't go any further with you until I have Claire's problem under control. I've thought all week about how tonight would bring us closer together. But if Claire is reacting this way to her mother's death and my neglect, I have to handle this myself. I can't impose on *you.*" Ragged emotion crept into his voice as he said goodbye.

Maggie stood in the hallway with the phone in her hand when her mother approached. "Honey, what's wrong?"

"I think Nick just broke up with me."

"What? Why do you say that?"

Maggie stood numbly, relating what Nick had said. "Why would he do that? We were all looking forward to tonight. What could be so bad that he couldn't tell me?" She blinked away a tear and turned to Jenny.

Jenny took the phone from her daughter's hand. "Give him time, babe. I'm sure he'll come around and explain." But her eyes shone with worry about what the explanation might be.

CHAPTER

TWENTY-FOUR

Claire didn't understand why she had to see Janet when she was supposed to be getting ready for Miss Jenny's party. She'd been waiting a whole week for this event and had even laid out her dress. *Daddy looked sad and scared at the same time. It's because I slipped when I said Gayle's name.* She stomped her foot, wanting to shout, "Darn it, Daddy. She's just a ghost. I want to go to my party!"

"Sorry, Claire, but it's more important that you see Miss Janet and tell her about your other friend. She needs to know." Nick ushered her to the car.

When they arrived, Janet insisted that Nick not sit in. "No, Nick. I understand how you must feel, but I think it's best if I talk to her alone."

"No offense, Janet, but when she said there was another friend, I question what we've accomplished here. I don't know what went wrong." He picked up a magazine and put it back on the table. He wanted to blame her or the therapy, but he couldn't. *It's my fault.* "I'm here for her now, and that's how it's going to be."

"Trust the process, Nick. You're being a great father."

"How can you say that when she's hallucinating and talking to people that aren't there? If I'd handled her grief, we wouldn't be here." He dropped into his chair, looking up at Janet with an unspoken plea. *Please help her. She's all I have.*

Janet peeked through the waiting room doorway, where Claire sat in the corner of the office, playing with a doll and mumbling. "Nick, I understand that you have regrets, and your impulse is to compensate by putting all your focus on her. It's admirable, but perhaps not practical. She needs to feel your support, but not that she's broken. Claire will get through this, and so will you. Have you talked to Maggie?"

"I canceled our plans for tonight and told her I had to stay with Claire. I know she was looking forward to seeing Jenny tonight for her tea party." He rubbed his palms on his trousers and stood.

"Let me talk with Claire and see where we are. If I think she's in crisis, I'll tell you. If she's stable, I see no harm in keeping your plans."

"I'm not sure what kind of company I'd be. I really don't want to let her out of my sight," he sighed heavily. "I'll try."

Janet gave his shoulder a squeeze. "Let me see what I can do."

Janet sat on the floor next to Claire. "Your dad is concerned about you. Can you tell me why?"

"Yes."

"Good. Do you want to tell me?"

"Not really."

"Okay, let's start with your friend Ron. Is he here with you today?"

"Sure, he's always with me; that's why he's my best friend." She saw Ron smile.

"Best friends are always there when you need them, right?"

"Yes."

"Is Ron alone or does he have a friend, too?" Janet rolled a ball to Claire.

Claire heaved a sigh, her thin shoulders sagging. "You're a grownup, Miss Janet. I don't think grownups understand."

"You're right, Claire. I am a grownup, and I don't understand yet. But I want to. If you explain it to me, then we could talk about it, right?"

"I suppose." Downcast, she picked threads from a pillow.

Janet waited for Claire to reply.

Studying her crossed legs, Claire said, "They're ghosts."

Whatever Janet expected, that wasn't it. "Ghosts? Okay, will you tell me about them?"

"Uh-huh." She picked at the rug with her fingers, then rolled the ball, glancing up at Janet.

"How do you know they are ghosts? Did they tell you?"

"Yes, Ron did, so that I wouldn't be afraid of him. But I was never afraid. He's really nice, and his job is to make me laugh so I don't stay sad about missing my mom."

"What about his other friend? Is she nice, too?"

"I don't see her much. She's here to help Daddy and Miss Sanderson."

Janet treated Claire through cognitive therapy, guiding her with feedback and support to help her reason through her experiences. Claire's responses were coherent and consistent, giving Janet little reason to suspect delusion or psychosis. Silently, she reviewed her approach. *Could this be Altered Perception Syndrome? Or just an overactive seven-year-old imagination?* Intrigued, she persisted.

"Help them how, Claire?"

"I'm not sure, but Miss Sanderson came to our house and went to church with us, and Daddy was really happy. They were supposed to have a tea party tonight, too. I'm supposed to spend the night at Miss Jenny's."

Janet grinned, understanding. "What does Gayle look like?"

"She's pretty with long blonde hair. She's nice, but she gets mad at Ron sometimes. I can't hear her like I hear Ron."

"Why does she get mad at him?"

"Because he's a new ghost and makes mistakes. But she fixed my tea party dress. "She rolled the ball back to Janet.

"I see. How did she do that?"

"Umm," she hesitated. "I know it sounds like magic, but it spun around in my room and kinda sewed itself up on the sleeve and the ruffle on the bottom, so I could wear it tonight."

Janet noted Claire's consistent body language and eye movements, suggesting she was recalling memories rather than imagining scenarios. *Remarkable,* she thought. *That's another level of interaction—with a ghost. I'll need to study this over the weekend.*

Claire continued. "When Miss Jenny called our house to invite me to the tea party, Ron didn't know which dress to pick, but Gayle did."

"Then Gayle fixed it?"

"Yes. She kinda moved her hands around, and it floated when it spun around."

Janet allowed herself a slight frown when Claire looked away. I suppose that could be verifiable. Could the dress provide evidence of the ghosts' existence? Doubt smothered her speculation. What am I saying?

"All right, Claire, I think we've talked enough for today. Thank you for telling me about your friends. I'm a grownup, and I understand what you told me. I'm proud of you for trusting me."

"Okay." Claire sat up taller, smiling at Janet's acknowledgment.

"Why don't you stay here a little longer and play while I talk to your dad about your next appointment, okay?"

"Okay. Are you gonna tell him?"

"No, that's between us. You can tell him when you're ready. I'll mention we talked about it, so he won't worry. Is that okay?"

"Okay." She selected a teddy bear and hugged it to her chest.

Janet rose from the rug and met Nick in the other room, where he paced like an expectant father.

"Is she okay? What did she say?"

"Nick, I believe we've made a breakthrough tonight. I assured Claire I would keep what she shared confidential until she wanted to tell you herself. For a seven-year-old, she is coherent and engaged. In my opinion, this is not clinical decline, though I recommend continued cognitive therapy to address the post-traumatic stress of losing her mother." She paused, watching Nick's reaction.

"That said," she smiled, and Nick stopped pacing to look at her. "I'd like her to speak with a friend of mine. It would expose her to someone with expertise in an area I think would benefit her."

"What area?" He crossed his arms, then let them drop to his sides.

"I don't mean to be cryptic, but I'd like you to keep an open mind. Remember, Claire confided in me, so I can't get into specifics. I believe she will talk to you in her own time. As her therapist, I think it's important that she reaches her own conclusions." She paused.

"I don't know whether to be intrigued or anxious."

Here goes. Janet chose her words carefully. "Nick, it's not uncommon for someone who has lost a loved one to have questions about life and death, the afterlife—questions that might raise spiritual concerns. I'd like Claire to consult with my friend who studies paranormal phenomena. I intend to do more research myself, and you might want to as well, so we can prepare for her curiosity." She watched his reaction, hoping he would consider her suggestion.

"Paranormal. Phenomena. Afterlife. Those are heavy subjects for a little girl. I don't know, Janet. It's a lot to take in. You really think it'll help?"

Good. He didn't freak out. "Yes, I really do. Let me contact him to see if he's in town. I'll text you his website, and we can discuss it later. In the meantime, I suggest you go about your usual business. She mentioned a tea party tonight. Is that right?"

"Until I canceled it to come here. I didn't know how long this would take, and I wanted to stay with her."

"I understand. Let's not make her think there's something wrong with her. She knows she's experiencing something different, but she's not afraid or obsessive. She's actually enjoying it. So, relax. Go with the flow."

"Go with the flow. Sure, my kid's imaginary friends might be paranormal phenomena. I'll just roll with it." He rubbed the stubble on his chin. "Are you really sure?"

Janet smiled. "You're a good dad. I have confidence in both of you. It will get better, trust me."

"Yeah, well, thanks again for seeing her—us—on such short notice. I appreciate it."

"No problem. Now enjoy your weekend. Play. But I have some homework for you." She motioned for him to sit and took the chair across from him.

"I want you to imagine a piece of wood carved by a father and his daughter. Each stroke of the chisel releases curls of wood, like releasing sadness. The father's steady hands guide his daughter's delicate ones through their shared journey of grief.

As they work, they smooth the rough edges, gradually revealing the beauty beneath the surface. Like how healing reshapes their hearts. That's the strength and resilience they discover within themselves.

When they work together, it's not about what's lost, but what's created. You're shaping your future and hers, one patient stroke at a time."

Nick stared at her for a moment, processing the metaphor. "Did you just make that up?"

Janet shrugged with a faint smile. "Sort of. It needs work, but hey, I've got my chisel. Try telling her a story like that. She'll get it. And if she's looking forward to seeing Jenny, I'd say take her."

Nick called Maggie from home, his voice uncertain as he asked if Claire could still come over, though he'd pick her up later. Maggie's voice faded on the other end, and Nick felt her disappointment echo his own.

"Can we talk about it, Nick? I want to know what changed your mind about tonight."

"I'm not sure I can," he admitted, his tone heavy. "I'm overwhelmed and have a lot to think about."

Maggie said softly, "I can think, too, you know."

"I know. More clearly than me, I'm sure." He exhaled heavily. "Janet told me to go about 'business as usual.' But it's hard, Maggie. I'm just a carpenter. This is over my head."

"You're not 'just' anything, Nick. You're doing your best for Claire."

"I'll get her ready, and we'll be over around 7:00, okay? Maybe we can talk."

As Nick hung up the phone, Claire trudged down the stairs.

"But why can't I spend the night, Daddy? We were having a pajama party after my tea party."

"I want to spend more time with my special girl. Is that so bad?"

"But you see me all the time, and I've never had a pajama party. I picked out my prettiest nightie with the little flowers on it, and everything is already packed. Is it about my friends?" She crossed her arms and pouted. "I shouldn't have told you."

Nick eased himself into a kitchen chair, then gently lifted Claire onto his lap. He wrapped his arms around her, his voice soft but steady. "You can always tell me what makes you happy or sad, okay? I'll try harder to listen." He paused, brushing a strand of hair from her face. "I'm glad you told Miss Janet about Gayle, and you can tell me more when you're ready." He tapped her nose with his finger. "Maybe you can teach me how I can be a better dad."

She rested her head on his chest, and Nick hugged her. "Can I tell you a story?" he said.

Claire listened quietly as he told the story of carving a sculpture for her mom, how sadness was carved away while happiness remained, smoothed and polished. A tear rolled down her cheek.

Nick thought, *Janet's right. She understands.* He glanced at her bag by the door. *What's wrong with me? Jenny and Maggie have always been there for us. You don't have to do this alone.*

"Claire, I'll tell you what. Let's take your bag with us, and after I talk to Miss Jenny and Miss Maggie, we'll see if you can spend the night. Okay?"

Sniffling, she looked at him with sad eyes. "Okay, Daddy. But I think I'm going to be really sleepy after our tea party and I might fall asleep on the couch."

Nick smiled. "We'll see, sweetie."

C H A P T E R

TWENTY-FIVE

Claire did not wear the dress that Gayle fixed. She wanted to show it to her dad, but not tonight. She put it back in her closet. When they arrived at the Sandersons' house, Maggie and Jenny met them at the front door. A somber Claire held a bright yellow bag, and Nick stood behind her.

Jenny took her hand. "Everything is ready, but I need your help to arrange the petit fours on the tray. You can take your gloves off if you'd like."

Looking at her dad, he nodded. Taking that as a yes, she smiled and followed Jenny into the kitchen, repeating 'petit fours' like Miss Jenny did.

Maggie watched Nick closely. "How are you doing?" she asked.

Nick saw the worry in her eyes. In a voice heavy with regret, he said, "First off, let me apologize. I was so upset and scared that I didn't think things through. Nothing makes sense. I'm sorry I let you down tonight. I'm drowning over here, and I don't know how to save her."

"Nick, you're scaring me. Please, tell me what's wrong. Maybe I can help."

With a deep breath, he encircled her in his arms. He felt her body tense, then relax.

"Let's sit down." Taking her hands in his, they moved to the parlor. "It was wrong to shut you out. I panicked."

"I'm here for you, Nick. Tell me what happened. Why did you call Janet?"

Nick recounted everything that had happened since Claire mentioned Gayle's name. The shock came when he explained what Janet said about the paranormal consultant.

Maggie's eyes widened. "No wonder you're freaked out. What do you believe, Nick? Do you think she sees these—people—spirits, or whatever they are?"

He looked at the ceiling, then back at her. "I don't know what to think. Janet's going to do more research and talk to this guy who deals with the phenomena. I'm out of my depth. I will research this, too. Maybe I can understand what she sees and what it means."

"I want to help, if you let me." Her sincerity moved him. He pulled her close, and she laid her head on his shoulder, rubbing her thumb back and forth on his hand. They sat in silence until they heard Claire giggling in the kitchen.

Nick swallowed hard, reviewing the feelings that erupted in him when Claire revealed her news about Gayle. "I don't even remember what she said. I felt like I was losing her to some force that would take her away, like Ann. I wanted to protect her, but against what?" He laced his fingers in hers, kissing her hand. "I shouldn't have pushed you away like that, Maggie. You've been in our corner all along."

She shushed him, cupping his cheek, and leaned in to kiss him. "I'm not going anywhere, Mister." They sat together like that when Jenny wheeled into the room.

Unbeknownst to Nick, Jenny listened intently as Claire described her friends, marveling at the vivid details. What a fascinating experience for the girl, she thought, considering the possibility that Claire could see and communicate with ghosts. Jenny promised Claire she wouldn't tell Nick, knowing it would likely worry him—or, more likely, unnerve him even further.

Jenny asked the couple, "We have a few leftovers from our tea. Would either of you like some?"

"None for me, thanks, Jenny. I'm not very hungry," Nick replied.

"I wouldn't mind a bite. Come on, Nick, keep me company while I nibble." She grabbed his hand and led him into the kitchen.

"Hey, Daddy. Look what we have! Are you hungry?"

Nick's stomach growled at the sight of a generous spread of tea sandwiches, cheeses, fresh berries, and glazed confections. "Hey, sweet pea, is there enough for us?"

Giggling, she replied, "This is all for me, but maybe you can lick the plate."

He crept menacingly toward her and pounced, tickling her. "Lick the plate, huh? I'm very hungry now!" He snarled, snapping at her fingers and nose.

Claire laughed and squirmed to escape. "Oh no! He's a big bad wolf, and he's going to eat me up! Save me, Miss Sanderson, save me!"

Maggie joined in the fun, trying to pull Nick off Claire. Laughing, he let her go and filled a delicate china plate with sandwiches, cookies, nuts, and berries. "We have to finish these before Claire eats them all."

Maggie sat down and held Claire's hand. "I think when we're not in school and we're all together like this, you can call me Miss Maggie. Miss

Sanderson is a mouthful, don't you think?" She popped a strawberry into her mouth.

"Really? Then it would be Miss Maggie, Miss Jenny, and Miss Janet. Am I a 'Miss' too because I'm a girl? Or do you have to be old?"

Nick snorted behind a mouthful of cookies. Jenny harrumphed, joining in. "Old? Who's old? I'll show you old." She chased Claire down the hall.

Nick watched them, a flicker of hope warming his chest. This could be our family, he thought.

As Maggie observed his expression shift from a smile to concern, she stepped closer, wrapping her arms around his waist. "Things will work out, Nick. We have to trust that God knows what He's doing. Maybe it's all happening for a reason. But she's happy. Just stay close. With Janet's help, we'll figure it out."

"I sure hope so, Maggie." He leaned into her, his daughter's laughter echoing in the hall.

Nick allowed Claire to spend the night, reassured by Jenny that she had things under control. He said goodnight, and after kissing them all, walked out with Maggie, lingering in her gentle company.

Driving home alone and weary, Nick wrestled with the hope that his life—and Claire's—might return to some version of normal, whatever that meant. As he parked in the driveway, unwelcome images of worst-case scenarios crept into his mind like shadows. Shaking them off, he glanced upward, murmuring a quiet prayer. *What do I do now?*

He let himself into the quiet house. He hadn't spent a night alone here since Ann was alive, when she'd taken their daughter on an overnight trip to visit a friend. Dropping his keys in the bowl, Nick thought of his late wife. Not wanting to sink further into sadness, he slipped off his shoes and sank into the couch, turning on the television to hear voices other than his own.

While the sports channel droned with predictions for the weekend's events, his thoughts turned to Maggie—should he rely on her for help and comfort? He knew he had strong feelings for her, and from the look in her eyes, she cared a lot for him. Hours ago, he was ready to abandon hope for a relationship. *I'm a mess,* he conceded. *I have to stop thinking that way. 'Go with the flow,' Janet said.*

Checking his work phone, he saw a text from Janet. He reached for his laptop on the end table and googled paranormal phenomena. Reading about documented sightings of poltergeists, apparitions, and spirits of the dead, he welcomed this distraction from his familiar world. Feeling less adrift, he typed in the URL of Janet's friend.

David Pearson's website described him as a paranormal investigator. A good-looking guy about his age, his photo gave Nick the impression of a young professor—bright eyes behind wire-rimmed glasses, hair falling on his forehead, not like the actors on ghost hunter shows. He clicked on a video, where his impressions were confirmed. An articulate description of his work, free from hype and dramatic flair, addressed Nick's suspicions with a calm, approachable demeanor.

Nick didn't believe everything but was drawn to the man's persuasive curiosity. He studied until his head rested against the back of the couch. With thoughts of Maggie, Claire, and ghosts, he sank into a restful sleep.

Gayle's form hovered over Nick's shoulder, her ethereal presence fluttering with irritation. *Now our cover is blown. Something else I'll have to fix,* she thought. *First, the psychologist, then Jenny, now this. Should we just show ourselves to the adults? Is seeing believing? Or would it cause more harm than good?* She sighed, considering her next move. *Maybe I should see The Boss.*

Gayle rarely second-guessed herself. In her former life, she had to make decisions all the time. Her husband changed his mind about everything, and she needed to have the last word. She'd always been a take-charge person, and she was doing her best to let others, even Ron, work things out on their own. But it still gnawed at her to ask for help.

Outside Maggie's guest room, she heard Claire and Ron talking. "Do you think I did the right thing, Ron? Everyone is worried about me, and I'm not sure why. Even Daddy's scared, and that makes me scared. I think Miss Janet and Miss Jenny believe me; should I tell him?" Claire addressed Ron's hazy outline in the dim light.

"Your dad loves you, and it scares him because he doesn't understand. Maybe he needs time to think about it. Some people think ghosts are evil or scary or aren't real, but if they see you are happier, even though your mom had to go away, they won't worry so much."

"I know you're helping me, and I like you a lot. It would be so cool if everyone liked you and Gayle, too." She smiled.

"I'm glad you're not so sad anymore. Sometimes you miss your mom, but that's okay. You learned your mom misses you too. She wants you to enjoy your life."

"But I don't know how to really make them believe me." She crossed her arms with a pout. "They can't see you like I can, so what should I do?"

Maggie leaned against the wall outside the guest room, listening to Claire's side of the conversation. It mystified her. *But who am I to judge? I don't have all the answers. And she's doing better. She's having a conversation. Maybe with herself, maybe not. Like billions of people, I pray, and sometimes I get answers. What about dreams? There must be an explanation, but I sure can't come up with one tonight.* She yawned, drained from the day, and went to bed.

-»⋇«-

The following morning, Nick arrived to pick up Claire with an assortment of muffins. Following Maggie, he joined them in the kitchen. "Morning, everyone."

"Daddy! Did you sleep all right without me in the house?" She ran to give him a hug, which made him happy.

"I did. But I missed your snoring." He hugged her.

Jenny and Maggie beckoned him to the table. Maggie poured him a cup of coffee. When she sat in front of him, he touched her hand and gave her a wink.

"I don't snore, do I, Daddy?"

"Oh yeah, you snore like a lumberjack."

"What's a lumberjack?"

Maggie jumped into the conversation. "Claire, I think your dad is pulling your leg."

Claire looked at her legs.

"Will you two stop teasing my girl?" Jenny scolded.

She patted Claire's hand. "Don't mind these two characters; they're just having fun with you."

After a laugh, Nick explained the expressions to Claire.

When Claire skipped upstairs to gather her things, Nick said to both women, "Thanks for having Claire over. I'm still trying to wrap my head around all of this. Last night, I did some research on the paranormal. Man, there is another level out there I knew nothing about. I watched a video recorded in an office after hours. Chairs moved by themselves, computers turned on and off, file drawers opened, and files flew everywhere. Then a woman fell for no apparent reason, as if something just pushed her down. I don't know how much to believe, but it sure looked real." He selected a blueberry muffin.

"The weirdest was at a video store. The guy was returning videos to a shelf, and as he moved to the next shelf, some would fall off the first shelf. He'd replace them and go back to the previous shelf, only to have more fall off. He kept at it and finally gave up and left the store."

Maggie looked suspicious and frowned. "Are you sure the videos weren't faked?"

"No, but the documentary seemed legit. There's something else." He sipped his coffee. "I visited the website of the guy Janet thinks Claire should talk to. He calls himself a paranormal investigator and goes to places to look for evidence of paranormal phenomena, like ghosts. I never believed in ghosts, but there was something about the guy. He was so matter-of-fact about the beliefs of different cultures and how most of the cases he took on had simple explanations. I didn't get the sense he saw ghosts everywhere he looked." Nick regarded the women who had become so important to him. "So, what do you two think? Are ghosts real?"

"Of course they are." Jenny scoffed in amusement. "Do you think we are the only beings in this little slice of time we call 'now?' Do you believe in UFOs and aliens, or that the entire infinite universe is just for us silly humans? Who's to say hunches or gut feelings aren't messages from the other side?" She rocked in her chair.

"Sometimes I know my Tom warns me to be careful. I never told you this, honey." She took Maggie's hand. "That day when I decided to be an amateur daredevil photographer and took the plunge down the hillside, he was there. He hadn't been gone long, and I didn't recognize the warning until it was too late."

Maggie stared at her in wonder. "I remember you calling to him when you were delirious."

"That fall may have broken my body, but it didn't break my spirit. It could have, but he helped me through the really bad days, too. So, it didn't heal right, and I'm here in a wheelchair. Maybe it saved me from getting hit by a car or something..." She blanched, remembering. "Oh, my goodness, I'm so sorry, Nick..."

"It's all right, Jenny. It's true, we never know. I wanted someone to blame for Ann's death, and sometimes I took it out on people who didn't deserve it. Now, it's comforting that Claire's mother may be watching over us from beyond, bringing people like you into our lives. Maybe when we remember someone we lost, their spirit lives on in a way."

Jenny nodded with a tight smile, her eyes misting. "I get a tickle on my neck just like when he used to blow a soft breath there just to see me shiver. And it still does. Trust me, I know he's around, watching over me." She paused and spoke softly. "Like Ann is watching over you and Claire."

Maggie looked at her mother, admitting she had listened at Claire's door last night and heard her talking. "It's uncanny that when she talks to her friend, she asks and answers questions. Like he's in the room."

Before anyone could comment, Claire came down the stairs with her backpack. "I'm ready."

"So, you are. Did you thank Miss Jenny and Miss Maggie for letting you stay overnight?"

"She sure did," Jenny said. "We loved having Miss Claire stay over. She is a pleasure to have around." Claire leaned into Jenny's arm.

"Then I guess we'll say our goodbyes. Thanks again." Nick leaned in and kissed their cheeks.

"Like they say down south, 'Y'all come back now, ya hear?'"

Nick chuckled as he took Claire's hand and walked to the door where Maggie stood. He brushed past her, inhaling her fragrance, perhaps lingering a moment longer than some might consider proper. "I'll call you."

Maggie waved goodbye and spun towards Jenny. "Mom, we need to talk."

"I thought we were." Jenny poured herself a second cup of coffee.

"You know what I mean. I didn't know you still felt Dad's presence here. What's that all about?"

"Join me for another cup?" Jenny peeled the paper from a chocolate chip muffin and broke off half for her daughter. She looked at something far away. "Let's sit on the deck; it's nice out."

Maggie opted for orange juice and sat next to Jenny, waiting. Leaves rustled and seemed to whisper secret things in the morning breeze, setting a surreal atmosphere.

"There were times even before Tom died that I sensed his presence, even when he was bedridden and in so much pain. I could be here, in the garden, even in church. We were always connected that way, Maggie. So, when he passed on, it didn't shock me that I could still feel him. I knew he didn't want to leave me and still felt a spiritual connection. He reminds me, when I need it, that he's nearby."

Jenny nibbled her muffin. "Sometimes, I notice the picture of us at the beach on my bedside table. It's moved a little and is facing the bed so I can see it while I'm lying down. I know you don't move things in there. It's your dad's way of reminding me I'll be okay.

"Once, I mixed a cake and couldn't reach the nutmeg, which we so seldom use. But the cake wouldn't taste the same without it. I was in this chair and tried to stand to reach for it, but I didn't have the strength or balance. I was determined to try again, and I forgot to set the brakes. I tried to stand, and the chair started rolling out from under me. I sat back down and cried; I felt so helpless. Then I watched the nutmeg fall off the shelf and land on the counter right in front of me. You tell me how that happened. I thanked Tom and finished baking the cake, which you said you loved for the spices I used."

"I remember that spice cake. We had company, so I see why you didn't mention it, but you never told me, either. Why not?"

"What would you have said? 'Wow, that's wild.' And that would have been the end of it. I got to keep it as a private moment between your dad and me for a few years. Now you know." Jenny took her daughter's hand, and they gazed into her garden, where spring vegetables and flowers bloomed in the rich soil she tended.

"I'm not imagining these things or making them up to feel better. They are as real as you're sitting there. So yes, I believe there is some other place where people exist after they leave us. We believe in Heaven, Hell, even Purgatory. We believe in angels and God. If He created all this, who's to say there isn't more out there that we don't know about? Levels of existence we're unaware of?

"People say, 'He was too young to die?' Sure, he had so much more he wanted to do. Maybe Claire's ghosts are here to do something so they can move on. I know Tom is near, and whatever form he's in, I know he loves me and is with me, hopefully until I can be with him, wherever we wind up."

Maggie studied her mother's face in the warm sunlight. She knew her parents had a great marriage, but this was a twist. "I see that it's a very personal thing between the two of you, and you're telling me my dad's a ghost? And Claire could really be communicating with one. Give me a minute to collect my thoughts. I've got memories revising all over the place."

Jenny took a sip of her coffee and paused. "Two ghosts, actually. Claire told me about Ron's friend last night, Gayle. But she doesn't talk to her much. And you can't tell Nick yet."

Maggie looked at her for a long moment and shook her head. "Okay, I guess I have some catching up to do. Mom, I can see Dad doesn't frighten you; he comforts you. But why do you think he's never visited me?" Her throat tightened as she recalled her father's crooked smile and weathered face driving her to college.

"You know how you feel right now? He's with you. For whatever reason, he's on a different wavelength. He doesn't speak to me or answer questions like Claire's friend. He warms my heart, dear. I feel protected and loved. I guess it's different for spouses. Sometimes a longing comes over me. I know when my time comes, we'll be together again. But I'm not rushing it."

Maggie teared up. "That's beautiful, Mom. I'm so happy for you. And I'm glad you're not in any hurry." She laughed, wiping at her tears.

"Of course." She touched Maggie's face. "I want my daughter to have a love so deep it lasts beyond your lives." They talked for two more hours, leafing through the photo album. Seeing pictures of her dad in a new light, she felt protected and loved.

The phone rang, and Maggie leaned over to give her mom a hug. She hurried into the hall and thought, *That's it. I'm getting a new cell phone, one that works in this area.*

"Hello," she said.

"Hi, Mags, I said I'd call."

"And so you have. Just the person I need to talk to."

"That sounds promising. What's up?"

"Are you done with your research on cell phones, plans, and coverage?"

"As a matter of fact, I am. Why?"

"I thought if you weren't busy, we could go shopping for one today."

"Sounds like a plan. What time would you like to go? We're not busy right now. Claire doesn't have homework, and I'm done trying to fix the furnace. I may have a theory on that..."

"Tell me about your theory later. I'm on a roll. I'm thinking I might even get one for Mom, too. How about I come pick you guys up, and we'll have lunch and then go shopping?"

"Better yet, why don't I pick you up since my car has the seat for Claire in the back? Would your mom like to get some fresh air and come with us?"

"That's a great idea. Wait a minute, do you have room for her wheelchair?"

"Sure, it'll fit in the back, and she can sit next to Claire."

"Perfect. Let me ask her." She laid the phone down.

"Mom, we're all going out to lunch and shopping, and you're coming with us."

"I thought you were going to ask me?"

Maggie laughed. "Always listening in, huh? Come on, it'll be fun. When's the last time we went out?"

"Sure, I'd love to go."

"Good!" She remembered Nick and went back into the hallway to pick up the phone. "Yes, we're both going. Can you be here around 11:30?"

"We'll be there, and Maggie?"

"Yes?"

"I'm really looking forward to spending time with you again." Lowering his voice to an intimate whisper, he continued, "I can't get you out of my mind. I want to be with you, alone."

"That sounds like a plan," she chirped, trying to keep Jenny from catching on. It didn't work.

"You two rescheduling your tea party?" Jenny asked.

"Mom! Would you stop being so perceptive?"

Jenny laughed. "I'll go get ready."

Jenny settled into Nick's car without hesitation, and he stowed the wheelchair in the back of the SUV. Claire was thrilled to sit with Jenny, and they chatted all the way to the restaurant.

Ron and Gayle flew above Nick's car, following them to the mall. Gayle circled the vehicle, her curiosity piqued by Jenny's confession to Maggie. "Now, come up with one of your bright ideas," she murmured, "so they don't think Claire is a whacko."

Ron winced at her bluntness.

"Oh, don't be so sensitive," Gayle huffed. "Listen, I'm heading upstairs to brief The Boss about our recent developments. Stay out of trouble." She added with a smirk, "Toodles," and disappeared.

After lunch, Jenny got her first real smartphone. Maggie suggested rigging a magnetic holder for her wheelchair so she could watch videos on the go. Nick chose a rugged cover for his phone, which the girls teased him about. "What? It's military-grade shock-resistant."

Once the old phones were traded in and the new plans, covers, and options added, Claire grumbled about not getting one. Maggie and Jenny promised to call her on her father's phone to FaceTime, which seemed to satisfy her. She didn't know that Nick planned to surprise her with one for her 8th birthday.

Parking in Maggie's driveway, Nick pushed the wheelchair to Jenny's side, opening her door with a flourish. "Your chariot awaits, madam."

Jenny settled into her chair, and Maggie gripped the handles. "I can take it from here."

"No way, I always see my dates to the door," he joked, pushing Jenny up the ramp. After some maneuvering, he surprised her with a kiss on the cheek.

"Thank you, young fellow. I had a lovely time. Maybe we can have a second date soon. Who knows, second date, second base." She winked.

"Forward much, Mom?" Maggie rolled her eyes.

"Hey, when you're hot, you're hot."

Nick grinned. "Just say the word, Gorgeous."

"Okay, you two, that's enough." Maggie pouted. "I'm feeling left out, and Claire's still strapped in."

"Sorry, Jenny. My heart belongs to another." Nick kissed Maggie's lips and returned to his car. He shook his head as Claire played a game on his new phone. *A normal day,* he mused. *How about that?*

Ron thought things were running smoothly enough. He wanted to know more about Jenny's late husband, Tom. *Is he one of us or from some other dimension?* He also intended to check on Janet and see what she was up to with her ghostbuster friend. *But first, I'll visit Albert's widow and see how she's doing.*

The three-minute flight to Rosie Cunningham's house was uneventful. Ron, in his former life in the LAX tower, preferred such flights—zero errors, no incident reports. He maintained a calm, even voice even when jumbo jets were only meters apart.

The modest two-bedroom home sat on half an acre of partially wooded land, six blocks from Nick's, edging the foothills. The grounds needed trimming, and the deck and porch required minor repairs and a coat of paint. Albert's workshop was cluttered with dusty, undisturbed tools and gadgets. He slipped inside to observe Rosie. The house was clean and orderly. She walked with a cane but didn't seem to be in much pain; he would report that to Albert. The TV was muted, and she hummed along with the radio while making herself a sandwich.

For several minutes, Ron watched her, smiling when she swayed to a tune. He noticed the piano in her living room and wondered if she still played. She replaced the sandwich fixings in the refrigerator and closed the door with her hip. The phone rang in her kitchen, and she answered, sandwich in hand, sitting at the table.

"Hello, Murray. How are you, brother dear? Yes, I'm fine. Have you seen the old gang lately? You moved? Oh, my. Tell me more."

Ron took his leave. He enjoyed being on his own for a change and flew to downtown Provo to see Janet. There was a minor incident with a bird that crossed his flight path, but he didn't feel the need to write it up. He paused midair; the sunset was beautiful.

TWENTY-SIX

Janet reached David Pearson, the paranormal expert, by phone. Without revealing her client's identity, she briefed him on Claire's experiences. They discussed Claire's descriptions of Ron and Gayle, focusing primarily on Ron. David explained that ghosts often appear to help people, and a common theme in ghost lore is their manifestation to settle unfinished business with the living.

"Assuming Claire saw the real thing, it's extraordinary that she interacted with them as you described. Children are often more curious than frightened by such phenomena. They tend to accept it easily, like magic, influenced by cartoons and fantasy movies. I also understand your concerns that they might imagine these visitations due to social withdrawal or post-traumatic stress."

"Of course, my client is my primary concern," Janet replied. "Personally, and professionally, I cannot evaluate her mental state based on the assumption that a supernatural event has occurred. These occurrences are quite rare and not scientifically accepted as fact, am I right?"

"Absolutely. Just like religious experiences, ancient pyramids, or UFOs. There are many aspects of our existence that scientists can't explain and, for various reasons, don't formally accept."

"Point taken, David," Janet said, glancing at the photo on his website. She was about to sign off and jot down notes for her next meeting with Claire when David asked a question.

"Has your client described any other observable phenomena?"

"She mentioned cold spots in her house," Janet replied, wondering if she should have mentioned it, but her curiosity got the better of her. "She also said that one ghost repaired her dress, like magic. That may be just fanciful..."

"Or quite significant, Janet. That's akin to a 'close encounter of the third kind' in my business." His voice rose slightly with restrained excitement. "Listen, I have a project in Salt Lake City next weekend. Keep me posted on this. If you talk to the father, let him know I'd be interested in observing the house and possibly conducting an interview. Tell him I'll give him a free evaluation of his heater. It's your call whether to involve the child, but I'd like to examine that dress."

"*Let* me think about it and talk to them. I'll get back to you."

"Please do. It... would be nice to see you again."

"Okay," she said. *Interesting.* They ended the call.

Janet recalled their time together on the last day of a Caribbean cruise. Relaxed and joking about returning to work, they had struck up a conversation before disembarking. After wishing each other safe travels, they unexpectedly met again in the airport lounge, bound for different cities. They spoke with easy camaraderie about navigating the world with more questions than answers and exchanged contact information. She hadn't expected to cross paths with him again—until now.

Ron noticed a grin spread across Janet's face as he considered this new development—a paranormal investigation—a chance to prove Claire wasn't delusional and that she truly did 'see dead people.' But which possibility was worse? Surrounded by Gayle's endless opinions and mortal Nick's limited perspective, Ron found himself wishing for a ghost buddy—a guy who could truly understand.

He blew a plastic ball from the play area in Janet's office a bit too hard. It bounced on the hardwood floor. She spun in her desk chair at the sound but returned to her notes. Ron figured he ought to head to Maggie and Jenny's before he did anything clumsier.

He believed that Tom, Jenny's late husband, might have the afterlife experience to give him advice about Maggie and how she affected Nick and Claire's life. As he cruised through their house, he sensed Jenny was upset about something.

"Margaret Ann Sanderson, are you up there?" Jenny called from the bottom of the stairs.

This time, Maggie heard her mother call. Rolling off the bed, she pulled off her earbuds and opened the door. "I'm here, do you need something?"

"What are you doing up there, dear? I've got a deck of cards and just opened a can of whoop ass. Would you like some?"

Maggie laughed and skipped down the stairs. "When you put it that way, how could I resist?" Pausing her playlist, she asked, "What diabolical game are you going to whoop me at tonight? You know you could have called me on your new phone."

At the Millers', Nick and Claire spent the evening in front of the TV. Claire loved watching movies with her dad on weekends, making popcorn together, and sitting side by side on the couch. Ever since Maggie and Janet had visited, Claire wanted to watch all the Harry Potter films. The plots seemed a little old for her, but Nick reviewed each one to ensure it wouldn't upset her, which struck him as funny. His normal daughter might be involved with the paranormal. The idea that Claire might communicate with the other side while still playing tea party made his head spin.

After the movie, Claire asked her dad if she could use his new cell phone to call Jenny. She was eager to try it out.

"Sure," he said, reaching into his back pocket and handing it to her. "Remember how to use it?"

"Yes, can I put in the code?" Nick showed her how, in case she needed it in an emergency.

"Okay, and just scroll down for Jenny's name."

"I know!" She grinned, too excited for instructions.

"Hello, Claire, how are you, dear?" Jenny answered.

"How did you know it's me?"

"It just felt like you." She chuckled. "And your dad's name is on the screen."

"Yeah, it's me. Isn't this cool? I'm not even close to our old phone. I'm on the couch. We just watched a Harry Potter movie, and I spilled some popcorn during a scary part. It was kinda funny; my hand jerked, and the popcorn flew straight up in the air. Daddy protected me, though. He put his arm around me and saved me from the popcorn." She giggled.

Claire whispered, "Ron and Gayle were watching, too. And you know what else?" Not giving Jenny a chance to respond, she continued, "I can go up to my room and still talk to you on the new phone. Isn't that cool? I never used his old cellphone; Daddy just used it for work and emergencies."

Jenny laughed, "I guess you're excited, huh? I hope your dad knows you're using his phone."

"Oh, yes, he gave it to me, and I know how to put the code in and everything, but I can't tell anyone what it is."

"That's how it should be, dear. So, what else is new with you?"

"Let's see... well, I made the popcorn with Daddy's help, then he made supper. It was spaghetti, but there weren't any meatballs. Daddy's not too good at making them, but it was still good. He took the plates out of the cabinet for me, and then I set the table. And, uh, oh yeah, I grew a half an inch! Daddy says we'll have to go clothes shopping if I keep growing. Isn't that silly? Of course, I'm going to keep growing."

Jenny beamed while talking with Claire, remembering Maggie as a chatty seven-year-old. "So, what do you say we get together before you're six feet tall and I have to strain my neck looking up at you?"

Claire giggled. "Will I grow that big? I'd be as tall as Daddy, huh?"

"Hmm. I have an idea. Wouldn't it be fun to go shopping with just us girls?"

"Can we do that? Is that like when I see Miss Janet and when you and I have our tea parties? Will it make Daddy sad not to go with us?"

"I don't think daddies get sad about clothes shopping. But ask him first."

"Daddy, Miss Jenny wants to take me shopping for new clothes before I'm six feet tall, and you won't get sad about it. Is that okay?"

Nick saw that one coming and asked if Miss Maggie would be going. "Daddy, Miss Jenny doesn't drive, and my feet don't reach the gas pedal 'cuz I'm not six feet tall yet, so I can't. That means Miss Maggie *has* to drive."

Nick teased, "Oh, so you plan on growing more than half an inch? Maybe I'd better wait until you get even taller before we get your new clothes. You might grow out of them before you get home!"

"No, I won't, Daddy. Miss Jenny and Miss Maggie want to take me *before* I grow more."

Nick thought about that for a while. It would be more fun for Claire with the ladies instead of him. She'd be perfectly safe with Maggie and Jenny. Besides, what did he know about little girls' clothes?

"Would it be okay if I talked to Miss Jenny?"

Claire jumped up to hand Nick his phone. "Hang on, Miss Jenny; Daddy wants to talk to you, and I am now walking over to him. Cool, huh?"

Shaking his head and smiling, Nick took the phone. "Hi, Jenny, what are you planning to do with my daughter? Is this some kind of conspiracy to leave me all alone, by myself, with no one to keep me company?" He glanced at Claire.

They joked while Claire twirled around, waiting for her turn to talk. They agreed that this Saturday, the girls would go shopping without Nick. He sadly announced he would stay home, all alone, by himself, with no one to keep him company.

From his spectral vantage point, Ron monitored the plan, quietly pleased that Claire enjoyed spending time with the women. But what if her young friends got involved, too? He considered his options. *Maybe I can arrange something with her playgroup at school.*

That Friday, at school, Ron could tell Claire was bursting to share news about her shopping trip the next day. She said nothing about it to Maggie in front of the class, but she'd told Ron about the mall, lunch, what she needed, and what the other girls wore. But Ron was still a man ghost, so it didn't count as much as telling another girl.

During recess, Ron asked Claire the name of her friend. She told him about Becky, mentioning that they didn't play much anymore. They used to have playdates and sleepovers, but not for a while. Ron knew Claire missed her and thought he could help. He scanned the playground from the air and spotted Becky playing catch with another girl, her laughter echoing across the yard. As the ball sailed between them, Ron blew on it, steering it toward Claire. Becky jogged over to retrieve it, still laughing. "Hi, Claire! I don't know what just happened—the ball went a little crazy!"

"That's okay," Claire replied. "Can I throw it, too?"

"Sure! You throw great."

"Okay!" She smiled at Ron and joined the other girls.

Ron grinned, feeling proud of himself. They had agreed she shouldn't talk about him with other kids. *But she needs to be with kids her own age.*

The three girls continued to play catch before moving on to hopscotch. From her spot on the playground, Maggie watched Claire enjoying herself with her friends. A small smile tugged at her lips—Claire wasn't off by herself this time.

When the bell rang to return to class, Claire, Becky, and Denise lined up to walk back to their classroom. Claire bubbled with excitement about her shopping trip the next day to get new clothes, carefully omitting Miss Sanderson's involvement. Her friends wanted to see what she got. Becky asked if she could come over to watch, and Denise chimed in, chanting, "Fashion show, fashion show!"

Claire smiled at the thought of her friends coming to her house to watch her model her new clothes, but she had to ask her dad first. It had been a long time since her friends visited. The girls exchanged phone numbers, and Claire gave them her new cell phone number. Once everyone left, she rushed to tell Miss Sanderson. Maggie wanted to hug her but held back, imagining Nick with three little girls in his house. She decided to call and give him a heads up. As the last student filed out of the classroom, she did.

"Hey, to what do I owe this pleasure? I'm just finishing up at work."

"I'm giving you a heads up," she chuckled.

"Uh-oh." He had a pencil between his teeth, measuring a wall for cabinets. "Hang on." He snatched the pencil from his mouth and wrote down the measurements. "Say that again?"

"You might be entertaining a gaggle of giggly girls tomorrow. Do you think you can handle that?"

"How many is a gaggle?" He picked up his pencil, grinning at himself. *Relax.*

Maggie told him about the girls planning Claire's fashion show. "She hasn't mentioned Becky in a while. Good for her. Um, how does one host a fashion show?" Nick tilted his head, a faint smile playing on his lips.

Maggie chuckled, launching into her explanation. "Assuming the girls' parents give the okay for them to come over, their moms and maybe a dad or two will want to stay for refreshments. It's a good thing, Nick; she needs friends her own age to play with."

"Okay, so two more girls and maybe three adults?"

"Plus me and Jenny." She paused. "I'll tell you what we'll do. I'll drive Jenny and Claire to the mall and drop them off at the southwest entrance so the students don't see me. Claire will call the girls on my mom's cell phone and make sure she writes their numbers down. She'll tell them to meet her at the Flashy Poodle. Don't ask; it's a trendy new store for girls. After they spend your hard-earned money, Mom will call me, and I'll pick them up at the drop-off point. The parents will bring their daughters to your house. I'll drop off Jenny and Claire before they get there, so it'll seem like you picked them up because you had to do something important for work."

"I did?"

"Yep, that's why you weren't shopping with them. I'll drive around the block and wait for them to go inside. It'll be after lunch but before dinner, so just have some iced tea or lemonade ready. Cookies are customary, but you won't have to bake them. Have some store-bought ones on hand. And remember, we're having that parent-teacher conference at your house tomorrow?"

"We are?"

"Yes, because you can't make it next week."

"I can't?"

"No. That's why I'm coming by your house tomorrow. When I see Becky and Denise's parents there, I'll just happen to have their girls' progress reports in my official Mapleton Elementary School folder. It'll save their parents a trip to school next week by holding their brief conference in your dining room, thereby maintaining my cover while the girls prepare for the fashion show."

"Uh-huh."

"You'll ask, and I'll say, 'Why thank you, Mr. Miller. I'd love to stay for the fashion show. But after the fashion show, I really must be going. Lovely to see you all. Your children are model students, yada yada.' I'll leave, and the parents will take their daughters home happy. While I'm gone, I'll pick up pizza and dessert for us. You call me when they leave, I'll come back, we'll eat, maybe sneak a kiss or two in the laundry room, and I'll drive Mom home. Easy peasy."

Nick was silent for a moment. "Did you just concoct this?"

"Buddy, when you're alone in a room with 25 seven-year-olds, you gotta think on your feet."

C H A P T E R

TWENTY-SEVEN

Saturday morning turned out to be a bright, breezy 68 degrees. The sky was blue, the clouds were white, and the trees were green—a perfect day for shopping. Claire woke up early and looked out her window, whooping for joy at the beautiful day. She threw back the covers, hopped out of bed, and pulled on her too-short jeans and a tee shirt. She donned a pretty red sweater, noticing the cold spots where her ghost friends had lingered. The three-hour countdown began.

Nick heard Claire skip down the stairs from the kitchen. He had cereal ready for her. "Miss Maggie will be here at 11 o'clock, so when you finish, go upstairs and clean your room for your guests. Don't forget to brush your teeth, okay?"

"Sure thing, Daddy-O." She smiled as she poured milk into her cereal.

He handed Maggie his credit card when she picked up Claire. She promised not to max it, teasing him with a wicked grin. Jenny waited in the car, ready for the plan. The mission was underway.

Nick had talked to the parents of the two girls, and not only did the moms want to attend the fashion show, but also one dad. This was turning into an actual production.

2 1 1

He did what any single dad might do to prepare for his daughter, her friends, and their parents to visit. He swept the porch, vacuumed, threw out a dead plant, and checked the bathrooms. He still needed to go to the store for snacks and lemonade but hesitated to revisit the market where Ann died. *Someday I will.*

Maggie called from the road at 2:30. The girls and their parents were on the way. After speaking to Nick, Maggie handed the phone to Claire, who excitedly tried to tell him about her new stuff. Nick laughed and said, "Surprise me when you have your show."

Now he waited to have company in his home for the first time since Ann died. He knew Becky's parents but hadn't met Denise's mother. The girls had been friends since kindergarten. *I really should be more involved.* He heard a car in the driveway and opened the front door to see Maggie's SUV. He hurried to help Jenny and pushed her into the house as Maggie drove away.

Claire dashed up the stairs to her room with some of her packages while Nick followed with the rest. "Do you need any more help, or can you handle this yourself?"

Claire's face flushed rosy pink as she scanned her room. She noticed Ron and Gayle were absent. "I'll be okay. Thank you for buying me all this, Dad." She hugged his waist. "You're so awesome!"

He hugged her back, his heart swelling with gratitude. "My pleasure, sweetie. I can't wait to see you in your new clothes!"

"See you later, alligator." She was already opening one of the bags.

"In a while, crocodile." He bounded down the stairs.

When Becky, Denise, and their parents arrived, Nick felt nervous at first, but Jenny engaged them with tales of her adventures and misadventures. Soon everyone was having a good time. The girls were eager to see Claire in her new clothes. They pranced and twirled, showing off what their parents bought them before rushing upstairs. They noticed Miss Sanderson, but the young ladies had a show to prepare. Nick noted how significant getting new clothes turned out to be. *Another girly thing I need to learn.*

The plan was progressing without a hitch when he asked Miss Sanderson to stay for the fashion show. He was improvising a question about Claire's progress report when she appeared at the top of the stairs. She smiled like a princess, and when she had everyone's attention, she slowly descended the steps, her giggling friends behind her. Nick stopped mid-sentence, staring at his little girl.

Her light blue dress with a white belt and full skirt fell just above her knees. A white cardigan with a lacy collar and trim matched the skirt's blue border. A blue bow in her hair complemented the ensemble. With her shiny black Mary Janes, she was ready to impress at church or a swanky tea party. She hopped off the last step and twirled, smiling and nodding as everyone oohed and aahed, shy and thrilled at the same time.

Nick looked over at Maggie and caught her eye. He raised his glass of iced tea and mouthed 'thank you' to her. She grinned and gave him a discreet thumbs up.

And so it went—dresses, tops, jeans, some classic, some trendy, and a little surprising to Nick. Bold graphics and colors that Maggie and the moms assured him were popular choices. New shoes, sneakers, boots, a jacket, and a new backpack. The nighties and unmentionables were not part of the show, but the girls admired them in Claire's room, jabbering like seven-year-olds.

Miss Sanderson said goodbye, and the adults discussed playdates. Nick arranged one for next Saturday, pleased that Claire would spend more time with Becky and Denise. As the parents and their girls piled into their cars, Jenny gave him a high-five, and Maggie returned with pizza and ice cream, like clockwork. After dinner and dessert, Claire led Maggie to her room to hang up her new dresses and put things away in her bureau drawers. They took pictures on Maggie's phone and brought them downstairs for Miss Jenny to see. Nick put his arm around Maggie's shoulder and pulled her close while she placed her hand on his chest, feeling his heart beat. "That was amazing. I couldn't have pulled this off without you."

"My pleasure. We had a ball, especially Mom." She nudged him toward the laundry room while Jenny entertained Claire. Following the plan, he leaned down and softly kissed her—twice. When they were together, he thought, everything fell into place; everything felt right.

Maggie sighed in his arms. He imagined them having coffee together in the morning, him mowing the lawn, her rewarding him with a cold glass of iced tea. Sitting around in the evenings, playing board games or reading. Watching Claire grow up and graduate high school.

After they helped Jenny to the car, Maggie returned to the house for her purse. Nick held up his index finger from the doorway, alerting Jenny that it might take a minute. Jenny grinned and played a game on her phone.

With Claire back in her room, he caught Maggie around the waist to show his appreciation. When they came up for air, remembering Jenny waiting in the car, Maggie choked on a laugh. "I'd better get out there before she comes looking for me."

Nick cupped her cheek and smiled into her deep brown eyes, almost blurting out his feelings, but he wanted to wait for a better moment. Sneaking in one more kiss, he turned her toward the door and walked her to the car. Feigning innocence, he grinned. "Sorry, her purse took *forever* to find. We lost track of time."

Jenny looked at them with a serene smile. "I bet." Nick stooped and kissed Jenny's hand. "Goodnight, Jenny, and thanks for spending my money. I hope you don't mind me stealing your daughter for a little while."

"Stealing? You better treat her like the treasure she is, or I'll roll all over you, mister." She tried to scowl, but her eyes twinkled with mischief.

Nick grinned, playing along. "Duly noted, ma'am. I'll be on my best behavior."

"For your sake, I hope so," Jenny quipped, flashing him a smile.

⁂

David arrived at Janet's office earlier than planned. They discussed possibilities to help understand Claire's experience. She admitted she had more of a problem with the presumed ghostly encounters than Claire did. The girl was unwavering about Ron and Gayle since she unburdened her secret, easily relating her interactions with the friends she now claimed were ghosts.

Janet wasn't sure she should include David in a session. She believed he was trustworthy and would not try to influence or exploit Claire, but his viewpoint might reinforce her belief and complicate Janet's job, perhaps even going beyond her scope of therapy. On the other hand, it would give Claire someone to understand and evaluate her story.

David looked at his watch and invited Janet to an early dinner. He'd flown in from a conference on the East Coast. Janet noted the time and declined. She had a session with Claire at 5 PM but promised to call him later with any developments.

During the session, Claire told Janet about her fashion show. Janet thought it was a good sign that she didn't mention Ron. Maybe having her friends over would help her stay grounded—interacting with kids her own age and stage of development. Imaginary friends usually tapered off among children around age seven. She pondered a paper she read by a specialist in that field when Claire mentioned that Ron wanted to meet Miss Jenny's husband.

Knowing the family, Janet said, "He passed away a few years ago." *Where is she going with this?*

"I know, but now he's a ghost, too. Ron wants to meet him so he can have a man friend. I think he doesn't have much fun with Gayle." She frowned. "I don't know what man-ghosts do for fun." She picked up a stuffed pig and pretended to make it fly.

"Daddy just works and comes home. Maybe Becky's dad could be his friend. Miss Maggie's his friend, but she's a girl. Would a man friend make my dad happier, like me?"

Janet observed Claire merging the characters in her unique world with the ordinary. Either Claire was having a remarkable otherworldly experience or a very serious 'disorder' they didn't even have a name for. It would be a case for the journals.

Janet wanted to talk to Maggie or Jenny about Jenny's husband. *How did Ron find out about him in the first place? Wait, I need to rethink this. Why does Claire think Tom's a ghost? Did Jenny talk to Claire about her late husband? Or Maggie? The more I talk to Claire, the more there is to discover.*

"Men like to have friends to do things with. Your dad wants to spend time with you now. It makes him happy. I think it also made him happy to see you with Becky and Denise, having fun with your new clothes. But if Becky's dad and your dad like some of the same things, they might be friends, too." They talked more about friendship until the session ended. Janet noted Claire's consistent inclusion of Ron in her social circle of real friends. *Fascinating. But I must take this further to help her differentiate between the two. I think.*

"Claire, let's talk about your ghost friend, Ron. What if I told you about a friend of mine who sees ghosts, too? Would you like to talk to him about Ron and Gayle?"

"He sees ghosts, too?" She wiggled a little in place.

Janet nodded. "Yes, and other things that are hard to explain. He might have answers for you that I don't know because I can't see ghosts. He said he'd like to hear about your friends and if anything is different about your house when Ron and Gayle are there."

"The house gets cold when they fly around. That's why I wear a sweater. Even Daddy does, but he thinks there's something wrong with the furnace. But I'll talk to him if you want."

"Okay," Janet nodded. *David can check that out. If he can find reasonable, ordinary explanations, maybe she'll question her belief that ghosts are influencing events and develop a more practical worldview.*

"Your dad will be here soon. I need his permission for you to see my friend. Have you told him that Ron and Gayle are ghosts?"

Claire bit her lip and looked away. "No, but I told Miss Jenny. I asked her not to tell my dad yet because he'd be worried." She thought for a long moment. "I guess we should tell him. Can you go first? I'll answer all his questions later, okay?" She sighed dramatically and picked up a doll from a basket on the floor, glancing at the corner where Ron usually waited.

Remarkable, Janet thought as she touched Claire's knee and rose from the floor. "Alright." She smiled. "I think that's a good idea."

In Janet's waiting room, Nick looked at her strangely when she asked about his furnace. "It's been on the blink for a while now. I can't find the problem. There's a draft from somewhere, but I can't figure out where. Why do you ask?"

"Claire says she knows. Do you want to know?"

"Yeah, I think so." He leaned back slightly on his heels.

"Remember, when I tell you about our sessions, it's with the understanding that we want Claire to come to her own conclusions, so I'll ask you not to challenge her belief. We'll make more progress that way. Agreed?"

"Agreed."

"Claire said it's because of the ghosts flying around."

"Ah, geez." Nick ran his fingers through his hair, turning his back to Janet.

"Nick, my goal is for Claire to develop skills to evaluate what's real and what's not. I would like your permission to bring in my friend David, you know, the paranormal investigator?"

"When? Where?" He turned back to face her, eyebrows raised.

"The sooner, the better. At your house. Claire could tell him, maybe show him things. David might prove that ghosts are not the cause of the cold spots in your house. If Claire sees that, she might evolve her understanding of cause and effect."

"I don't know, Janet. I'm not too crazy about him coming to the house, but the maintenance guy told me the weatherstripping and the furnace are fine. Are you saying he can tell if it's ghosts making it cold? What if he can't explain it either?" He looked at her, then at the floor. "What does Claire say about seeing David?"

"She said okay. I think it would help her. He's very bright and doesn't believe everything is supernatural."

"Yeah, I got that from his website. He seems level-headed. But after watching those videos on unexplainable strange happenings, I want to know more. You think we should?"

"Yes, I do," she said.

"Would you come, Janet? I'd like another witness." He paced, conflicted. "I'm still a skeptic about this paranormal stuff." He sighed. "I can't believe we are going through with this."

"I understand, Nick. I'm skeptical too. The important thing is to acknowledge Claire's current reality. It's a bit like when a parent comforts a child by checking under her bed for monsters. We don't believe the monsters are real, but we want to help them through it. Yes, I'll come," she said. "I want to observe her reactions and the questions she asks."

"I'm willing to try anything to help Claire. All right, set it up. Maybe it'll scare off these so-called ghosts." As if on cue, a sudden chill raised goosebumps on his arms.

Don't bet on it, Nick. You ain't seen nothin' yet! Gayle zipped over his head, messing up his hair.

Janet gasped, her eyes darting around the room. "What the hell was that?"

Nick smoothed his hair and shrugged nonchalantly. "A draft?"

"In my waiting room?" Janet blinked, trying to steady her voice. Hearing her own shrill tone, she cleared her throat, blushing.

"Welcome to my world," Nick replied, his tone almost amused.

Twenty-Eight

That night, Nick called Maggie to update her on Claire's session, feeling conflicted about a guy coming to his house to investigate the presence of ghosts. "She thinks it'll help Claire and wants him involved. What do you think, Mags?"

On her cell phone, Maggie smiled at his request for advice. "He's the paranormal expert, right? Janet is using all her psychological expertise to help Claire. If someone experienced in the paranormal can investigate, maybe you'll learn what's going on in your house."

"Damn, Maggie. I can just see the TV cameras in my yard, reporters at her school. People will look at my little girl like she's nuts. We're getting along so much better, but I'm the one worried. Claire is happy as a lark." He paused for a moment. "Pearson doesn't seem like a publicity hound, but I should make it clear—no press conference, just a visit."

Setting her pen down, Maggie stood and stretched before sitting on her bed. "Nick, I think you're on the right track. If this guy can discreetly prove or disprove ghosts in your house, great. But can you accept either answer? Maybe you should prepare yourself. If he proves you have ghosts, how will you handle it?"

She felt a twinge of guilt as she spoke, not revealing that Claire had already confided in Jenny, and Jenny in her, about the ghosts. She thought it would be better if he evaluated for himself.

"I have no idea." Hesitating, Nick asked, "Do you think it's possible? That Claire really sees ghosts? Would that mean my house is haunted?"

He heard Maggie sigh before she spoke. "After Mom told me how my dad reaches out to her from the other side, I'm leaning towards 'it's possible.' She feels she can communicate with him, and it eases her pain, so I'm all for it. In Claire's case, she was unhappy and needed a friend. Since Ron came into her life, your relationship with her has improved. She's a happier child. I can't explain it with certainty, but I don't think she's making all this up."

Nick looked around his living room for clues, finding none, and replied softly, "I don't think she is either." He smiled, hearing Claire's faint voice in a conversation upstairs. "Maybe I'm evolving, Maggie. Janet said she would be here when he comes. Will you come too?"

"I'm certainly interested, but let me check with Janet first. I don't want to get in the way."

"Honey, you're never 'in the way.' You belong here. Without you, we wouldn't have come this far. I want you to be there."

"Okay, consider me there. When?"

Relieved, he said, "I'm not sure yet; Janet said she'd call."

"Okay, I'll touch base with her too. We'll make this ghost party happen. Woo hoo! Sorry, I just hope it's not like that movie where the little girl's toys spin around the room, and the TV goes wacky, and she says, 'they're he-re.' That would be creepy."

"Stop it, Maggie," he laughed. "You're freaking me out a little." *More than a little.*

Listening in, Gayle considered ways to meddle in David's investigation. *Should we mess with his equipment or leave the house so he couldn't prove anything?* As Nick ended the call, she dimmed a little, forcing herself to ask, "What do you think, Ron?"

"How about we fly around and move things? Slam doors and stuff? That would be fun," Ron suggested.

"Yeah, but if we go all poltergeist, they'd know for sure we're here. Then what? There would be complications, don't you think?" Gayle paused, considering the consequences.

"I guess so. But Nick would know Claire's not making it up. Then again..."

Gayle flew figure-eights on the ceiling, thinking. "If we disappear and Nick and Maggie stay together, and Claire is happy, we could wrap up here, and then I can get my wings. But Claire wouldn't have you around."

"Right. I know we can't stay here forever. But they should know she's not sick. She has a gift. What if...?"

"I think we should watch him and see if his equipment can find our ghost DNA or whatever, or if he's a quack."

"It's your call, Gayle," he grinned. "I don't know our exit strategy, but I want Claire's dad and the others to know she's okay. Can you pervade their thoughts or something?"

"No. No pervading. The Boss said so." Gayle listened to her conscience. "I don't think we should manipulate anyone, as much as I'd like to. Lord knows, if people did things my way, everyone would live happily ever after. But I'm supposed to let things work themselves out. Be a team player and all that. Ugh." She sighed, and her form flickered in the light. "Oh, no.

Ron!" She darted around the room in a panic, her face a mask of horror. "I... I just can't decide!"

Ron stared at her, taken aback by her admission. "It's okay, Gayle. Let's just decide to play it by ear." He paused, "I'm going to get some air; I'll be back in a bit."

Ron flew to Jenny's, thinking, *maybe Tom can help.* He looked around to see if her late husband showed up. *This kitchen always smells good. Sometimes it's the flowers from her garden, and other times it's her baking. I do miss a good meal.*

He saw Jenny in the backyard with a dreamy smile on her face. *Could it be...?*

Ron floated over to Jenny's wheelchair and noticed a shimmer hovering near her. *I can't quite make it out. It's like a current of air is holding a pattern around her shoulders.*

"Tom? Is that you?" Ron said, waiting. "Tom? I'm a friend of your wife and daughter." He noticed Jenny open her palm as though she held someone's hand, breathing softly. *Yeah, it must be Tom. Why doesn't he answer me?*

"Because I'm with my wife, Ron. Now, what's on your mind?" a deep voice drawled in Ron's mind.

Ron gawked at the space that spoke to him. Delighted, he blurted, "You *do* exist."

"Of course I do. Don't you?"

"I can see myself and Gayle. But I only see a shimmer where you are. And you're talking in my head!"

"That's because we're on different planes. Mostly, I watch over my wife and daughter. It's a phase in my journey. You're the first caseworker I've talked to."

Caseworker, I kinda like that. "This is so cool. I hope we can be friends, Tom. You know, we're both dead—and ghosts—and guys." He thought out loud.

"I know what you and your lady friend have been doing. I appreciate how she's helping my Maggie. It's high time she met a nice fella."

"Oh, then you must know I've been helping that nice fella's daughter."

"Jenny loves that girl. She knows Claire can see and talk to you. So, Ron. Our paths have now crossed. What can I do for you?"

"I don't know how long I'll be here, and I only have Gayle and sweet Claire to talk to. I figured it would be nice to get a man's point of view on a paranormal investigation."

"One of those TV ghost hunter shows? I'm not sure how much help I'd be. I don't fly or do tricks. I just sort of occur when Jenny needs me."

Ron chuckled. "It's not a ghost show; it's a guy who might prove we exist coming to Claire's house. But he seems legit, and we're not sure if we should reveal ourselves."

"Ah. To reveal or not to reveal. I see. You're worried if the adults learn that Claire really sees ghosts, they'll treat her differently. If the guy doesn't find evidence, they'll worry about her mental health. There's no telling how the adults will react."

"Exactly, Tom. I've been sent here to make her happy, and I think I've done that. But the adults might not understand, and she would be sad again. Can you, um, occur at Claire's when the paranormal guy does his thing? Maybe you can help read the situation. If we can't resolve it, things could get worse. Can you help us?"

Jenny reached from her chair to snip a budding rose. They saw a shadow of sadness cross her face as her eyes scanned the distance.

"I'll do my best, Ron. You'll know when I'm there. Now, I should attend to my wife."

Ron thanked him. With new hope and a new friend, he flew back to the Millers' house.

C H A P T E R

TWENTY-NINE

Saturday afternoon, a full-size black SUV came to an abrupt stop in front of Nick's house. For a moment, Nick imagined somber government agents flashing credentials and rifling through his belongings before questioning him and his daughter.

He shook his head as Janet opened the passenger door. David rounded the hood, tucked a lock of brown hair behind his ear, and removed his wire-rimmed glasses. Wiping them on his maroon golf shirt, he squinted, and his focused brown eyes met Nick's. They shook hands. Nick liked his grip but felt a bit uneasy.

"I needed something big enough for my gear," he grinned, sweeping his hand toward the vehicle. "That's all the rental place had left."

Nick smiled. "Let me help you." They unloaded several heavy cases.

Maggie arrived with Jenny, who insisted on joining them.

"I'm not missing this show for anything. You couldn't keep me away with a Neutron Wand." Sizing up David, Jenny raised an eyebrow. "You have one of those, right?"

"No, ma'am. That's just in the movies," David chuckled easily. "I'm only here to observe. Unless they get really feisty." He winked at her.

Once inside, Nick introduced Claire, who stood close to his side. David explained a device that picked up electromagnetic fields and recorded levels of interference. His specialized infrared thermometer could indicate rapid temperature changes; a cold spot in a room might signal shifting energy. "That could be an unnatural weather phenomenon or a glitch in the HVAC system." He paused. "Or... something else," he grinned.

He demonstrated a variable frequency voice recorder capable of analyzing ambient noise patterns and sweeping AM, FM, and shortwave signals. "In case any spirits care to comment." He glanced around.

"We could go for hours without hearing an entity reaching out from beyond. But some spirits are playful and arrive when you least expect them. So, please be patient, but watchful. You might be surprised." He clicked a button on the audio device, and feedback squealed through the room.

They flinched, captivated by the drama. Janet and Nick exchanged glances, rolled their eyes, and laughed, watching David the showman have a little fun with them. They settled into their chairs around the kitchen, murmuring with curiosity.

"I'm going to check the draft around the furnace first. I'll be right back." He directed a camera toward the basement door. Nick moved closer as David descended the stairs.

Nick noticed Claire squirming and bouncing in her seat, covering her mouth as if wanting to say something, when a draft whooshed by him. Ron and Gayle zipped up the stairs to the second floor.

Janet leaned over and whispered for Nick not to say anything to David that might influence his findings. The skeptic in Nick wanted to understand the drafts; he just wasn't sure he wanted them to be ghosts.

Jenny and Maggie waited, whispering to each other and glancing at Claire. Nick could tell they cared about how this would affect her.

The ghosts hovered at the top of the stairs, waiting to see what would unfold when David took his readings. Gayle didn't believe he could detect them. She decided they would have some fun messing with David, but not give him anything conclusive—just enough to show him she was in charge, but not enough to prove anything.

David swept his special thermometer in an arc as he returned from the basement, checking the kitchen and then the dining area. He squinted with concern as he approached Claire, scanning her with the temperature wand. He gasped, and the wand shook in his hand. Claire's eyes widened, and her mouth dropped open. David chuckled, letting her in on the prank.

"No significant abnormalities yet, folks." He approached the stairs and turned to the group. "Claire, would you mind if I checked your closet?"

She glanced at Janet and shrugged. "Sure, that's okay," she said to David, remembering the dress Gayle had fixed for her. She looked at her dad, but Nick shrugged.

Gayle fluttered at the top of the stairs, suddenly anxious. Then she remembered, with a chill of concern, *Claire's party dress.*

David set up another camera and tucked an EMF detector under his arm. He retrieved a device that Gayle suspected might be an ectoplasm meter—something she had only read about but never seen. She hovered at the top of the stairs, worried he would detect her ectoplasm. Her anxiety spiked, and forgetting herself, she soared down the stairs to avoid detection, ironically creating an icy jetstream as she passed by David, the ghost detective.

David's digital thermometer flashed when the temperature dropped from a comfortable 72 to 45 degrees. Realizing what she did, Gayle beckoned to Ron, then held up a hand to stop him, and returned to the top of the stairs. The reading returned to normal. David tapped the device, shaking it with a sheepish grin. The spectators gasped and murmured as David's hair and clothes began to ripple in the wake of an unseen wind, wobbling his knees. He picked up the devices he dropped, clipped them to his utility belt, removed the camera from its tripod, and climbed the stairs like a high-tech handyman. Claire giggled and gave Ron a thumbs up.

The group watched intently to see what would happen next. From above, Gayle frantically blew wind down the stairs, and David stumbled backward, gripping the banister with his free hand. He turned to the group below and calmly stated, "I seem to be encountering some resistance." His hair flying behind him, he trudged up the stairs against the wind.

Claire leaned over to Janet, cupping her hand near her mouth. "They're just having fun with him. He's going to find my dress." Janet looked at her with wide eyes, tugging uncomfortably at her sweater and smoothing her jeans. She patted Claire's hand as if to reassure her. Claire's voice was soft but certain. "It's okay, Miss Janet. You can hold my hand."

Janet watched David, knowing part of her wanted him to find ghosts. If he did, it would prove Claire right. But how could she— a seemingly rational psychologist—reconcile that with reality?

The others spoke in hushed tones, posing questions with few answers. Nick wanted to follow him but stayed at the foot of the stairs, listening. After what seemed like twenty minutes, David started down the stairs, holding the white party dress with purple flowers draped over his arm. He gripped the banister with one hand and mumbled notes to the camera in the other. Hair disheveled and eyes distant, deep in thought, he approached the table.

More out of habit than necessity, because she didn't want to lose, Gayle continued her irrational attempts to thwart the man who might prove her existence to the group at Nick's dining room table.

David looked at Claire, holding up the dress. "Is this the one?" She sat with her hands in her lap, smiling and nodding. To Nick and the ladies, he mumbled, "I need to run a few more tests." Clearing his throat, he continued, "Ah, as you can see, things can get rather unpredictable. If anyone wants to leave..."

The overhead lights flickered, and the blender on the kitchen counter whirred to life. David walked over and unplugged it, still holding the dress. "... for your own safety. I would understand." His voice was even and sincere; no one thought it was an act.

Jenny spoke up, "Are you kidding? It's just getting spooky!" Maggie and Nick exchanged glances and nodded, albeit with some hesitation, in agreement. Janet was not as enthusiastic. David winked at her and examined Claire's dress on the kitchen counter.

Gayle tried to distract him by activating the microwave and the electric can opener.

David sighed, disconnecting the other devices. "It's not uncommon for kitchen appliances to behave strangely," he deadpanned, closing drawers as Gayle opened them. Nick watched, mesmerized, as did the others.

He turned to his daughter, who wore a peaceful grin and sat on her hands, quietly as if she had been asked. He so wanted to believe her, and heaven help him, the proof was happening right before his eyes.

Janet knew David was one of the best in his field and admired his cool demeanor. He knew what he was doing. Their previous meetings had gone well, and he addressed her ambivalence without being pushy or condescending. He was easy on the eyes, too. His hair flopped over his forehead, and he would sweep it back with his fingers, only to have it fall again as he got caught up in an explanation. *I wonder if it falls in his eyes when he—Easy, girl. No time for fantasies. This could benefit Claire.*

Jenny studied the faces, enjoying herself. She believed Claire the moment the girl confided in her about her ghost friends. A true believer since Tom died, she supported her wholeheartedly. Now, she hoped the others would believe her too. *This could have a huge impact on Claire's life. Her gifts could help so many people.* As for Nick—Jenny could tell he had doubts, but after today, he'd have to see the light.

A subtle movement of air stroked Jenny's neck. *That wasn't Claire's friends. Nope, I know that feeling.* "Hello, my dear," she whispered, recognizing her husband's familiar presence. "Are you here to join the fun? I'll bet you're getting a kick out of this, aren't you?"

As Gayle considered her next volley, eyeing the refrigerator, Ron noticed the stirring of air behind him, a shift in pressure. It must be Tom. "Glad you could make it, buddy. Have any ideas?"

"Looks like y'all are making a little mischief," Tom said.

His deep voice resonated like a bass guitar in Ron's head. *That's so cool when he does that.*

Gayle turned sharply, sensing Tom's presence. "Who are you talking to?" she asked, scanning the room. As if on cue, the freezer door opened a few inches and then closed again. The group noticed but seemed indifferent, already accustomed to the strange occurrences.

"Tom is here," Ron confirmed.

"Oh, he is?" Gayle replied, narrowing her eyes as she continued her search, feeling a shift in the air.

"Yeah, but he's from a different level, so he doesn't look like us."

"Right, I knew that. I can sense him." She turned toward the faint shimmer. "Welcome, Tom. Are you here to help?"

"If I can. What are you trying to do?" Tom asked. "I think they suspect you're here. Do you want to blow their minds?"

He wants in the game, Ron mused. "What do you say, Gayle? They know we're here now. We should really blow their minds, don't you think?"

Gayle hesitated. "I just wanted to mess with him, but I forgot about the dress. I—I tried to distract him with the small appliances." Her form flickered and dimmed, realizing that her efforts to remain undetected only confirmed their presence. "My decision...that is...I was..."

"Say it, Gayle. You can do it." Ron chuckled.

"Wrong. I was wrong, Ron." She glared at him.

"Now, that wasn't so hard, was it?" He smiled mischievously.

Gayle narrowed her eyes. "Don't say it. Don't you—"

"Wrong Way."

"Ugh, you just couldn't resist, could you?"

Winking at Gayle, Ron turned to Jenny's late husband. "Moving right along, how should we make *real* believers out of them, Tom?"

Tom glanced at David, who was waving a device over Claire's dress and dictating notes into a handheld recorder. "He's got some nifty gear," he remarked, then added, "I know Jenny's a believer, but the others might rationalize what they saw. You should do something spectacular."

"Yeah. If we leave no doubt that we exist, they'll have to believe Claire."

Tom said, "Can you materialize? That ought to be convincing."

"No one knows what we look like except Claire," Gayle replied. "Obviously, we're not very scary."

"Can your bodies handle such a transition?" Tom asked. "No offense, Gayle, but you're looking a little peaked."

Gayle shrugged. "None taken. I am kind of worn out. And I've never tried it before. But I need this form to get my wings. I can't mess that up."

"I'll do it," Ron said.

"What if you can't get back, Ron?" Gayle asked. "What would happen to you? More importantly, what would happen to me if The Boss found out? It's too dangerous." She crossed her arms. *I'll get blamed for it, and my wings will fly off without me.*

"Oh, hold on, guys. I think The Boss is calling me." She put her hand to her ear. "Yes, sir? I'll be right there. Gotta fly, boys. Be back in a jiff, I hope." She vanished.

Tom turned to Ron. "What was that all about?"

"She wants to cover her butt if anything goes wrong, so she pretended he called her."

Gayle returned, a bit rattled. "The Boss says we can try it. But just you, Ron. Time is running out, so be very careful. If you get stuck halfway through, I'm not sure I can fix it."

Ron looked at Tom. "Well?"

"It's up to you, Ron. I wouldn't want my idea to put you at risk, but it would certainly get their attention."

CHAPTER
THIRTY

David checked his recorder and replaced his camera on the tripod, focusing it on the stairs leading to the second floor. Gayle hoped Ron could pull it off, and that David's camera would capture the transformation, but she had her doubts. She and Tom tried to boost his confidence as Ron shook off his nerves, eager to prove himself.

David rolled his shoulders and adjusted the camera lens, muttering into his voice recorder. Inside, his heart thumped as he steadied himself. *This is the real thing. My equipment doesn't give false positives, and the data is sound.* He double-checked the readings and scanned the room, bracing for the unexpected.

He swept his camera toward the ladies, who whispered excitedly at the table, then to Nick, who paced the kitchen, eyeing the countertop devices warily. He duct-taped the knife drawer shut, then turned, hands on hips, sizing up the refrigerator as if it were a potential projectile.

Jenny, Maggie, Janet, and Claire sat with their chairs facing the stairs, the adults ready with their cell phone cameras. Janet had captured a video of

David trudging up the stairs like a mountain climber battling a windstorm. She couldn't explain it, but she could still tease him about it.

Everyone heard what sounded like a drum roll—its origin was anyone's guess—but it captured their attention, eyes fixed on the staircase. Claire couldn't sit still, obviously thrilled. She took hold of Maggie's hand on one side and Janet's on the other. Her legs swung back and forth so hard that her chair slid noisily on the tile floor.

David noted Claire's excitement, sensing she was in contact with the entities, and lifted the camera to his eye, scanning the area. *Something big is about to happen.* The air pressure seemed to shift, stirred by something formless. The recorder on his belt confirmed the sonic disturbance. *They're communicating! Goosebumps raised the hair on his arms as a cool breeze swept from the stairs into the living room.*

The sun hung low in the western sky, its light streaming through the window blinds over Nick's sofa. Bright stripes illuminated dust motes in the air. David trained his camera on a spot that appeared disrupted—the dust moved as if displaced by a shape, an empty outline between him and the group. Three women and Claire stared at the same space.

A static hum accompanied the shimmer. As it grew louder, shadows shifted, and overhead lights dimmed, then brightened. Jenny nudged Maggie and pointed to her teacup, the contents rippling.

The air buzzed as the outline took shape. A form resembling a head and shoulders gathered space into itself, less than ten feet from the mesmerized guests. David circled the apparition and crept closer, chuckling nervously as a pale gray, blurry head came into view.

Ron concentrated so hard that when his eyes appeared, they were squeezed shut with strain. The group watched, transfixed, until Claire squealed his name, giggling and nudging Janet with her shoulder. Janet rocked side to side with Claire's movements, gaping as Ron's eyes opened and a nose formed between them. Effort puckered the lips that appeared next, breaking into a toothy smile. The head swiveled toward Claire and winked.

Gayle murmured, "Well, I'll be damned," and Tom breathed a sigh of relief.

David kept filming, his body operating on autopilot while his mind swirled with theories and possibilities. Ron's head and shoulders were life-size and becoming denser; the staircase was barely visible behind him. Everyone realized they were in the presence of an actual ghost.

Ron was so tickled that he got distracted, and his face faded. Claire yelled, "No!"

Ron's eyes widened, and his mouth formed an 'O.' His image wavered, but his head and shoulders returned. David zoomed in, recording every moment.

He panned the camera to capture the ladies' expressions and took a selfie with Ron's head just before the image blinked out with an audible 'pop.' Just for fun. Glancing at Nick, David grinned. *I've got to get this shot of him sliding down the wall with that dumbfounded look on his face.*

Pandemonium erupted at the kitchen table. Cheers and hugs for Claire, wonder at what had just transpired. Even Janet couldn't entirely refute what she had witnessed.

Claire glowed inside, warmth spreading through her. *Ron proved to her family and friends that he was real.* People could finally believe her. She had a friend who happened to be a ghost. They had only seen part of him, but their excitement matched hers. But now she couldn't see or hear him. Ron had disappeared, and she didn't know where he was.

Gayle swooped down the stairs, and something blurry moved behind her. "Come back, come back! You nitwit!" She flew in circles, spinning and searching for Ron.

Tom tried to calm her down, but Gayle was frantic. *Oh, no. It was too much for him. He must return to his regular body. If anything happened to him, I'll be in so much trouble. The Boss will, uh, kill me.*

David noticed it first. While sliding a fresh battery into his camera, a needle spiked on an analog meter. He snatched his headphones and heard static crackling as the energy field flew through the front door and around the kitchen table, ruffling the curtains.

Gayle, Tom, and Claire heard Ron howl, "Whoop-de-doo!" as David's recorder displayed the subsonic pulse.

Claire cheered, jumping out of her chair and throwing her fists in the air. The adults stared at her and each other, clearly processing the recent events.

David conducted interviews, ending with Claire's matter-of-fact description of a ghost repairing her party dress. As he filmed her, his mind drifted. He knew that when edited for viewing, more trolls would bash the video than believers would support it. It was the nature of his business. He was more interested in his peers' reviews than accolades. But he wouldn't mind a partner to share his rare discoveries with. Compatible partners seemed as scarce as ghosts these days.

He could tell by looking at her that Janet needed time to think. David didn't expect her to dive into the deep end with him. He hoped to see her again, perhaps to find common ground between their professions and personalities. She intrigued him, and he was a man in search of intrigue.

CHAPTER

THIRTY-ONE

Jenny, Maggie, and Nick milled about the kitchen while David packed up his equipment. Animated, he gushed about compiling the data and video into a documentary.

"Not like those cheesy shaky-cam jump-scare shows," he said, trying to engage Janet, who now looked like she needed a nap. "I'd love to get you on camera with a psychological perspective."

Janet remained silent and declined the after-event interview. She helped load his gear, and they left together. David continued his excited chatter, but she tuned him out, studying the twilight from her window, trying to make sense of what she'd seen. He dropped her off at her car, and she agreed to talk later.

Nick carried Claire, asleep on the sofa, upstairs and tucked her in. He returned to the kitchen, where wine and snacks awaited.

"So," Nick said.

"So," Maggie replied.

"Yup," Jenny added.

Nick took Maggie's hand, turning to Jenny's warm smile.

"How about them apples, huh?" Jenny said. "Claire has been telling the truth all along. Her gifts are beyond me. What an extraordinary child."

"That she is. I'm amazed—but how do we help her? And what's next?" Maggie asked.

Maggie glided to the kitchen counter, filled the kettle, and set it on the stove. Taking three cups from the overhead cupboard and three tea bags from a canister, she grabbed spoons from the silverware drawer, closing it with a flick of her hip. She turned to Nick, ripping the duct tape from the adjacent drawer, smiling. "I think we're safe from spontaneous flying cutlery now. Right, Nick?"

"I think so." He nodded, watching her, comforted that she seemed at ease. He wanted her near, wanted her in their lives.

"Oh." She stopped, grinning at the cups on the counter. "We have wine, too. I guess I'm a little distracted."

Nick poured the wine. "I know what you mean. I'm glad she's not hallucinating, but what if this is worse?"

Jenny laid her hand on his wrist. "Don't be silly, Nick. She's a normal seven-year-old with a bonus, an amazing ability. Start there, grow with it, learn from it. Treat it as a blessing."

The trio paused, each reflecting on the day's events.

"You know, they had Tom's help tonight," Jenny said, sipping her wine.

"What? How did you know, Mom?" Maggie gasped, setting the hot kettle on the stove with a clatter.

She shrugged. "The way I always know. The little things that get my attention."

Nick looked at Maggie, then at her mother. "Have you always believed, Jenny? In visits from the other side?"

Jenny considered his question. "I believe that when I have a vivid memory of someone who has passed away, it feels like a visit from the other side. When I recall their words, the scents, and the sounds, it's as if I'm receiving a message. It's like they left something behind for me, and I've discovered it. As I've grown older and lost more people, I take a moment to be grateful for those memories. Who knows, I might run into them on the other side." She sipped her drink while the younger pair contemplated her words.

Jenny smiled wistfully and shared a memory of the first time Tom contacted her. "It was about something private that only Tom and I knew. We were young, driving back to our little apartment after a weekend in the mountains. We'd made glorious love that morning..."

"Mom! Eeew!" Maggie teased, scrunching her face.

Jenny patted her hand. "Missy, I know they teach about these things in school."

"Anyway, I'll spare you the details," Jenny continued. "I shivered, like when someone touches that spot on your neck. I kept thinking about it while your dad was away on a job for a few weeks. Let's just say I made a discovery. I clearly remembered a story my mother told me at our kitchen table before she died—almost 30 years ago. I can still smell the biscuits she made.

"Someone was waiting to be born into this world," she said, placing her hand on Maggie's. "And she had a great adventure ahead, filled with beauty and pain, love and loss. She embraced it all because when she left, she would become memories for those she left behind."

Nick watched them closely as Maggie pondered her mother's words. She rubbed her fingers, her eyes defocusing as if lost in a vivid memory. "Mom, I remember Dad swinging me by my hands when I was a child."

With the vision clear in her mind, Maggie said, "I think I understand what you mean, Mom—the things I remember about Daddy." She stroked her fingers with her thumb. "I'm still shocked about what happened today. I'm pretty sure this memory is going to stick with me." She glanced at Nick, calmness in her eyes.

"I know Janet is going to have a hard time with it," she chuckled. "You think I'm stubborn; David has to convince my favorite by-the-book psychologist that she saw a ghost today."

Nibbling on cheese and crackers, they discussed what each of them had seen and felt. An apparition had appeared, and Claire called him Ron. The three talked into the wee hours until Jenny yawned, and they decided to call it a night.

Nick helped Jenny settle into Maggie's car and placed her wheelchair in the trunk while Maggie cleared the table. Inside, Nick wrapped his arms around her waist, clasping his hands. "Leave those things, sweetheart. You've done enough tonight."

Maggie leaned back against his solid chest, covering his calloused hands with hers. "I hope you like roller coasters, Miller. Looks like you have a wild ride ahead."

Nick agreed, his heart thudding with the risk he was about to take. The kitchen offered a cozy refuge from a world that shifted beneath their feet. In the stillness, Nick savored the moment of intimacy. "I hope you like roller coasters too. Because I can't imagine navigating Claire's world without you. I don't want to do this alone."

The moment of truth tightened his throat. Images of Ann and their ten years together filled him with a newfound peace. It was now simple and clear. "I love you, Maggie, and I want us to be together. I hope you feel the same way."

Maggie turned in his arms and reached around his neck to pull him closer. They held each other, and time lost its sway. When they pulled apart, she searched his eyes. "Nick, I've never felt this way about anyone. The truth is…" She paused for a few agonizing moments, "I love roller coasters." Her mouth twisted into a grin. "And I love you too. Let's do this already. I'm in."

Nick cupped her cheek. Lost for words, he ached for more of her. "Soon," he said.

Maggie smiled and repeated, "Soon." She took his hand and led him out his front door to her car.

He kissed her again before she slid into the driver's seat. "Text me when you get home, okay?"

"Sure thing, now that I can take my phone to bed with me," she replied as she pulled away. Maggie's gaze lingered in the rearview mirror as she drove off, seeing Nick still standing there, the image seeming frozen in time.

Nick locked the door behind him, stretched his arms overhead, yawned, turned off the lights, and walked up the familiar steps to his bedroom, pausing near the top. The surreal events of the staircase still baffled him, but he was too tired to ponder them. As he passed Claire's room, he stopped and listened. Silence, except for her breathing.

While undressing for bed, Nick replied to Maggie's text, a simple message confirming their shared feelings. He noticed a hatbox on the shelf of his closet, and for the first time in over a year, he opened it while sitting on his bed, dwelling on a photo of Ann, himself, and Claire as a toddler. He offered a silent prayer of gratitude for all that she brought to their lives and asked for her blessing. Inside the box, among the jewelry and souvenirs, he found a forgotten heirloom that assured him she did. He held it up to the lamp, remembering the conversation with Ann in this room and the light in her eyes. Feeling at peace, he knew what he needed to do.

2 4 4

C H A P T E R

THIRTY-TWO

The next morning, Claire threw off her covers, slid out of bed, and kneeled to say her prayers, asking God to include Ron and Gayle, and a new ghost she didn't know yet. In the hallway, she noticed her dad's bedroom door ajar. She peeked in and saw him asleep, and she was hungry. She skipped downstairs to make herself some cereal. Usually, her dad helped, but everyone—even Ron and Gayle—slept late today.

They kept the cereal and bowls in a lower cabinet so Claire could reach them. She retrieved two bowls and chose corn flakes because Daddy didn't like her having too much sugar. The milk carton was heavy, but she managed. She found two placemats and positioned a bowl on each, folding paper napkins in triangles and placing a spoon on each napkin, just like Jenny showed her. Admiring the pretty table, she sat down to eat, even as her mind wandered.

I'm so glad everyone got to see Ron, even if it was just his head. The silly ghost. He sure scared me for a minute. I thought he disappeared. Does Daddy believe me now? Will I still go to Miss Janet's office? Will everyone still like me?

Just then, Ron zoomed down the stairs, twisting in and out of the newels. He slid onto the countertop on his stomach, hands on his chin, singing, "Good Morning!"

Laughing, Claire replied, "Good morning to you, sleepy head. You're in a good mood today."

"Yes, I am. After last night, I feel like I can do anything!"

"It was awesome. Have you learned any other new tricks?"

Ron floated up from the counter and somersaulted to the couch. Claire laughed as he zoomed around the living room, flipping while she ate her cereal.

Nick lumbered down the stairs in his pajamas, yawning. He watched Claire giggling, looking around the room. *Ron must be entertaining her,* he thought. *But first, coffee.* "Morning, honey girl. You're up early." Noticing the set table, he smiled. "Hey, did you make me breakfast?"

"Morning, Daddy. Yes, if you want cereal. But I didn't put milk in so it wouldn't get mushy. Watch out for Ron; he's flying all over the place." She giggled but gave him a wary glance.

"Is he now? That's nice." He tousled her hair, thinking, *Be cool, Dad. Just another day at the Millers.*

"What shall we do today, Claire? Have any ideas?"

Finishing her cereal, she rose from the table and placed her bowl and spoon in the sink. "I don't know. What do you want to do?"

Nick started the coffeemaker and put a slice of bread in the toaster. He paused, considering the consequences, but plugged in the other appliances. Turning around, he grabbed Claire by the waist, tickling her. "I don't know, what do you want to do?" She laughed, to his delight. "We stayed up late, so we'll miss church today. What if we go see Miss Maggie and Miss Jenny?"

"Sure, that's okay with me."

"Then help me put milk in my cereal because...oh, no! My hands!" He lunged toward her again, his fingers clawing the air as she squealed. "We'll call them and see if it's okay. Then I guess we'd better get dressed, what do you think?"

Claire ran, posing for her dad at the foot of the stairs. "I don't know, what do you think?"

Ron knew he'd made a difference in their lives. They were comfortable with each other. *I'm kind of proud of myself. They've come a long way, and so have I.*

Gayle joined him at the kitchen window. "I gotta give you credit, dude. What gets me is you did it all on your own." In a pang of self-reflection, she added, "What rattles me more is that I can't take the credit—I kinda bungled my part of your grand reveal. Nick and Maggie fell in love all by themselves. I moved a few utensils around and got them talking, but sheesh!" She swirled around Ron, changing ethereal colors, and faced him. "Maybe I'm just much better than I thought! I'm kidding. You did good work, Ron. Now, if we can finish up with this merry bunch, maybe we can blow this pop stand."

"Thanks, Gayle." He contemplated what that would mean. "Things seem to be working themselves out. But I don't know how I'm going to leave Claire. If I had a kid of my own, I sure wish she was like her."

"She is a cutie, all right. Listen, my motto is 'do a little more than they ask for.' Let's make sure we give it our best to wrap things up. Impress them, and The Boss might give you another assignment."

Ron blinked. "I never thought of that."

"Well, think of it. I've had some amazing jobs, Ron. I've seen the world and changed a few lives. But it's up to The Boss. I suggest that whatever he wants done, you do."

Ron shrugged. "Okay."

As Nick and Claire drove to Maggie and Jenny's, he asked her about the ghosts. She told him about first seeing them on the ceiling at home and what they did at the school picnic. He now understood why she laughed so hard. Ron cheered her up just by fooling around.

Nick glanced at his daughter, thinking, *I guess I should thank him for that. What would I say? 'Hey buddy, I appreciate ya?' Claire said he's here to make her happy, and I certainly needed help in that department. I'm learning, anyway. My sweet child has a gift. It may be a burden or a calling. I'm so glad Maggie's in this with me.*

Jenny and Maggie's house evoked warm, dormant memories for Nick. His childhood home, which inspired his love for craftsmanship, came to mind. Both structures were created by artisans long since passed, leaving behind their work for others to enjoy for generations.

Approaching the front door, Nick envisioned a proper porch and ramp for Jenny, improving the path over a platform step, a threshold, and an awkward maneuver into the foyer. *I can build that.*

Claire knocked and ran ahead, leaving Maggie and Nick at the front door. She made a beeline for Jenny, who opened her arms to greet her. "How's my special girl?"

"I feel terrific, Miss Jenny. I'm so happy you got to see Ron!" She glanced over at her dad, who was whispering to Maggie. Then she whispered to Jenny, "They like each other a lot, huh?"

"I hope so. They sure kiss a lot, too. Don't they?"

Claire giggled. "Yeah. It's a little weird."

"Why is that, honey? Do you think it's okay that they're kissing?"

"I remember Dad used to kiss Mommy all the time, and now he's kissing Miss Maggie. I'm not sad; it's just a little weird."

"I understand, sweetie. Well, it was nice meeting your friend, Ron."

"Ron said they love each other now." Claire's smooth forehead wrinkled. "Miss Jenny? If I love Daddy and he loves Miss Maggie, and she loves you, does that mean I can love you both, too?"

"Sweet girl, there's always room for love. You can bet your bottom dollar that Miss Maggie and I love you to pieces, and your dad's not too bad either." She laughed.

Claire snuggled on Jenny's lap. "What's a bottom dollar? I don't have any dollars. I don't even get an allowance."

Jenny answered, "It comes from a card game called poker. When someone thought for sure they were going to win, they put their last dollar underneath their bet. So, they called it betting their bottom dollar."

"Okay, I guess." Claire frowned, and Jenny said she'd show her at their next party.

"How about some cookies and a nice glass of cold milk? Does that sound good?"

"Sounds better than a mean glass of milk!" She giggled with Jenny. "And your cookies always sound good to me." Nick and Maggie entered the kitchen.

"Daddy, do you have a bottom dollar?"

Nick looked sideways at Jenny. "What have you been teaching my daughter?"

"How to bet at poker, of course," Jenny grinned.

They sat outside on the deck overlooking Jenny's garden. Nick studied the rear deck and ramp to the backyard, which had been added with attention to the period design. He noted the ramp's structure and incline while Jenny coasted downhill to gather three blooming roses from a well-tended bush. She ascended with the flowers in her lap and a few firm pushes on her wheels. Maggie carried a tray of cookies and a pitcher of milk from the kitchen. Claire helped arrange the roses in a vase, mindful of the thorns.

They snacked and talked about ghosts, with Claire providing details. Maggie and Nick were shocked when Claire told them Gayle's job was to help get them together.

They remembered the strange occurrences not only at Nick's house but also at the school picnic and Maggie's barbecue. Claire recounted how Gayle kept moving and hiding things the first day she met Miss Janet.

Maggie gasped, laughing at herself. "I thought I'd lost my mind or something! That sneaky ghost—then Nick started helping me find things."

They enjoyed the day together like a normal family: games, lunch, a movie—nothing out of the ordinary—except for a brief chill that made Maggie cuddle closer to Nick. They exchanged glances as Nick put his arm around her and grinned. *They might've done some tricks to get our attention, but I know we have something special.*

As Nick and Maggie said goodbye, Jenny rolled to the door with Claire on her lap. Jenny turned to the trio. "I think it's time to schedule a Special-Event, Girls-Only, Overnight Tea-and-Pajama Party."

Claire looked at her dad, eyes wide. Maggie looked at Nick, and Nick looked at Jenny. "What?" Jenny said, eyebrows raised. "Can't an old lady have a party with her favorite young friend?"

"Maybe Gayle the Ghost isn't the only one helping us along," Maggie said, smiling coyly at Nick. They made plans for Claire to spend Friday night with Jenny, which meant she and Nick could finally have a "real" date with the possibility of their own sleepover. This time, there shouldn't be any otherworldly interference. Hopefully. Maybe.

CHAPTER
THIRTY-THREE

Claire filled her backpack with a nightgown, toothbrush, hairbrush, and extra clothes for Saturday. *I'm so glad Daddy loves Miss Maggie. I wish we could live with her and Miss Jenny. Miss Jenny would be like my grandma, and we could have tea parties all the time. I could even call her Grandma.*

Claire pondered this. *Would that mean Miss Maggie would be like my mom?* She decided to ask Miss Jenny when she arrived because she was really smart about those things. She sang softly in the back seat for the rest of the ride, smoothing the dress that Gayle had fixed. This time, she didn't turn to Ron for the answer.

Later, at the restaurant, it turned out Nick and Maggie both liked teriyaki. While she loved the sushi, Nick didn't. After their early dinner, Nick drove to Bridal Veil Falls, a popular destination at the south end of Provo Canyon. He'd thought about it all week and had a purpose in choosing this particular spot. He parked, and they hiked the short, shady trail to the foot of the falls.

"I haven't been here in a while. It's so beautiful," Maggie said, brushing foliage with her hand, her other hand in Nick's.

The roar of falling water grew louder as they approached, cascading over a 600-foot drop. A few teens scrambled on the rocks below them. The tram and restaurant had closed because of an avalanche and later a fire, but the sight of the falls was worth the drive.

The late spring day brought warm sunlight into a small clearing, where they could enjoy the mist on their faces. "What a surprise coming here, Nick. This is a wonderful idea. Too bad we're not dressed for hiking," she smiled.

"I didn't really plan on hiking."

Maggie turned toward him, a mischievous twinkle in her eye. "Just what did you plan on, big fella?" She put her arms around him.

Butterflies took wing in his belly. "Hold that thought," he said, holding her close as hikers passed on a narrow section of the trail. He tried to think of something to stall the moment, feeling fear, pain, loss, and finally, the boldness of love. He reached into his trouser pocket and pulled out a small black box, concealing it in his hand. At the same time, a dollar bill fell from his pocket and fluttered to the ground.

She noticed it first. "I'll get it."

"No, wait. Let me." He dropped to his knee, retrieving the dollar. *Gayle, or whoever you are, I've got this. Now that I'm down here, let me finish.* "Maggie," he said, "When my mother passed away, I inherited this. Ann and I always thought we would give it to Claire when she was old enough, but I found it in a box of memories the night of our ghost encounter. That night I knew in my bones you were the only one for me, the only one I want to take this journey with, and that Claire's mom would welcome you to our family."

Maggie gasped, her hands flying to her mouth, eyes wide as Nick opened the box and raised it toward her. She listened to the rush of the water and felt the spray on her face, moist with tears. Trembling, she touched the ring with one finger as if it would disappear, lifting the box in her hands.

"We've had a remarkable beginning, and I hope we have a long way to go. I love you and pray that you will do me the honor of becoming my wife. Margaret Sanderson, will you marry me?"

Maggie knew she loved him, and Claire, even the ghosts. This was the family she wanted. She had only one answer. "Yes!"

He stood up, taking the ring from the box and placing it on her finger. "Oh, my God. It's beautiful, Nick. I love it." She turned her hand to see the diamond sparkle in the sun. She threw her arms around his neck and kissed him, to the amusement of the hikers, who gave them a wide berth. The burble of the water traversing the rocks sounded clearer, more intimate, where they stood. She would always associate that sound and the fresh smell of water with this day, when Nick proposed.

Nick's tension and doubts released in her arms, transforming into a sense of trust and certainty. Grateful for this second chance at love, he realized they could face any obstacles together, building a life for Claire and for each other. No more 'what ifs.' *And we will be whole again.*

Nick's heart swelled with gratitude, weakening his knees. He leaned into her and turned his eyes skyward in silent thanks. They walked, enjoying the falls. Maggie had many questions: "When did you know? Does Claire know? Where will we live?" Nick groaned. "Slow down, woman," he chuckled. "Let me catch my breath."

When they returned to the car, Nick opened the passenger door and kissed her as she settled into her seat. He got behind the wheel and noticed her gazing at her ring with tears in her eyes. "You like it, don't you?"

"Of course I do! I'm so happy, Nick."

"My mother was special to me, and now your mother is part of my family, too. Our family. I want Claire to think of you as a mom. I'm certain Ann would approve. Claire's ghost friends aside, I believe Ann helped us find this path too. I hope I'm not saying this wrong."

"No, Nick. I understand. It's a lovely sentiment. I feel at peace about it."

Nick smiled and held her hand, kissing the ring on her finger. "Good. Hold that thought. We have another stop to make." He drove into historic downtown Provo and parked at the Hines Mansion, now an upscale Bed and Breakfast.

Maggie caught her breath and turned to Nick. "Are we staying here?"

"If that's alright with you."

"Are you serious?" she squealed. "I've always wanted to stay here! I've seen photos of the rooms and the garden. Oh, I've heard breakfast is to die for. My goodness, Nick, you're going to make me cry again!"

Nick's lips turned up into a grin. "It's okay then?"

"Yes, Nick, it's more than okay. Our first night together! Now, let's go check it out!"

The mansion boasted a luxurious B & B with nine guest rooms, most featuring Victorian-era decor. Maggie's eyes were drawn to the polished marble fireplace in the main parlor. They were greeted by a friendly woman with dark brown hair streaked with gray, braided down her back, who wore a floor-length emerald-green gown.

She shook their hands and said, "Welcome to Hines Mansion! We are so glad you've joined us." After checking in, she escorted them to their room. They admired the oak staircase to the second floor and followed her down the hall to the Kitty Hines suite.

The room was decorated in French provincial style, featuring shades of pale blue and cream. Maggie beamed when the hostess pointed out the jetted tub set in a bay window. The original stained glass colored the evening light. She explained that this suite existed in the original structure. Maggie almost clapped her hands in delight.

Nick thanked their hostess, who left them to enjoy the room. Maggie took it all in, touching the Baroque lamp by the canopied bed and moving to the bureau where a crochet lace doily accented a vase of fresh flowers. She touched the silky, light blue scarf that twirled around the column near the tub, cascading down the other side.

"This is so beautiful. I'm amazed at how thoughtful and sneaky you are." She stood on her toes and locked her lips with his. Nick returned the kiss with a gentle promise of things to come.

He suggested they walk around the garden before dark and retrieve their bags from the car. Maggie agreed, and they descended the oak staircase, Nick's hand sliding over the railing as he admired the craftsmanship. Outside, they meandered through the garden, enjoying the beautiful spring flowers and herbs, some reminiscent of those her mom raised in their own backyard—Blue Mist, white hydrangeas, and Miss Molly Butterfly bushes.

As if on cue, a kaleidoscope of butterflies fluttered from the foliage. The couple retrieved their bags and walked inside to a formal parlor showcasing period furniture. More stained glass caught the light, casting a glowing palette of color. A charming marble table with two needlepoint upholstered chairs created a cozy niche in front of a window with lace curtains. They rested in the warm and elegant atmosphere, both silent, contemplating how their lives were changing and what the future held for them.

In their room, Maggie noticed two fluffy white robes hanging in the closet. Her nerves tingled as anticipation rose. No house phone, cell phones turned off, no television—just peace, quiet, and the man she loved. After their dinner, neither felt hungry, not even for freshly baked cookies and strawberries with cream.

They sat on the bed, side by side, pillows cushioned by the ornate headboard. They had much to discuss, and they did until Maggie yawned. Nick leaned over, placed his arm around her shoulder, and drew her closer to his chest. He took her hand and kissed her ring. Looking into her soft brown eyes, he whispered, "I'm so glad we're together. I love you." His expression said it all.

Placing her hand on his chest, she whispered, "I've been waiting a long time for you, Nick. I've wanted us to be together." Her eyes averted, and she continued, "I hope I don't disappoint you." Her insecurities threatened but subsided.

Maggie's words humbled him. "I'm sure you won't disappoint me. Besides, we can work on it till we get it right." She giggled, just as he'd hoped. He kissed her, conveying the depth of his desire in that kiss and those that followed.

Birds sang outside their window in the morning light. Nick felt her warm body next to his. The night they shared replayed in his mind, vivid and surreal as a lingering dream.

They explored new territories together—sometimes tentative, overwhelming, or downright immodest. One surprising moment, a soothing warm breeze enveloped them in their private cocoon. They exchanged an intimate smile, and Maggie whispered, "They wouldn't dare, would they?"

Nick remembered speaking into the darkness, "Some privacy here, please." They mused that their love made waves in another dimension.

She stirred, and he caressed her hair, combing his fingers through it as it spread over the pillow, framing her face. God, she's beautiful. Though a part of him remained with Ann, Maggie healed him, restoring his damaged heart.

Her hand caressed the stubble on his cheek, her ring reminding her of the promise and hope he brought into her life. Her foot stroked his. Secure and loved, she snuggled closer.

They lolled in bed, each with their betrothed. This new chapter of their lives had begun.

After showering and donning their fluffy robes, Nick retrieved a cart outside their room with freshly brewed coffee in a silver carafe. They bantered about calling home but decided to surprise Jenny and Claire in person. Leisurely, they dressed, sipping from porcelain cups. Maggie wore white jeans and a multi-colored top with short sleeves. Nick's gray slacks and light green button-down shirt complemented the sage green of his eyes. Hand in hand, they walked downstairs to breakfast.

Breakfast. They stared for a moment, admiring the artful selection of herbed eggs, strawberry-stuffed French toast, roasted potatoes, and fresh fruit and juices. Warm muffins with honey butter and cookies nestled in woven baskets. They sampled each other's dishes and chatted comfortably. After Nick savored a second helping and Maggie couldn't resist one more delicious macaroon, the conversation slowed as they lingered over tea, together as a couple.

When they pulled into the driveway, Maggie bounced in her seat, eager to show Jenny her ring. Nick had other ideas. He leaned over to find her lips. The sweet kiss reminded them of the passion they shared the previous night, and she returned it—fully committed, fully his.

When they stepped into the house, Claire ran towards them, hugging her dad around the waist and grabbing Maggie's hand. "Hi! Did you guys have as much fun as I did last night?"

Nick chuckled and picked her up, smacking a kiss on her cheek. "You bet your bottom dollar we did, sweetheart. Where's Miss Jenny?"

"Comin' right up, people! Comin' right up." She wheeled herself from the kitchen into the hallway. Eying her daughter, Jenny recognized that look. Nick had it, too. She feigned disinterest, waiting for them to say something. They gazed at each other with silly grins. Jenny couldn't wait any longer. "Well?"

Nick put Claire down but held her hand. Maggie strode to her mother, thrusting her hand under Jenny's face. "Oh my! Oh my goodness." She took hold of Maggie's hand for a closer look at the ring. She looked up into her daughter's eyes, tears brimming, and said, "It's about time."

Maggie burst out laughing and stooped to kiss her mom's forehead. "Thanks for watching Claire, Mom. It gave us a wonderful day out."

"I'll bet your night in wasn't too bad either," Jenny teased.

"Ha! I'll never tell." Nick joined them with Claire, who asked what happened. Maggie turned from her mom and took Claire's hand in hers. Nick nodded as if to say, 'You've got this.'

Maggie led Claire to the couch. "Honey, you know how much your dad loves you, right?"

"Sure. Is this about my dad kissing you?"

Maggie's eyes darted up at Nick and her mom. "Yes, it is. How do you feel about us kissing?"

"It's okay because he loves you. That's why people kiss."

"Is it okay with you that I love your dad, too?"

"Really? That's cool. Are you going steady now?" She grinned, swinging her legs.

Jenny and Nick chuckled. Maggie replied, "Kind of, but instead of going steady like in high school, we're engaged. That means we plan to get married in the future. Would you like that?" She held her breath.

Claire looked up at her dad and Jenny, her face pinched in thought. After a moment, she asked, "Would Miss Jenny be my grandma then?"

A burst of joy caught in Jenny's throat. "Dear girl, you can call me Grandma now if you want. I would love it."

"Okay, but what do I call you, Miss Maggie? Does that mean you'll be my mom?"

Maggie glanced at Nick and smiled at Claire. "I will never replace your mother, Claire. She will always be with you in your heart. But I would like to be your second mom. Would that be okay?"

"Can I call you Mommy at school?" Claire grinned mischievously.

"No, you may not, young lady. Are you teasing me?" Maggie chuckled, sighing with relief.

"We-lll." Claire drew out the word and smirked. "Do I get to be a flower girl and wear a pretty dress?"

Maggie embraced her. "You most certainly will. When the time comes, we'll all go shopping, and you can pick out the best flower girl dress in the store."

Claire hugged her side and said, "You'll be an awesome second mom, Miss Maggie." She noticed the engagement ring on Maggie's finger. "Whoa, Dad. You did good!"

"This calls for a tea party! What do you say, Claire? Want to help me in the kitchen?"

"Okay...Grandma. Let's roll."

Gayle and Ron circled the Sanderson home. "Mission accomplished! Beam me back home!" cried Gayle.

"Go for it, Gayle. I think I'll stick around for a while. Claire will want to talk about this."

"Hey, knock yourself out, but I've got plans." With the ghost equivalent of a peck on the cheek, she said, "See ya when I see ya," and disappeared with a whoosh.

Ron had plans as well. His thoughts turned to Rosie Cunningham. *Albert seemed satisfied with my last report. But I can help even more.*

He felt a satisfaction that had eluded him in life. He once expected perfection from himself and others, which never happened. Now, he made mistakes, but their successes bolstered his confidence. *I'm learning to care about others. It's not so bad. Maybe I really can do this.*

Claire and Nick returned home from the Sandersons'. Ron zoomed to Claire's side and said, "Gayle has gone back home. Her mission is accomplished."

Claire looked at her dad. "Gayle isn't here anymore, Daddy. Since you and Miss Maggie love each other, she finished her job."

"I think Maggie and I did our jobs too, honey. But I agree she helped. So, she's not here anymore?"

"Nope. Ron says she's gone back."

"So, is Ron still here?"

"Yup," she giggled. Ron made a face over Nick's shoulder.

Nick sat down on a kitchen chair and motioned for Claire to come closer, lifting her onto his lap. "Honey girl, you said Ron came here to make you happy, right?"

"Yes, and Gayle came for you and Miss Maggie."

"So, are you happy that Maggie and I will get married?"

"Oh, yes! I think it's terrific! I'll have another mommy and a grandma."

"Are you happy in school?"

She nodded.

"Do you think Ron finished his job too?"

Claire hesitated. "Yes, but he's my best friend, Daddy."

"I know. Becky's your best friend too, right?"

"Yeah, but she can't do tricks or fly like Ron."

"Maybe so, but can Ron jump rope, play catch, or go shopping with you and have an ice cream cone?"

In a small voice, Claire answered, "No, I guess not. But can't I have them both?"

"You can decide that, Claire. When you visit Miss Janet, why don't you ask her what she thinks?"

"Okay, Daddy. I didn't think I would see her again after she saw that Ron's a real ghost."

"I think you should visit her for a while longer. She is your friend too because you can talk to her about Ron and anything else. Would that be okay?" Nick's thoughts turned to the new issues they would work through together.

"Okay. Can I tell her about you and Miss Maggie getting married?"

"Sure, you can. I'll check with her to see if Tuesday's still on."

"Thanks, Daddy. I love you." She gave him a hard hug around his neck with her thin arms. "You're the best Dad ever."

Nick responded as expected, swallowing a rush of emotion as he held her tight.

Janet confirmed Claire's next appointment and ended the call with Nick. She had been seeing David almost every day since the revelation at Nick's house. David tried to involve her in his paranormal world while she countered him with human psychology of belief. It was a tug of war to find enough common ground to build a relationship. Janet found him attractive, a pleasant distraction in her career-driven life. David found her downright sexy and challenged him on several levels, but he didn't seem to make much headway. During their dinner meetings, he was a perfect gentleman, pulling out her chair, a soft touch to the shoulder, a smile. She enjoyed his persistence and patience.

When Nick and Claire arrived at Janet's, she bubbled with excitement to share the big news. Nick spent the hour at the coffee shop mulling over the events that had changed his life. He pictured Maggie as his wife. He knew Claire loved her and Jenny, a bonus grandma who adored her too. The four of them made a family.

Nick wondered where they would live. *Would Maggie want to move in? Should he and Claire move in with them? Or buy another house? Jenny's downstairs bedroom suits her well. I haven't seen their basement, though. Is it big enough for my workshop?*

He stirred a packet of sugar into his coffee. *What about Ron? Would he be moving in too?* He sighed, grateful for Maggie, Jenny, Janet, and even Claire's advice. They would hash it out together.

In Janet's office, Claire fidgeted in her chair. "Yes, Ron is here. He always comes with me. But you haven't let me tell you my good news!"

"And what's your good news, Claire?"

Claire bounced. "Daddy and Miss Maggie are getting married!"

"Well, that is good news. Are you happy about that?"

"Oh yes! She's going to be my new second mommy, and Miss Jenny is going to be my grandma! Miss Maggie said my mother in heaven will always be in my heart, and I'm going to be their flower girl and get a pretty new dress."

"It sounds like things are going well, then. Right?"

Claire's eyes darted to Ron, who hovered in his usual spot, and she frowned. "Not everything."

"Oh? What is it?"

"Daddy thinks Ron might be done with his job. But he's wrong. I still want him to be my best friend."

"Why is that, Claire?" Janet reached for Claire's hands. Smiling gently, she asked, "How does it make you feel?"

"Sad. I've had so much fun with him, and now that all you guys know about him, I can talk about him, and you won't think I'm weird. Why does he have to go away?" Claire looked towards Ron, who gave her a little wave. She thought he looked tired, as if he didn't feel like goofing around.

Janet said, "Claire, some friends don't stay, and it's not your fault. But when we were with them, we had fun. When we think of them, we can have happy memories, right?"

"Like when I think of my mom, I get sad. But sometimes I remember her, and it makes me happy."

"That's right, Claire. It's okay to feel sad when we miss someone we love. But when we think about why we love them, we can feel better. When we make new friends, we learn about what makes us happy too. What do you think?"

"Yeah, but...am I being selfish because I want to keep Ron as my friend?"

"What if Mary had a party dress she really liked, but she didn't wear it often; it just hung in her closet. But her friend Beth really liked the dress and couldn't buy one. Mary saw how she could help Beth. Mary wanted to keep her dress, but she gave it to her friend so that she could be happy too.

"But we can't keep people for ourselves, Claire. We make new friends, and we help each other grow and learn. You said Ron makes you happy, and I can see that he does." Claire looked towards the place where Ron waited. Janet looked in that direction too.

"What if Ron could make someone else happy too? Would he want you to make other friends? Would you want to 'keep' him if someone needed him more?" Janet paused, observing Claire and considering her own words and what she had seen.

"You said your mom is in heaven and wants you to be happy. You still love her even though she's not with you now. Sometimes it hurts, and you miss her, but you know she loves you, and it makes you happy when you remember her. Now, Miss Maggie can be your second mom, and she will love you and take care of you. And Miss Jenny can be your grandma, and she'll love you too. We keep making new friends because there's enough love for everybody, even if sometimes they have to leave."

Claire thought about that for a long while. She looked over at Ron, her eyes filling with tears. She really, really didn't want him to leave, and she sort of understood what Miss Janet meant, but... "Do I have to choose right now?"

"No, sweetheart. Think about it, and we'll talk some more next time, okay?"

"Okay." Claire wiped her eyes with her fists and, looking at Ron, said, "Ron looks sad too."

Janet thought about the resilience of children. How it feels to care for someone deeply, even if it doesn't make sense. Even if they leave. *Maybe I should try harder with my friend David. Because you never know...*

Janet held Claire's hand and led her out of her office to meet her dad. She told Nick that their session had gone well and that she wanted to stick to their schedule. Nick agreed and hoped Janet understood her as well as he wanted to.

CHAPTER

THIRTY-FOUR

Gayle stood confidently in front of The Boss, though a sense of concern lingered. She had done well with Maggie and Nick, accomplishing her mission, but The Boss could be unpredictable. A panel of seven serious specters sat behind a long table. She didn't recognize all of them and suspected they were the welcoming committee for new angels. As she faced The Boss, she thought of Ron—how she had pushed him out of his comfort zone. Smiling to herself, she reflected on how far he had come, thanks to her guidance.

"So, here we are again. Nick and Maggie are engaged. Your mission seems to have succeeded. Well done."

"Yes, sir. Thank you." *So far, so good.*

"Where's your student? Did you leave him behind? After that trick of showing his head, I'd think he'd be here to boast about his success."

"He's not really the boastful type these days. Sure, he's happy he pulled it off, but he wanted to stay a while longer to tie up loose ends."

"Yes, yes, I suppose he would. He's taken quite a liking to that little girl. He did right by her. In fact, he did so well that I'm considering giving him another assignment."

Shuddering inside, Gayle maintained a straight face and managed a smile. "Oh, that's wonderful for him." *Please tell me you don't need me for that job. But enough about Ron. Let's talk about me.*

"In the meantime, let's discuss you. You have proven yourself a competent mentor more than once, Gayle. However, regarding this last mission, tell me what you've learned."

"What I've learned, sir?"

"Yes, explain why you chose the strategy of taking on the couple's happiness while Ron worked with the child."

Gayle was taken aback, and several exaggerated responses came to mind. *Well, sir. My well-researched cost-benefit analysis indicated that, statistically... No, that won't work. 'I considered myself uniquely qualified to manage the complexities of their romantic dynamics...' Meh. 'Under my direction, Ron would gain valuable experience by...' Aaah, who am I kidding?*

"Sir, the truth is..." Gayle glanced at the panel, their expectant faces urging her to continue.

"The truth is that Ron was better with Claire than I could ever be. He was patient and caring. He let her be herself. About all I did with Nick and Maggie was hide the silverware and condiments at the barbecue. I nudged them a time or two, but they did the rest. I think they would have fallen in love with or without me."

"I see," said The Boss, and the panel's eyebrows raised in unison.

She thought she should stop, but the words kept flowing. "I suppose I learned I don't have to be in control all the time. People can make their own choices, and some may not reflect well on me. Sometimes, it isn't about me at all..." Her shoulders sagged, feeling she had said too much.

"Gayle," The Boss interrupted. "When you repaired that party dress for little Claire, David, the P.I., ran tests and published his findings. We'll get several more cases from that. It was good PR. Good teachers learn from their students. Sometimes it's best to leave well enough alone—let nature take its course. But I'm afraid that..." He looked at the panel on his left and right, holding back a sneeze.

Gayle floated uncomfortably before them, hoping that telling the truth wouldn't cost her the wings she had wanted for so long.

He finally sneezed. "...I'm afraid that many in your position might have tried to embellish their role or throw their student under the bus, hoping for a promotion. But you didn't do that. I admire your honesty.

"Some good people die and go straight to Heaven—babies, folks too old or sick to commit bad deeds. The ones who choose to do evil travel in the other direction. Then there are those who left their lives too soon to wrap things up. We are one of many levels of existence, just a stepping stone to the next." He broke into a solo rendition of "What a Wonderful World," in a voice uncannily like Louis Armstrong's.

Gayle's eyes widened in surprise. She opened her mouth to speak but found no words.

The being on The Boss' left floated toward Gayle. His flowing robe morphed into a fashionable suit and tie. "While he's serenading us, let me introduce myself." He handed her a silk-laminated business card. "I'm with Heaven Sent. We're the premier guardian angel organization on the next level. I appreciate your humility, Gayle. It's vital in the work we do.

I've looked over your files, and I think you'd be a good fit for our team." The Boss finished his ditty, and the room fell silent after a smattering of polite applause. All eyes were on Gayle.

"Gayle, if you'd like to join us, it would give me great pleasure to award you your wings."

She did a little dance where she stood. "Woohoo! When do I start?"

He smiled and swooped behind her. Gayle glowed with excitement when she felt a tickle on her back. "Your training starts Tuesday morning. We'll send you the details. Meanwhile, get used to these. They can be tricky at first."

Gayle shrugged and felt their weight. Extending her new wings, she squealed like a young girl. The Boss nodded his congratulations and winked. "Go ahead, Gayle. Take them out for a spin. You've earned them." She thanked them with a curtsy and flapped awkwardly out of the room, knocking out the exit sign above the door.

The ancient intercom at the table where The Boss sat crackled and shrieked with feedback. "Boss, we've got incoming. 62-year-old female, Statesville, North Carolina."

Keying the microphone, he replied, "Thank you, Larry. I'll be there directly." He turned to the pale specter on his right. "Fred, ask Albert to have Maintenance replace this intercom and get me his new schedule for the other upgrades. For goodness' sake, we need to keep up with Earth's technology."

The Boss turned to his team. "All right, folks, let's get to work and find another candidate to replace Gayle."

-»›※‹«-

Ron flew alongside Nick and Claire as they drove home from her session, where Janet explained how friends come and go. He thought, *When we make new friends, we learn what makes us happy. Claire, and even Gayle, helped me learn that and feel better about myself. Most people aren't bad at all.* This mission taught him he could help others and atone for those he had hurt while alive. It filled him with purpose.

When Nick pulled into his driveway, Ron veered off. *I'm not done here yet. There's someone else I need to see. It could make a difference.*

Nick did not attend Albert's funeral, but unbeknownst to him, Rosie Cunningham attended Ann's. She felt responsible for sending Albert on an errand that led to Ann's death. She mourned for Mr. Miller and his young daughter, who had their whole lives ahead of them. She learned where the Millers lived and wondered if visiting would help or do more harm than good. They lived nearby, but she no longer drove and had lost her nerve in daily living.

The announcement in the Orem-Provo news of Nick Miller's engagement caught her by surprise. The page she rarely read lay open on her coffee table, as if staged. Memories flooded back—her husband, her sadness, her regret. It soothed Rosie's conscience that Mr. Miller now had someone to love and help raise his daughter. *I wonder if he would accept a call from me. What's to lose? If he hangs up, at least I tried.* Before she could hesitate, Rosie dialed Nick's number with trembling fingers.

Nick's house phone rang as they entered. He didn't get many calls on it anymore. He answered, figuring it was probably someone asking for a donation.

"Mr. Miller?"

"Yes, may I ask who's calling?"

Taking a breath, she replied, "This is Rosie Cunningham."

"May I help you?"

"We've never actually met, but I'm Albert Cunningham's widow. He passed away when..."

"I know who you are now." Nick swallowed the mixed feelings rising in his throat. "What can I do for you, Mrs. Cunningham?"

"That's kind of you to ask. I'm calling to see if you and I could meet and talk. I don't drive anymore, but I could take a taxi or..."

"Excuse me," Nick interrupted, his tone sharpening with unexpected emotion. "But what is there to talk about? I don't mean to be rude, but your husband and my wife are both gone. End of story."

Gathering her courage, she said, "Pardon me, but hearing your voice, it doesn't seem like the end of the story. I believe it would benefit us both to talk about the accident and our spouses. Please consider it. I'm hoping it will help. Perhaps you could bring your fiancé; I read about your engagement in the paper." Softly, she added, "Please."

Rosie waited, sensing Nick's struggle to respond. He hesitated. "Mrs. Cunningham, would you mind if I discussed this with my fiancé? Give me your phone number and address, and I'll get back to you. Will that be all right?" He paused. "This is sudden for me."

"Of course, I understand. I appreciate this, Mr. Miller." She provided her information, hoping it wouldn't take too long before he returned her call. She needed to clear the air sooner rather than later.

At the Sandersons', Maggie and Jenny made plans for a winter wedding. The dining room had become their command center, cluttered with magazines, pamphlets, and brochures. Laptops and cell phones buzzed with activity, while a dry erase board displayed a line drawing of a seating arrangement beside a corkboard pinned with photos and business cards.

With so many decisions to make, Maggie felt a surge of gratitude for her mother, who kept her grounded. They had booked the ceremony at

Nick's church but had yet to confirm the reception venue for size and availability. The guest list was a work in progress. *Is 100 too few or too many?* Colors, flowers, favors, food—the list seemed endless. Just then, both of their phones chimed simultaneously.

Nick arrived at their house and, assessing the situation, chose to stay out of the way, believing the ladies could handle the decisions better. He had been in a tricky negotiation with the mother of the bride regarding expenses but had finally agreed to split the costs under one condition: Jenny would pay for Maggie's gown and Claire's dress, and that was final.

Maggie finished her call and snuggled with Nick. "Let's take a walk, babe. I need a break from wedding plans." They strolled to a nearby spot where they could watch the sunset.

Nick shared Mrs. Cunningham's phone call with her. "What do you think, Maggie? She may want to apologize on Albert's behalf, but it wasn't her fault. I'm not sure what we have to discuss."

"Honey, she probably needs to set things right in her mind. She's in her eighties, right? It would be kind of you to let her apologize. The poor woman feels guilty when it wasn't anyone's fault. I think you should talk to her. I'll go with you. Call her and set up a time for a visit."

"Yes, dear." He relented, his eyes reflecting sadness.

"Oh, stop it." She bumped his shoulder playfully.

Mrs. Cunningham sat heavily in her rocker, relieved that Nick returned her call. They agreed to meet the following day while Claire stayed with Jenny. Nick and Maggie walked from his house, just a few blocks away. She welcomed them in, leading them to the living room and offering lemonade, which they accepted. Ron perched on the mantel over the fireplace.

Rosie sat in a chair facing Nick and Maggie on the flowered sofa. "Maggie, you are lovely and will make a beautiful bride," Rosie smiled. "I read about your engagement in the newspaper."

"Thank you, Mrs. Cunningham, that's very kind."

"Please call me Rosie, dear. Mr. Miller, Nick, if I may, I'm so sorry. I can't imagine how you and your little girl managed the loss of your wife. I know my Albert caused her death, and I'm sure he would regret what happened as much as I do." Rosie dabbed her eyes with a tissue before continuing. "Now I'll stop that. It's not my intention to make you uncomfortable, but it is a relief to finally tell you in person."

Nick replied, "Rosie, I never believed it was your husband's fault. I never blamed him." Maggie reached over and took Nick's hand. "I won't say it hasn't been hard for us, but it's almost two years, and I'm blessed that I can remarry. My daughter is going to have a second mom and grandmother." He brought their clasped hands to his lips.

"Maggie, and others have helped us, and we are doing well. Ann will always be in my heart, but we have moved on, as we must, and will soon be a family." He looked at Maggie. "We are at peace. I hope you can be, as well."

Rosie's features softened. "Albert and I had a good life. After over fifty years together, I know he would have wanted to make amends somehow. But I don't know what I could do for you. I'm not sure what to do with myself anymore. May I share something with you?"

"Please do, Rosie," Maggie encouraged.

"I've told no one this, but it's troubled me. Albert loved his old Cadillac. At our age, we were content to just take a drive or have ice cream." Her voice trailed off, her lips tightening.

"What is it, Rosie?"

"That's just it, Nick. I sent him to the store that day for pistachio ice cream—something so insignificant that affected so many." She looked at the couple, searching their faces.

Nick sat in thought for a moment before returning the old woman's gaze. "Thank you for sharing that, Rosie. It's strange, really. You and Maggie will be the first to hear this: After the accident, I spoke with the woman who held Ann's place in line while she ran back to get olives for me. She didn't even like olives." He rubbed his face, recalling. "I guess we know they loved us." He blinked several times. "Let's hold onto that instead of our sadness. It was a cruel twist of fate, but we were the last people they thought of. They knew we loved them, too. Isn't that something?"

"It certainly is, to think of it that way." Rosie wiped her eyes and offered Maggie a tissue. "It certainly is."

They sipped their lemonade and chatted about the world and the weather. "Albert loved Utah with its snow and mountains. I've cherished this house and the memories here, but it's become more than I can handle alone. It's odd," she said, looking around as if searching for clues. "Lately, it's been drafty."

She chuckled, "Oh, I'm going on. Thank you for visiting. You've helped me decide, Nick and Maggie. It's time I 'hang on,' as you said, to the fond memories and leave the rest behind. I would like a warmer climate." She smiled, patting the arms of her chair. "My brother, Murray, lives at an assisted living home in Florida and tells me he's very comfortable there, with new friends. I believe I've decided to sell this old house and join him."

Drafty. Nick and Maggie acknowledged this without speaking. He took Maggie's hand and stood. "Rosie, I don't mean to presume, but if you need help preparing to move, please call me. I'm fairly handy, and I know people who could assist with repairs to get a better price for the house."

Maggie smiled and took Rosie's hand. "Trust me, he's being modest; he's far more than 'fairly handy.' Please keep us in mind, okay?"

Rosie showed them to the door. "Thank you both; you've been so kind. I will keep you in my prayers."

Satisfied, Ron left to update Albert about his widow's plans and her newfound peace with Nick Miller. He also realized he should be more careful stirring up drafts in people's homes. But it gave him another idea.

As summer approached, school would soon close for the season. Claire played with her friends Becky and Denise on the playground and even had a sleepover at Becky's house. One Saturday, Nick and Maggie took all three girls to a matinee and out for ice cream afterward.

When Claire interacted with other children, she never mentioned Ron, and he didn't linger during class. She missed talking with him, but he always hung around after she said her prayers. They would chat about her girlfriends and, of course, the wedding.

Nick, passing by her room and hearing her voice, no longer worried about it. But sometimes, he couldn't help but wonder how long Ron planned to stay.

Ron, hovering nearby, recalled how Claire had told him he was her best friend, but she now spent more time with her girlfriends. *That's a good thing, right? Maybe I've completed my mission, and it's time to move on. I hope I can visit her once in a while. I should check in with The Boss. Soon.*

Summer arrived, and the school year ended. Nick saved his vacation time for the wedding and their honeymoon, but Maggie's schedule matched Claire's, so Nick dropped her off on his way to work and picked her up afterward. Claire still saw Janet, but only twice that month. Sometimes they had dinner afterward; other times, he and Claire drove straight home or to Jenny and Maggie's.

To Nick, they were creating a family, and he loved it. Claire blossomed under the female attention. Thrilled to be part of the wedding plans, Claire made more decisions without consulting Ron. During a spirited debate about centerpieces, Nick heard Claire call Maggie 'Mom' for the first time. It stopped him mid-sentence. He and Jenny exchanged goofy grins.

Maggie carried on to prevent Claire from getting embarrassed, but Nick noticed her tearing up as she put her arm around Claire's shoulders. She glanced at Nick with an expression that moved him, conveying her feelings as if speaking to his heart.

Later that night, the family decided that Nick and Claire would move in with Maggie and Jenny until, or if, they wanted a bigger house. Until then, they would alternate while organizing the move. Nick agreed, pleased and surprised by how well things were working out.

The next morning, Nick heard Claire giggling in her room and knew Ron was still around. Gathering his daughter and a few things to take to what would soon be their new home, he felt a sudden urge to visit Rosie Cunningham. First, he needed to start his crew at a new job less than a mile from her house.

It turned out the wealthy developer who hired Nick's company for the job had reconsidered the custom cabinetry they made for his house. His wife thought the materials were, as she put it, 'too cold.' Not too modern, but 'drafty.' She felt the same about the high-end fixtures and appliances, the flooring, and the red cedar pergola. She couldn't explain it, and her husband didn't care. He had just closed a deal that would allow them to buy a sprawling 5,000 square foot home in the foothills with a tennis court and indoor pool.

The developer parked the trucks in his driveway and wrote a check to Nick's firm that doubled their profits. On the way back to the shop, Nick stopped by Rosie's with a measuring tape and photos, and they struck a deal later that day. His boss, the owner, was happy to donate cabinets, appliances, and even the pergola, enlisting a friend to film the story for the media. The crew would complete Rosie's remodel in less than two weeks.

While overseeing that job, Nick prepared his own home for sale. Rosie stayed with the Sandersons during the noisier work on her house. She and the ladies planned the wedding and chatted like old friends. Claire didn't know Rosie's story but treated her with kindness and youthful exuberance that delighted her.

One afternoon, while Nick was building a new ramp at Maggie and Jenny's, Maggie joined him on the upgraded porch with cold drinks, holding his hand.

"You're not so bad after all, Miller."

"No?" He returned her smile.

"Yeah, I think I'll keep you." They heard Claire and Rosie laughing at one of Jenny's stories.

"I'm glad we could do that for Rosie. It feels good, like it's healing part of me."

"It should. You've helped her heal, too."

"Funny how it worked out. The cabinets fit perfectly, along with the appliances. Even the timing. It was almost, uh, how can I put it..."

"Supernatural?" Maggie suggested with a wry grin.

"Yeah, that." Nick agreed, just as his work phone pinged with a text message. "The guys are done, so I can take Rosie home. I'd like to check out the work."

"Okay, I'll get her. Dinner at six."

Rosie stood in her new kitchen, turning slowly to take in the details. The transformation moved her. Albert had maintained their home with an eye toward preserving and repairing rather than buying new. The little quirks a homeowner accepts as part of the home's character—a replacement tile that didn't quite match, the stain on the floor that never came out—were now fond memories she could cherish. She knew the improvements would hold greater value for the new family that would soon continue the house's history.

"Nick, it's wonderful." They walked to the backyard and stood in the shade of the pavilion roof, admiring the landscaping, which had improved with simple touches. The siding had been power washed, and perennials were planted in front.

"I think it's about ready to list, don't you?"

"I do. I can't thank you enough." She placed her hand on his arm as they turned toward the house. "Oh, I've been meaning to show you this." She guided him toward the garage.

"This is Albert's workshop. I'm sure he would want you to take anything you like. The rest will go into the estate sale. It's the least I can do."

He was prepared to decline but saw the hope in her eyes and thought it better to accept her offer. He wanted her to benefit from their good fortune without feeling like she was receiving charity. "Thank you, Rosie."

Her eyes brightened, and she shared stories about her husband's hobbies and inventions. The gadgets and equipment intrigued him. "He loved to tinker with electronics—cameras, radio transmitters, and such. He also built mechanical devices."

"This is amazing, Rosie. I can think of so many projects—for Jenny's accessibility, Claire's play area, even school projects for Maggie's class."

"Come back with a truck when you're ready." Her smile confirmed to Nick that this was indeed a stroke of good fortune for both of them. They were recovering from their losses and moving on.

C H A P T E R

THIRTY-FIVE

Later that summer, Claire celebrated her eighth birthday. Maggie and Jenny wanted to make it special for her and took a break from wedding plans. They hosted an outdoor party for Claire's friends from school, along with Janet and David. In the backyard, balloons of every color hung from the trees and fence, brightening the space. Claire helped Jenny bake her own birthday cake. Ron showed up, and to Jenny's delight, so did Tom. Nick hung a colorful piñata from a branch of the big oak tree. The kids had a blast, cheering when it finally broke and candy spilled out. They didn't mind, or even know, that it was sugar-free.

Claire eagerly tore into her presents and jumped for joy when she opened Jenny's gift—her very own apron with her name embroidered on the bib. Helping her grandma in the kitchen was a treat for both of them. Maggie's gift complemented the apron: a tall white chef's hat and oven mitts. Claire wore the toque for the rest of the day because it was the coolest hat ever. Nick made her a polished wooden treasure box for her keepsakes. When she solved the lock and opened it, she squealed, "My very own cell phone, yay! Thanks, Dad! Now I can call all my friends every day..." Nick, standing beside Maggie, gave her such a bewildered look that the room erupted in laughter.

The summer sped by. Maggie finally found her perfect wedding gown. She modeled it for Jenny and Claire, and they immediately approved. Claire clapped her hands and smiled at her second mom, saying she looked like a princess, all white and sparkly.

Maggie marveled at the find. The sweetheart neckline and three-quarter length sleeves in soft velvet were just what she had envisioned. Standing on the platform surrounded by mirrors, she saw her mother's eyes fill with tears. They had waited a long time for this.

Amidst the primping and posing, Claire found a lovely dress for the flower girl, her eyes gleaming with excitement. Since Maggie wouldn't let Nick see her gown, Claire decided to keep her dress a secret too. They kept it very hush-hush; there were lots of giggles and whispers in their house.

Since the wedding would take place in mid-December, the church would be decorated for Christmas. Maggie planned her own touches with boughs of pine on the windowsills and red poinsettias in her bouquet, complemented by holly berries adorning the altar.

At home, Jenny couldn't resist dressing in her new holly green satin gown with long sleeves and a white velvet short cape for the cold weather. She called Claire into her bedroom to see how they looked together.

Claire's eyes sparkled as she admired her first long dress, feeling very grown-up. The colors matched the mother-of-the-bride's gown. When Jenny teased her, saying they looked like twins, Claire couldn't help but laugh.

C H A P T E R

THIRTY-SIX

By September, Maggie and Claire were back in school. This year, Claire had a different teacher. Becky and Denise were in her class. They knew about the wedding and asked about her dress. Claire teased that they would have to wait for the wedding to see it, but she couldn't resist describing it—down to the minute detail. She pictured the way it would shimmer under the lights, the lace so delicate it felt like it might crumble with a touch.

As October weather cooled, the leaves transformed from green to shades of orange, yellow, and red before drifting to the ground. People bundled up for the crisp days, raking their front yards. Claire looked forward to Halloween. Costumes were for sale in stores, along with an abundance of candy and decorations. Ghosts and skeletons hung from trees in the neighborhood, while fake graveyards and tombstones adorned front yards.

She was excited to have fun with Ron since he was a ghost, after all. She knew he didn't like to be scary, but wouldn't it be cool to do 'fun scary'? Grandma Jenny wanted to trick-or-treat at their house.

Nick and Claire helped Jenny set up an assembly line for caramel popcorn. Claire worked the microwave; the recipe called for about nine cups for each batch. Nick poured the hot bags over a cooling rack while Jenny melted butter and brown sugar on the stove. Meanwhile, Maggie placed mixing bowls on the counter and lined cookie sheets with wax paper. Jenny added vanilla and baking soda to the butter mixture.

Ron hovered above, unseen by all but Claire. He wanted to join in the fun, but Claire grinned and put her finger to her lips, so he only blew a single puffed kernel astray.

Nick poured the caramel over the popcorn and helped Claire toss it with a wooden spoon until all the popcorn was coated. Then Maggie emptied the bowls onto the cookie sheets to cool. Once it cooled, they all broke the popcorn apart, filling resealable plastic snack bags.

They made several batches, some with nuts and a few with drizzled chocolate that somehow got set aside. They prepared at least fifty bags for trick-or-treaters. Jenny figured they would have to eat the leftovers, and everyone liked that idea.

Claire asked Ron, "Since it's Halloween, it's okay to scare trick-or-treaters a little, right? It's just teasing."

She thought it would be fun if Ron made the bags rise off the tray. She could already picture the trick, imagining the popcorn floating in front of the trick-or-treaters' eyes.

Jenny, listening in, furrowed her brow. "Something scarier," she said, her voice more serious.

Maggie, joining them, rubbed her hands together in wicked glee. "I have some sound effects—groans, eerie music, and screams that I can play. That'll scare the little monsters." Her eyes crinkled with mischief.

Claire and her family won Ron over, and he agreed, his ghostly form seeming to perk up at the idea of having some fun. Claire relayed the plan to the adults. Maggie, always practical, suggested covering Ron with a sheet. Claire nodded enthusiastically, but Nick shook his head. "It might fall off while flying around," he said, amused but skeptical. They decided on a test run to see if it would stay in place.

Jenny, ever the optimist, figured they could get away with it; people would think they used a wire. Ron, hovering nearby, suggested to Claire, "You could throw it over me."

Maggie handed a white sheet to Claire, knowing exactly where he was. With Nick's help, they threw the sheet like they were making a bed, and Ron made himself denser, swooping under it. They talked over each other, laughing. *Why didn't we think of that before?* Now they could at least look in his direction.

The group decided Ron would fly to the kids and drop the bags of caramel popcorn into their trick-or-treat bags. He would be an actual ghost pretending to be a fake ghost by wearing a sheet—like people thought ghosts should.

Nick couldn't believe he was taking part in this, his mind still trying to wrap around the absurdity of it all. But as he looked over at Claire, her face beaming with excitement, he couldn't help but smile. It seemed harmless enough, and it had pulled the whole family into the fun, ridiculous as it was.

Claire dressed after dinner to be ready. She wore a pink ballerina tutu with white leggings and pink slippers. A pink t-shirt and a tiara atop her head completed the ensemble. She stayed inside to answer the door.

Maggie figured if she was answering the door with Claire, she should be in costume too. She made herself up with green face paint and a flowing black gown, complemented by a pointed witch's hat and long green fingernails. Claire held Maggie's hand, jumping around, impatient for the night to begin.

When the doorbell rang, Maggie's heart raced with excitement. She turned the volume up on the music, and the howls and groans began. Ron, covered in his sheet, hovered quietly behind her, ready to spring into action. Maggie opened the door to three kids about five or six years old. Behind her, Jenny and Nick exchanged glances, chuckling as they touched each other's arms, eager to see the kids' reactions.

Claire held the tray of popcorn bags with a very solemn face. Maggie moved to the side, and Ron flew overhead, dropping the bags into the children's buckets. They screamed and ran back to their parents, who waited on the sidewalk. The father called out, "Neat trick!" and off they went.

They closed the door and burst out laughing. The joy was contagious, and their laughter filled the house. As the evening progressed, it seemed word had spread throughout the neighborhood—more kids and even some adults began showing up at the door. A group of teens thought it would be fun to pull Ron's sheet, which fell to the floor, leaving the popcorn hovering in midair. They dropped their bags of candy and shrieked, fleeing into the night. The tricks were a hit, and the treats were gone. Maggie shut off the outside lights and closed the door, smiling. *Best Halloween ever.*

They thanked Ron—Claire happily, Nick sheepishly, and Maggie matter-of-factly. The sheet spun a somersault before dropping into a laundry basket. Jenny grinned. *My kind of family.*

C H A P T E R
THIRTY-SEVEN

Ron stood before The Boss and his executive staff, who sat behind a long mahogany table. His summons was a mystery, and the serious expressions on their faces did little to calm his nerves.

"Hello, Ron."

"Hello, Boss."

"Do you know why you're here?"

Not really. "Is this about Halloween?" Ron asked, trying to lighten the mood.

The Boss chuckled. "No, but that looked kind of fun. How would you describe your mission? Do you consider it successful?" He scribbled on some papers, passing them to an aide who left the room in a hurry.

"Yes, sir, I think we met the objectives. Claire's happy, and her father's going to marry Maggie. Is there anything else?

"Well, yes. Gayle submitted a positive report about you."

"She did?"

"You're surprised. I was, too. That's not like her. Nonetheless, here we are. Tell me, what did you learn?"

Ron thought for a moment. "A few things, sir. When flying, if I use my hands like the flaps of an airplane, I get more lift..."

"No, not about flying. We'll get you into a class for that. What did you learn about yourself?"

"Befriending Claire was new to me. I didn't have many friends when I was alive. I guess I was obnoxious, but I'm getting better."

"Yes, I agree. Did you go off mission to help anyone else?"

"Um, just for a little while. I swirled around a lady so she'd get cold. I thought it might help...someone."

"Hmm. That little stunt created ripples in our work here."

"It did? Oh, I'm sorry. I didn't know." *What ripples?*

"Not to worry. They were good ripples, caused by good deeds." He pressed a button on the new intercom. "Joey, roll that tape we talked about."

"On it, Boss." The screen behind the ghosts lit up, showing Ron flying around the developer's wife as she inspected her custom kitchen cabinets, appliances, and building materials. She shivered and trotted away in expensive high heels.

The Boss leaned back in his chair, nodding. "Albert spotted this from a surveillance camera in the building. He said he asked you to check in on his widow, Rosie. When Nick and Maggie visited her, you helped them both heal. She also got a remodel and made new friends and a plan for her remaining years. Albert's thrilled—he's been busy engineering new systems around here because of it. You didn't just chill the lady; you made ripples!"

"We need more operatives like you, Ron. You went above and beyond. You—" The Boss got a faraway look in his eyes.

"Here he goes, Ralph." One of the executive ghosts leaned closer and nudged the ghost next to him, chuckling.

The Boss stood up, striking a pose like Frank Sinatra, holding rolled-up papers like a microphone, singing, "You did it yooour waaaay." The execs clapped politely. The Boss grinned sheepishly. He cleared his throat and sat down.

"As I was saying, you have talent, Ron. We're sending you on a solo mission. It's a little different—well, it's completely different from your current one, but it'll help round out your skill set."

"Thank you, sir." He was eager but sad. "Will I have time to say goodbye to Claire?"

"Of course, son. Wrap things up well, and report back for your orders."

"Why, Ron? Do you really have to leave right now?"

Ron's ghost heart ached. They had anticipated this day, but that didn't make it any easier. "Yes, Claire. There's someone else who needs my help. You know I have to help them, right?"

Claire wiped her eyes with her sleeve, her voice small. "I know. But will I ever see you again?"

"I don't know when, but I will try my best."

"Okay." She sniffled, trying to be brave. "I hope you have a nice time on your next mission. I wish I could give you a hug goodbye."

"Me, too. You're a special girl. Be a good friend to Becky and Denise, okay?" He disappeared.

Claire sat in bed and pulled the blanket over her head. She cried, then got up and went to her daddy's room. Silently opening his door, she walked to his bed and crawled under the covers, snuggling against him.

Nick felt her curl up next to him. He squinted in the morning light. She hadn't crawled into bed with him since Ann died. He reached out, smoothing her hair with his hand. "What's up, honey bun? Bad dream?"

"He's gone," she moaned.

"Hmm? What's gone?" Nick blinked away sleep.

"Ron. Ron's gone."

"Where did he go? Did he say when he'd be back?"

"No, Daddy, he's *gone,* gone."

Claire was bereft, and Nick needed to console her. "Did Ron say why he was leaving?"

"Yes. He said he needed to help someone else."

"Okay. That's a good thing, right?"

"Yes. But it makes me sad because I need him, too."

Claire quieted, save for a few hiccups. Nick waited, holding her.

"I know he made me happy when I was sad before, and I'm still happy, so I guess he did his job. I love you and Grandma and Mom, and Maggie Mom. But it hurts, Daddy. What if I never see him again?"

"I know, sweetheart. We are all here for you. Do you want to talk to Miss Janet about it, too?"

"Maybe," she sniffed.

"Tell you what, I'll call her in a little while. Let's get dressed and go out for breakfast. Maggie Mom can come, too. How does that sound?"

"Okay."

He called Janet first, then Maggie. As soon as he told her, she asked, "Do you want me to come with you?"

"That would be great, hon. I'll pick you up in half an hour, okay?"

"Sure, see you then."

When they arrived at Janet's office, Nick thanked her for coming in on a Saturday. Janet wanted to talk to Claire alone first but told the couple they could join them later. Janet saw the gratitude on Maggie's face for being included.

Claire clutched the tissue Janet handed her, twisting it in her fingers. "He waited for me to wake up, and he looked sad."

"How could you tell?"

"His eyes were kind of droopy. He said somebody else needed him."

"So, he's going to help someone like he helped you, right?"

"I know. But I want him here; I miss him already." She sniffled.

Janet passed Claire another tissue. "Remember when we talked about how some people come into our lives for a reason, and we remember them for it? He has helped you so much. Won't it be nice if he can help someone else?"

Claire said, "I guess so."

They talked more, and Janet asked Claire if it would be all right to have her dad and Miss Maggie join them. "Okay," she answered, blowing her nose.

The couple joined Janet and Claire. Maggie suppressed a smile when Nick sat in the small chair, recalling their first parent-teacher conference.

The therapist explained that Claire understood why Ron had to leave, and as parents, they could help her work through her feelings with their own stories of absent friends. Even though she wanted him to stay, now it was someone else's turn. She would always remember him and Gayle, too. Because of the two ghosts, Claire now had a family with a mom, a dad, and a grandma. Wasn't that a wonderful gift from her ghost friends?

As the door clicked shut, Janet exhaled, her shoulders slumping. She replayed the session in her mind, marveling at how she'd just explained how two ghosts—sent from who-knows-where—had helped this family come together. A chuckle escaped her. "Maybe I'm the one who needs a therapist," she muttered under her breath, shaking her head.

Gazing out her fifth-floor window at the city below, she thought, *I know what I saw, but how can I justify therapy for something I can't fully believe?* She imagined herself at a professional conference, *'Yes, I'm a ghost psychologist. No, I don't treat ghosts; just people who see them. Well, yes, I have seen one.' Arrgh! I'm sure David would get a kick out of that. She checked her watch. Oh, we're having lunch in 45 minutes. I'd better get ready. And he better not smirk.*

CHAPTER

THIRTY-EIGHT

Nick, Maggie, and Claire ate a late breakfast at a country diner, then returned home. Jenny waited to hear how things went. She asked Claire to come into the kitchen with her while Nick and Maggie settled on the couch.

Jenny took Claire's hand in hers and smiled. "Do you want to tell your grandma what happened this morning, honey?"

Claire sat on a kitchen chair, leaning towards Jenny so they could hold hands. "Ron has gone away, Grandma. I miss him, but he needs to help someone else now. Miss Janet thinks it's good that he can do that, and I should remember him as a special person in my life. I am, but it's hard."

Jenny sympathized with her and said, "I have a story to tell you. My husband's name was Tom. He was Maggie's daddy. We loved him very much, and he got sick. When he died, it was very hard for Maggie and me, but together we managed. Sweetie, I know God made this beautiful world, but He didn't explain everything. There are many things we can't always understand, and your Ron is one of them."

She poured milk into two cups and opened a sleeve of Oreos. "My Tom is another. You know how I love to sit in the backyard? Well, that's one place my husband comes to visit me. Not like Ron, but I know it's him when he's there."

Claire rose from her chair and leaned on Jenny's arm. Ron told her about Tom, but she didn't know the whole story, just that he had helped them that night at her house. "That's really cool, Grandma. Can you talk to him like I talk to Ron?"

Jenny smiled. "I can talk with him, but I don't hear his words. I just know when he's there."

"Oh." Claire tilted her head, frowning.

Jenny shivered and smiled. "Like just now—he tickled the back of my neck with a tiny puff of air, and I can feel him near."

Claire peered over Jenny's shoulder, her whisper filled with wonder. "I feel him too, Grandma. And the air behind you looks kinda squiggly."

Now Jenny frowned. "Dear child, what are you saying?"

Claire dropped her arms and stepped away from Jenny. "Shh, please be quiet, Grandma."

Claire heard a rumbling voice say, "Tell her I love her."

"Oh, Grandma, he says he loves you!"

Jenny looked at Claire with shock in her eyes. "You can hear him?"

"He's very serious and quiet, but I heard him. He doesn't look like Ron or Gayle; he's just kinda...there."

Nick and Maggie joined them in the kitchen, concern etched on Nick's face. "What's going on?" he asked.

Jenny turned to Maggie, clutching her hands, her voice trembling. "She said she can hear your father."

Nick and Maggie shouted, "What!?"

Claire grinned from ear to ear. "Hush, everybody, please. He talks really softly."

Maggie kneeled in front of her mother. "Are you all right, Mom?"

Catching her breath, Jenny looked at Maggie, then at Nick. "Oh, my word. I don't know what to say."

"Tell him you love him back, Grandma, tell him."

"Sweet thing, he knows. I tell him all the time."

"I know," Claire said, hopping in place. "But tell him now."

Maggie took her mother's hand. "Mom?"

Jenny brushed the tears from her cheeks and said, "You know I love you, you old coot."

Nick rested his hands on Jenny's shoulders, offering silent support. A sudden draft brushed past his neck, sending a chill down his spine.

Claire broke into a wide grin. Dropping her voice to a low, serious tone, she mimicked, "Who are you calling an old coot, you young chicken?"

Jenny gasped. "That's what he always called me." Tears flowed. "Oh, my goodness, do you realize what this means?"

Nick walked from behind Jenny's chair and looked down at Maggie. She released her mom's hand with a gentle squeeze and put her arm around his waist. They watched Claire tilt her head to the side, listening. Nick nearly groaned. 'Oh no, here we go again.' But Jenny's miracle was happening, and he didn't want to taint it.

Maggie leaned against Nick for support. Her father was communicating through Claire. "This is wonderful! Mom? Nick?" Jenny beamed at Claire. Nick looked about to be sick.

Claire laughed. "Grandpa Tom says, 'Just roll with it,' Daddy." She tilted her head, as if listening, then spoke again in her low, "Tom" voice. "Maggie, remember that song we sang together when I drove you to college?"

Maggie's breath caught as a memory surfaced. Claire giggled, clearly amused by her reaction.

Maggie whispered, "Don't worry. Be happy. Oh, Daddy, thank you." The tears spilled with her laughter as she buried her face in the crook of Nick's neck. He held her close, gazing at his daughter.

Claire looked toward a place only she could see. "Grandpa Tom said, 'I gotta skedaddle. Catch you on the flipside.'"

Maggie and Jenny gaped at each other, sharing a memory of Tom in his hat, winking on his way to work. "Wow," Jenny said.

"Yeah, wow." Maggie wiped her eyes.

It took a while for them to calm down. This opened so many possibilities. They sat, astonished. Claire couldn't sit still, so happy she could help her grandma, and now she had a ghost grandpa.

Nick could only shake his head, caught between disbelief and wonder. As his gaze lingered on Claire, he sighed and muttered to himself, 'Just roll with it,' right, Tom?

Nick called Janet and handed the phone to Claire. Janet acknowledged the words tumbling from Claire's mouth, validating her emotions and assuring her they would talk more next week. She sighed when Maggie took the phone and confirmed Claire's account of the event.

"What was that all about, Jan?" David asked, scooping a bite of cheesecake from her plate. He grinned, his eyes twinkling in that annoying way, as she considered her career choices. She must open her mind to possibilities more spiritual than scientific. Didn't she?

She deadpanned to her lunch date, "Sorry, it's confidential. Just between us mortals." She reflected on whatever-this-was with David as she finished her dessert, playfully rapping his knuckles when he reached for another bite. Recoiling in mock humiliation, a lock of hair fell into his eyes. *It's not logical that would be so sexy. Dammit, it's just a dopamine release from the cheesecake. Because I love cheesecake. Right?*

CHAPTER

THIRTY-NINE

November brought flurries of early snow and wedding details. Nick confirmed the church and reception hall. The caterers were on board with the final menu. Nick ordered his tux with a holly green cummerbund and boutonniere to match Claire's and Jenny's dresses. Jenny would roll alongside Maggie up the aisle, allowing them to proceed side by side into Maggie's future.

Even with preparations for the wedding, Thanksgiving was a tradition everyone wanted to celebrate. Jenny took charge of the turkey and let Claire mix some craisins into the stuffing. Nick placed the prepped and trussed turkey in the oven and sighed heavily, flexing his muscles.

"My work here is done," he proclaimed, drawing guffaws and fake coughs from the kitchen. Maggie squeezed his bicep and cooed in falsetto, "My hero," fluttering her eyelashes. Janet and David arrived with dessert. Rosie Cunningham was invited but had already agreed to join friends from her church.

Six family and friends gathered around the dining room table in relaxed company. They bowed their heads for a moment and reached for the food.

Claire looked at her grandma and smiled, "Grandpa says everything looks lovely."

Across the table, Janet's head snapped up. "What did you say, Claire?"

Claire turned to face her. "I told you about my grandpa."

"Yes, you did. He's here? *Now?*"

David fidgeted in his seat before standing abruptly, his thoughts clearly on his work. "Don't you dare," Janet said sharply, grabbing his wrist. "This is a private thing, no pictures."

"Yes, he's here," Claire answered. "He said, 'David, take her word for it, please.'" She still giggled when she used the deep voice.

Everyone put down their bowls but David, who squirmed in his chair, springing to his feet. He looked at the faces around the table, a bowl of mashed potatoes in his hands. "This family has not one, not two, but three ghosts in your lives, and you won't let me record it for history? Think of the...the science. Ow, that's hot." He replaced the potatoes on the table.

Nick stood up. "Relax, David. You've got plenty of science at my house. You've published a video that got thousands of views. We don't want Claire to get more internet attention. Tom is Jenny's husband and my fiancé's father. This is their time with him; please respect that."

"Of course, Nick. I apologize; in my excitement, all I thought of was my work. Jenny, Maggie, I'm sorry." He sat down, glancing at Janet.

Jenny smiled. "I understand your enthusiasm, David. It's all still new to us, and we're trying to keep Claire's gifts safe until she's older."

Claire looked around the table and laughed. "Grandpa says, 'Chill out, everybody. Eat your food before it gets cold.'"

Nick reached for a roll, then asked Claire, "Honey, exactly where is your grandpa?"

Maggie looked at Nick, wondering what was on his mind.

Claire said, "Grandpa is next to Grandma, on this side, Daddy." She pointed.

Nick put down the roll and stood next to Jenny. Everyone at the table stopped, bowls once again replaced on the table, and forks clinked on empty plates. Maggie clasped her hand to her mouth as she realized what was happening.

Nick didn't feel the least bit foolish as he looked straight ahead. "Sir, I've spoken to your wonderful wife, but now that I have this opportunity, I would like to have your blessing and permission to marry your daughter. I love her; my daughter loves her, and we want her in our lives. We're a package deal, Claire and I. Same with Maggie and Jenny. We want us all to be a family."

Maggie and Jenny were silent, and Janet wiped a tear from her eye. David just stared—what a moment. Claire tilted her head.

"Grandpa says, 'Nick, I'd say my daughter has found herself a good man. Tell Maggie...oops." Claire turned to Maggie and said, "He's better than a good parking place at the mall." Maggie squealed in delight, recalling the moment.

Claire waited, listening. "Nick, I know my Jenny loves you, and Claire does too. You both have my blessings, son."

Claire stopped translating from beyond and grabbed her father's hand. "Isn't this cool, Dad? Can we marry Maggie now?"

Nick scanned the room, his gaze resting on Maggie, his friends, and Jenny. A wave of gratitude swelled within him as he knelt beside Claire, pulling her into his arms. "Thanks for being you, sweetie," he whispered, his voice thick with emotion.

Jenny spoke up. "Well, this is a Thanksgiving we won't soon forget. Now, as my Tom said, 'Let's eat before it gets cold.' Otherwise, you know where the microwave is."

They filled their plates, quietly at first, then the meal sparked lively conversation and finally the giving of thanks. They were all aware of how blessed they were.

Janet gave David an arched eyebrow and stole a glazed carrot from his plate.

CHAPTER
FORTY

The music started. Nick stood at the altar, relaxed, except for his hands, which clasped in front of him, then behind, then at his sides. Claire walked up the aisle, spreading candy cane amaryllis petals on the white runner. She grinned when a few petals fluttered from her basket. Ron floated in front of her, cheeks puffed out as he blew the petals. She put her hand in the basket, pretending she did the tossing. She was so happy he came to the wedding and wanted to talk to him about his new mission.

Claire noticed her grandpa standing on the other side of Maggie, who seemed unaware of his presence. He hovered near her mother, ready to accompany them.

Maggie and her mother walked up the aisle, with Tom hovering behind. Nick watched his bride approach, graceful in her gown, her serene face illuminated by sparkling eyes. He mouthed, "I love you." Smiling, she whispered back, "I love you, too." Jenny mimed, "You'd better."

At the reception, Claire found Ron in a quiet corner. "I'm so glad to see you, Ron," she said with a smile. "Wasn't it beautiful?"

"Yes, it was. I'm glad you're officially a family now."

"Yes, we are. Guess what?"

Ron grinned. "What?"

"I can talk to my grandpa, Tom, now."

"Really? No kidding?"

"No kidding," she laughed. "He's here today; you can see him over by Grandma."

"I see him now. Oh, here come your parents. I'll talk to you later, okay? I want to tell you about my new mission."

"I want to hear all about it," she called back.

Claire chatted with Ron, her quiet murmurs unnoticed by most guests. However, Janet and David exchanged a glance, and Janet nudged his side to get his attention.

"Oof, what was that for?" he asked.

"Just don't say anything."

"I didn't say anything."

"Well, you were thinking about it."

"Oh, so now you can read my mind?"

"Shut up."

"Okay."

"Do you have to be so accommodating?"

Janet nudged him again, grinning, her playful gesture catching him off guard. Despite his vast knowledge of the paranormal and ability to debate the most learned skeptics, David felt adrift in navigating Janet's mysterious charm.

So, he did the only thing he could think of to make his point. He leaned over and kissed her. Janet gasped and started to push him away, but when her hand went to his chest, she grabbed his tie and pulled.

Maggie and Nick were making the rounds, visiting their guests. Her entire school seemed to have turned out, even Mrs. Gates. They had just talked to Rosie Cunningham and were now approaching Janet. "Hey, you two, enjoying yourselves?" Nick grinned.

David took his time releasing Janet's lips and looked up with a grin. "I am now." He swung away from Janet before she could poke him again, but she lightly backhanded his arm.

Looking a little dazed, Janet greeted them. "Hi, Mr. and Mrs. Miller."

"Has a nice ring to it, doesn't it?" asked Nick.

"Speaking of rings," Janet said, grabbing Maggie's hand to admire her wedding ring.

Nick shoved his hand next to Maggie's. "Twins," he said. A confused frown rippled across Janet's face as she looked at the obviously different rings and then sharply between them. Nick and Maggie laughed out loud. "The rings. Okay, they're fraternal twins. Geez, Dr. Janet."

Janet sighed in relief and blushed at her faux pas. Changing the subject, she asked, "How's your mom?"

"She's great, thanks. Holding court with some of Dad's old employees. It means a lot to her that they came."

"Right, from the newspaper," Janet said, recalling how Tom was the major stockholder when they were acquired. His shares kept Jenny afloat. "Good for her. I bet she's glad to see their old friends."

Nick said, "She's got their attention, showing off her new granddaughter. You've been wonderful with her, Janet. We're so grateful." He kissed her cheek in appreciation.

"Thank you. I'd say, 'Just doing my job,' but it's been more of an adventure."

"Here, here." David added, "Now, if we could just get the good doctor in session with some of my, um…"

"Don't even say it, ghost boy," Janet shot him a look.

"I'm not gonna touch that one," Maggie said. "We're going to continue making the rounds, so we'll see you later. Love you guys."

"Yeah, continue your—conversation," Nick winked.

David put his palms out toward Janet in a surrender gesture. She tried not to grin.

Claire chatted with Becky and her family. Denise and her mom were there, too. The girls skipped to the dance floor, giggling as they jumped around. Claire danced with her dad after he had danced with her second mom as a married couple. She spoke with Ron again, and he told her about the homeless woman he was going to help.

"She lives in Florida. It's much warmer there, even for me. She has a little dog for company. But something bad happened at her work, and now she has to live in her car, and her family doesn't know."

Claire believed Ron could help the woman. "I know you can fix things, Ron. Like you helped me, Daddy, and Maggie. Be careful flying, okay?" Ron nodded. She was trying hard to be brave and not cry. "Goodbye, Ron. When you learn new tricks, will you come back and show me?"

"You can bet your bottom dollar." With a smile and a flip in midair, he disappeared. Claire walked back to the party and her grandma. She needed a hug, and her grandma gave the best. She was sad she wouldn't see Ron as often as she wanted, but happy he'd be helping someone else. *Maybe she could help him with his next mission. Wouldn't that be cool?*

EPILOGUE

Ron soared through the clouds, the windless expanse caressing his ethereal form like a warm tide. He was halfway to Florida when a familiar thought tugged at him, pulling him off course. His buddies, Joey and Larry, were likely holed up in the Ghostland control room. He hadn't seen them since his training days when they delighted in sharing embarrassing rookie tales. Curiosity and nostalgia spurred him onward, and in a blink, he transported himself into the humming chaos of the Intake area.

He found them sorting through piles of new equipment—fancy optical headsets, controllers, even a new hologram projector.

"Hi, fellas. How's it going? Wow, looks like you're upgrading."

"Hey, Ron, good to see you, pal," said Joey.

A familiar voice broke through the squabble of electronic alerts. "Well, look who's here!" Larry popped up from behind a tangle of cables, his wild grin unmistakable. "I guess they're letting anybody in these days."

Ron chuckled. "Hello, Larry."

"Ron," Joey said, "this is Magnus." Joey motioned to a man with long blonde hair and white coveralls, who said nothing. He glanced at Ron, then the cables, then left the room. "He's from IT—helping with the installation." Joey rolled his eyes. "You know how they are."

"Ron, my boy," Larry beamed, rubbing his hands together. "We are moving up in the world, so to speak." He flicked a switch on the hologram unit. "Dim the lights, would you, Joey?" Larry tapped a few icons on a tablet, and a video cube about the size of a small refrigerator flickered into view.

"So, Albert stopped by for a beer after his shift the other day—" Larry said. A flicker of light expanded into a holographic projection, and Albert's head and shoulders materialized inside the cube. He waved enthusiastically. "Hiya, Ron!"

Albert's grin widened. "Remember what you pulled off at the Millers'? This is kinda like that, only...um, here."

Ron stared at the image, both amused and impressed. "Wait, didn't I do that myself?"

"Yeah, that was all you, Ron," Larry continued. "But when you did that little parlor trick, it opened up new possibilities for all of us..."

"Really, how?"

"The Boss saw you had skills and the nerve to try them out. So, he let you 'show yourself' to the adults. They saw you were real, and David collected evidence and made a video. See, the more people believe, the more we can help." He swept his hand toward the equipment. "So, we upgrade."

Joey glanced at Larry, and Larry glanced at Albert's image. Ron's eyes flicked between them. "Wait a minute—are you telling me you guys have beer?"

"Hey, Magnus," Larry called into the server room, smiling at Ron. "You can knock off for the day. See you in the morning." Magnus grunted, grabbed his bag, and left.

Albert grinned. "I'll be there in a jiffy."

Joey turned to Ron. "Okay, just keep it quiet; we don't want The Boss to catch us."

Larry handed him a cold bottle. "Ron, you deserve it, buddy."

Albert floated in and gave Ron a high five while accepting a beer from Larry. "Remember how I handed you that paper file on the Millers? Well, look at this."

Ron watched in wonder as the hologram took shape, showing Rosie Cunningham helped into an airport shuttle. "Ah, there's my Rosie." Albert paused. "Ron, you really did me a solid there." He smiled and clinked his bottle with Ron's. "Scroll back, Joey. Please."

He did, and scenes appeared of Nick and his crew's remodel of the Cunningham house, the busy estate sale, and a new family moving in. "You'll see Rosie and her brother at their place in Florida when you start your new mission." Albert sipped his beer.

"Go forward, Joe. Watch this, Ron." Maggie ran to her family in the kitchen, whooping and waving a positive pregnancy test.

They watched David on the road, giving interviews and investigating paranormal claims, and Janet tending to her practice, studying files alone in her apartment.

Ron's gaze lingered on the projection as warmth spread through him. He hadn't realized how far-reaching his small acts of kindness had been. The Millers, Rosie, even Albert—all of it rippled outward, touching lives in ways he couldn't have imagined. A smile tugged at his lips. *Ripples.* The projection flickered out.

"I'll try to reboot," Larry said, turning to the controls. "Still a few bugs to work out."

"But how? When did... or does all this happen? I don't get it," Ron stammered in confusion.

Albert beamed like a proud papa. "Most of it has already happened. But Earth time and our time can run at different speeds. We're figuring out how to see further into the past and even slightly into the future. You know how we track our Incoming, right?" He gestured to the wall of monitors that once displayed the events leading to Albert's own heart attack and Ron's fall.

"The system shows the moments leading up to someone's demise and alerts us to prepare for them. We can apply that idea to significant events in someone's life. Once we get the programming right, we'll be able to pull up scenes from people's past incidents to better help them."

"You mean, like what humans or even ghosts need to resolve to move on?"

"That's right, Ron." They fell silent for a moment, processing the possibilities. "We hope to have it worked out by your next mission, but no promises." Albert watched as the system rebooted.

Larry held up a tangle of wiring. "We have lots of work to do. But go forth and do good, pal. We've got your back."

Ron raised his bottle with a grin. "I will do my best, guys." The cold beer was a nostalgic comfort, but what truly warmed him was the camaraderie of this moment.

The projection refreshed, revealing an image of Claire and her friends. Nick shoveled new snow from the garden path while Maggie and Jenny sat on the porch, Tom's shimmer between them. The girls threw snowballs, and Claire fell back, laughing, to make a snow angel. Ron smiled.

As he watched the joyful chaos unfold, a quiet sense of peace settled over him—something he hadn't felt in a long time. In life, his job carried the weight of countless lives with unwavering precision, each decision a delicate step along the knife's edge of perfection. Now, as a ghost, his challenges were different, yet no less daunting. He had navigated this strange afterlife, learning and growing in ways he never thought possible, in a world that demanded more from his heart than his skill.

In this ethereal existence, he discovered a truth more profound: the power of love and the strength found in letting go of perfection. Ron realized that true mastery lay not in controlling outcomes but in embracing each moment with empathy and presence.

Watching Claire, Nick, and their friends, he understood more about the human spirit. Life's true beauty resided in its imperfections—in the snow angels and laughter, in the shared warmth of friendship and family. These were the ties that bound souls together, transcending the boundaries of life and death.

In that moment, Ron felt more alive than ever. He learned that moving forward required courage and acceptance. It was about finding connections and allowing peace within oneself. As they toasted the scene before them, Ron vowed to carry this lesson into his next adventures, a guardian in service of love and support.

And so, in the gentle fall of the snow, Ron found his purpose—a reminder that the heart's enduring journey lies not in holding tight but in learning to let go.

THE END
(For Now)

RON'S JOURNEY CONTINUES

We hope you have enjoyed Book 1 of the Nearly Departed series. Here is a preview from Book 2 - Ghost On a Mission, coming soon:

Julie scratched her dog's ears, its head in her lap. "How did this happen, Tulip?" Her eyes scanned the parking lot, searching for answers. "We'll get through this, don't you worry." Tulip's tail thumped on the floor of the van, the beagle's encouragement shining in her dark eyes. "Yes, we will, baby." A furry kiss. "I better find us something to eat." Julie winced at the thought of dumpster diving for expired food behind Walmart. She thought of her children, strong and stable. *They would be so disappointed in me.*

Julie wondered if someone could do this to her, and they were probably watching. She'd have to contact her son Brad soon; he would help her. She didn't want to rely on her kids, but this situation had to end. Another apartment was out of the question now. She would need first and last months' rent plus a cleaning deposit, and she was down to her last $200 in cash.

Poor Tulip was hungry, and it had to be done. Degrading? Yes, but necessary. *I could lose a few pounds, but I will not let my dog go hungry.* Waiting until dark, she walked behind the store to check the dumpsters for discarded food. There was always something edible from the in-store deli or bakery. She removed a deli bag from the bin, searching for food containers. The best finds were takeout boxes that someone forgot to take.

"You give them nine years of hard work, and they don't even investigate before letting you go. *Who does that?*" Tulip whined softly at her distress. *Like I would transfer money from a resident's account to mine? I wouldn't be that stupid. After all these years, they assume I'm guilty and freeze my accounts. Who has the authority to do that? I have thousands in that bank. But how do I prove it?*

Until recently, Julie was a resident care supervisor at Greenhaven, an assisted living facility in Destin. She loved her job; the residents were like family to her. But someone had set her up to take a fall, depositing a resident's funds into her personal account.

Ron, the ghost, had work to do. His mission was to solve the crime and help Julie get her life back. His primary responsibility was her safety. She affected many people, some of whom Ron knew. It was his first solo mission, and he had to admit he was a little nervous. He floated invisibly behind her as she searched for dinner, saving her money for a greater emergency.

She returned with sustenance for the night: day-old cookies and unsold deli sandwiches. A resourceful and optimistic problem solver, lately she had struggled to just get through the day's challenges. But something she couldn't quite place, a faint notion of hope, gave her a moment's relief. "It'll get better. Just you wait, Tulip." They ate in silent camaraderie, resigned to an uneasy sleep.

***

"What do you mean her service is disconnected? When was the last time you talked to her?" Brad grilled his laid-back brother Roger, part owner of a bar and grille in Clearwater.

"I don't know, man. Six or eight weeks ago? When did *you* talk to her?" Roger knew he was annoying his older brother but wouldn't betray his own worry yet. "Was it my turn to keep track of her?"

Exasperated, Brad knew he was tired and hungry after a long day running his security company, but he didn't let up. "Okay, *man.* Maybe we should call *Jan*—did you think of that, genius?"

"Let me check my calendar, hmm... do you have her num—"

"Roger!"

"Okay, okay. I'll call her and get back to you. Jeez."

Roger called their sister and, without preamble, asked, "When was the last time you talked to Mom?"

"Hello to you too, big brother. What's going on?"

"Sorry, Sis, but Brad and I haven't been able to get in touch with her."

"Do you mean she hasn't returned your calls?"

"No, her number is no longer in service."

"That can't be right, Rog. She's never without her cell phone. Did you try Greenhaven?"

"Uh, yeah. Of course we called, but all we got was the runaround. 'She's out of the office. She's away from her desk. Please leave a message.'"

"Well, that sounds fishy. She would have at least returned your messages. Do you think she went on vacation or something?"

"She would have group texted us for that, don't you think?"

"Yeah, you're right. Can you ask Brad to drive down and check out her apartment? He's the closest. If he can't, maybe he'll send one of his guys."

"Maybe you should ask him. I think he's kind of annoyed with me right now, though I can't imagine why."

"You can't imagine, huh? Brother, dear." She chuckled. "You knuckleheads are why I got into child psychology. Okay, I'll call him. Keep in touch."

"You bet, Jan. But seriously, I don't feel good about this. Something's not right."

"I hear you, and I understand." She hung up.

An incoming text lit her phone. *David.* She frowned. *Yeah, you are not on my agenda right now, ghostbuster.* She didn't reply; her session with Claire started in a few minutes.

ABOUT THE AUTHOR

Teri Petzold is a passionate voice in literary fiction, drawing readers into stories rich with depth and introspection. Her journey as an author began in the spring of 2020, when a closed Senior Center and her son's recovery from knee surgery sparked a creative partnership and the birth of her first book. Since then, Petzold has published multiple works, including a mystery and several collaborative projects with her son David. An accomplished art teacher, Teri remains active at the Senior Center, engaging with peers and inspiring others. At 86 years old and a proud mother of five, she brings wisdom and creativity to every page. Teri continues to write and collaborate, always exploring new ideas and narratives for future literary adventures.